THE SALIGNAC LEGACY

The Salignac Legacy

Caenys Kerr

RED AVENTURINE PRESS

Cover Art by Erica Christensen

Logo design by Courtney Taylor

Dedication

For my husband, David, who accidentally spawned a romance about chicken livers.

Contents

Dear Reader

Dear Reader,

Sometimes we don't recognize how much our lives are shaped by those who go before us until something or someone stands up to threaten what we hold dear—whether that's the sports club we've been a member of for five years or a secret society our family has been a part of for a hundred years.

Cat and Lachie's story is the first in The Priceless Heritage Series revolving around family traditions and legacies. My critical friend calls the themes the Four P's: Pâté, Perfume, Parures, and Pottery. I hope in time, you'll enjoy all four. They are closely related to Lachie's family, the McKells, with links to newcomers who bring their own centuries-old traditions that need to be guarded and developed for the changing times.

Each of the stories has a connection to places I've been—Australia (my home base), the UK, Italy, Egypt, India and Ireland. Learning about specific traditions has kept me entertained in the writing of these stories, and I hope you'll enjoy that too.

I'd love to hear your stories of the places and people you find in the stories, or your own family legacies. I can be contacted through my website https://caenyskerr.wordpress.com/contact

1

Chapter one

"Scotland! You want me to travel halfway 'round the world with you because your great-aunts liked my pâté?"

"You know it's more than the pâté itself. Elspeth and Alethea recognized the flavor was the one known only to the McKells. I've confirmed it. Unless you've somehow stolen the recipe or whoever taught you stole it, you must be the last person who knows how to make the pâté this way."

"I'd watch what you're saying, mate. In Melbourne, we don't take kindly to being called criminals by random strangers." The giant in front of Catriona dragged his hands through his thick, coppery-red mane and across the base of his throat. His face put his age at early thirties. The seriousness of his concern made him appear older.

"Ach. We canna talk here, lass. Yer boss keeps giving me the evil eye."

"Because I'm meant to be working, not arguing with the customers."

"Can we meet later?" he asked.

She screwed her mouth to one side. Apart from him all but calling her a dodgy character, and the absolute size of the man, she didn't see any threat. Her head told her not to get involved. Who'd call you a thief to your face and expect you to meet for coffee? She wavered. His sheer magnetism and those sparkling blue eyes sent the butterflies in her chest into a little happy dance. They wanted to know him better.

Her heart said to give him a go. A beverage, a chat, and go on home. What's the harm?

"There's a coffee shop in Collins Place," she said. "It's open later than most. I'll meet you there at five-thirty."

"Aye." He scowled and strode into the busy foot traffic outside the shop. His expression was reminiscent of a child not getting his own way, it made her smile. He appeared to be a man who expected things to travel on the lines he set and was unused to being challenged.

"What was he on about?" her boss demanded. His gaze followed the big man's retreat.

"Nothing much, Charles. It seems his aunts liked my pâté. He wanted to check it out."

"It's not your pâté when it's here in the shop. It's mine. Don't let him get any ideas he can do anything more than buy it and eat it here." He flicked the cloth he was carrying against the counter's edge and stormed to the kitchen.

Not for the first time, Catriona sensed her employment at this boutique café in Melbourne's Paris End was nearly done. The recipe did not belong to Charles Sopworthy. It was hers; or rather it was passed to her safekeeping from her mother. It was definitely her secret to protect.

Shortly after five, she strolled from her workplace, skipped across the tram tracks, and walked into the semi-enclosed Collins Place.

The big man was already there, in the only café left open in the food court. He sat in the area partially covered by the mezzanine level above. The dark wood and black décor suggested a nightclub venue. Instead, it was open to the forecourt, in full view of passers-by. The place catered to early theatre- and cinema-goers, or those who wanted an after-work drink, with or without alcohol. At this hour, there was a scattering of other patrons present.

The Scot got to his feet when Catriona approached. He bore the fit build, size, and barely-leashed energy of a powerlifter performing at the Olympics. "You're early," she said.

"I have nowhere else to be until I convince you to come home with me."

"You make it sound more like a proposal than a proposition," her laugh skittered. She took the seat he held for her.

"Aye, it may be." A flirtatious smile lit the man's face, sending her heart into a two-step beat. He appeared much younger than the scowling giant she encountered at lunch time. Then the smile was gone.

It seemed he'd forgotten himself for a moment.

She laughed anyway. "You're quick off the mark. Can I get you a coffee?"

"No, lass, I'll do it. What will ye have?"

"A large, long black, please."

"No milk or sugar?"

"No thanks. I was weaned years ago. Plus, I'm sweet enough without extras."

"Aye, I can see." The grin peeked out again.

She followed his progress to the counter. He gave the impression he was usually the one in command. *But not so arrogant he can't order his own coffee.*

He was gone long enough for the coffee to be prepared. Catriona wrapped her fingers around the porcelain mug he passed to her to hold her hands steady. "Okay, tell me your version of the story. I'll see if I can make sense of it."

He took his seat. "It's not my version, lass. It's the truth. That recipe has been passed through my family since the early 1800s."

"Kiddy-whispers. Like that game children play," she said. "Every time a story is told, the message changes until there's no semblance of the original and no truth left."

"I can't agree. My forebears were meticulous in recounting the history. We Scots have depended on accurate storytelling." His brow furrowed.

"Scots aren't necessarily my favorite people." She sipped her drink. "Don't look so shocked, get on with your story."

"Why is it you dinna care for the Scots?" he asked.

"Another story for another day. You were saying?"

Looking like he wanted to press the point, he scratched at his cheek with the back of one finger. "In 1790, my ancestor traveled from France with her father to meet with my great—I've lost count how many greats—grandfather, Malcolm McKell. Malcolm fell in love with Simone on sight. They planned to get married. She returned to France to gather the things she would need to make a life in Scotland."

"Hang on, the highland clearances were happening then, weren't they? What woman in her right mind would give away a cozy life in France to risk it for a Scot with the English banging on the door?"

"I take offence with yer sneer when ye mention my countrymen, lass."

"My name is Catriona, not 'lass.' When you call me lass, I feel like a five-year-old and you're as old as Methuselah."

The man's frown shifted to a grin. "Ye might be fifty, I'd still call ye lass. It's what we do. I know who ye are because my great-aunts described yer appearance to me, along with the name of the café where I would find ye. Today, I read the name on yer badge ye're wearing."

Her hand touched the plastic rectangle on her blouse, unpinned it, and slipped it into her bag.

"I don't know yer surname. I can't call ye Miss or Mrs. anything."

"It's Miss Cameron. I'm not married. Catriona is fine, or Cat. I guess I can handle the lass bit. What do I call you? Laddie?"

A laugh cracked from him. "Oh aye. I've not introduced myself, have I? Laochailan McKell, at yer service, Miss Cameron. Please call me Lachie." He pronounced the name as a guttural, throat-clearing "Locky". He extended his hand.

His fingers touched hers and she jerked as a spark flashed along her arm.

"Oh, static electricity, sorry," she said.

His grin was back. This time there was a knowing edge to it.

"Go on with your story. Your ancestor went back to France and…? She must have survived because you're here to tell the tale." Catriona feared she was hooked on the sound of his voice. She wanted him to go on speaking in his lyrical tones.

"Oh aye. She survived, and indeed, prospered." He rested his elbows on the table and leaned toward her. "Simone sailed back to Scotland with a shipload of haberdashery, crockery, chickens, goats, cognac, vegetables, even some French variety lavender. It didn't last in the Scottish winters, so she got some English stuff, instead. Simone chose to make Scotland her home and loved it."

"She was from a wealthy family?"

"Aye, and marrying into one, too. My family tried to keep the peace with the English. We weren't always successful." Lachie flicked his right hand. "It depended on who was troop commander at any given point in time. Usually, though, Simone was able to charm them with her style and her cooking. She explained it would be pointless for them to steal our vegetables because they wouldn't know how to use them. The chickens were too small to feed a man. Once they were gone, there were no replacements. They should let them be too." There was more than a hint of pride in the smile he let loose.

"They bought it? It seems incredulous that hungry soldiers would be so easily dissuaded."

"Not all of them, as you suggest, but Simone was clever. She kept a chicken run in the basement of the house, releasing a quarter of the chickens at once. They were the only ones the English saw or stole. The next time the English officer came to dinner, after she'd lost some of her flock, he was served tough mutton and no sweets. Simone's explanation was that with few chickens left, she would have to breed them again to have eggs. There would be no delicacies until then. It seemed to work. The raids would stop for a while."

"She sounds like a character," Cat chuckled.

"She was. The women after her have been the same." He took a sip of his coffee.

"What does any of this have to do with my pâté?" She tilted her head to one side.

"Simone loved pâté. The chickens she bred not only produced enough eggs to keep the family satisfied, every part of the chicken was used. Because they were small, several were needed for a meal. The meat was carved off and the frames used to make soup. The feathers were used to line the bottom of her garden beds when she planted her crops. The livers, which normally would've fed the dogs, she kept for making the most amazing pâté."

Cat wasn't sure whether to chuckle or be inspired by his furrowed brow and earnest expression as Lachie recounted events from centuries past as though they happened in the streets of Melbourne just yesterday.

He scratched the side of his cheek with the back of one forefinger. "She started with a basic recipe, I'm told. From there, she made adjustments. When the cognac ran out, she used the whisky my family produced. She infused it with herbs, lavender mostly, and some wild juniper, I think, to soften the flavor. Whatever she did, however she made it, the flavor was superb, distinctive. The recipe was never written down. It passed to the daughters of each generation with the strict instruction it was to remain secret."

He sat back in his seat, holding his coffee mug. "It's the way it has endured. The McKells built our fortune on whisky. Demand for Simone's Pâté grew too. Both products worked side by side. It remained so for nearly two hundred years."

"What's the problem now?"

"The last of Simone's female-to-female descendants, whom we know of, was killed in a car accident a year ago." Lachie's gaze focused on his coffee mug.

"You've lost the recipe?" Cat sighed.

"More, we're losing a big chunk of our livelihood and our workers' jobs." Lachie frowned. "Our customers are not happy with our best efforts to reproduce the flavor. Our research and development people have been working on it, day and night, without success. We've laid off men and women who have worked with us for years. It breaks my heart."

She felt the emotion rolling from him. One thumb rubbed against his collar bone and the look of anguish on his face was almost tangible. He cared.

Goosebumps rose on her arms as if his distress jumped across the space of the table to grab hold of her. She swallowed to clear her throat. "You haven't explained where I come into things."

"Ye're right." He passed a hand along the side of his face. "Let me explain. A month ago, my great-aunts came to Australia and happened to walk into yer café."

"It's not my café. I work there." She took a sip of her brew.

"They shared a few dishes, trying new flavors. One was the pâté. They asked their server who made it, and she pointed to ye. Do ye remember?"

"Yes, the old ladies were lovely. There was a small communication problem because their accent was so broad," she shrugged, "but I got they liked my chicken livers."

"They didn't only like it. They recognized it as Simone's recipe. How did ye create it?" Lachie asked.

"My grandmother and my mother taught me. They've never committed it to paper, either, but I don't know anything of your Simone. I can't see there would be any connection there at all. Who was she before she married into your family?"

"Comtesse Simone de Salignac. One reason she was keen to leave France was because it was the time when the revolutionaries were seeking the nobility. If she'd stayed in France, her life was definitely in peril. She would have decided it was more likely she may survive and raise a family in Scotland, even though she wasn't completely safe.

There was her husband, too, her much-loved Malcolm. Ye've gone pale, lass. Are y'alright?"

She swallowed. "I'll be fine in a moment. Probably hungry. I'll go get a Florentine. Would you like one too?"

"Let me do it for ye. I don't want ye to faint on me."

Her gaze tracked his movement from the table to the counter, but her mind was elsewhere.

De Salignac! Everything slipped into place for her. Didn't she have the old name as part of her own? Her recipe was passed to her with total secrecy, too. The way the whisky was blended with the herbs and the way she used goat's milk to prepare the livers.

She held Simone's ancient recipe in her head. She was one of them.

Did it make her duty-bound to help the McKells? Wasn't this the family who tossed out her beloved great-grandmother because she fell in love with an Englishman? Damn! What should she do?

She knew nothing of this man's family apart from what her mother and grandmother told her, and it wasn't very positive.

Her mother died of cancer when Catriona was eighteen. Her grandmother's mind slipped in and out of focus. The chances of building on the knowledge of her family's history were slim to none. Still, she would try to talk to her grandmother.

Lachie resumed his seat, glancing across at her.

"Will ye come?" He placed the plate with two biscuits on the table.

"I can't afford to take off at a moment's notice. I have a job, responsibilities." She nibbled one of the cornflakes and chocolate delicacies.

"Ye're not married, ye said. Do ye have children?"

"No, I don't have children. You'd better watch it. You're getting way too personal for someone I've just met." She took a ferocious bite of the confection and chewed determinedly.

"Ach, lass, I'm trying to find a way forward here. My people need the recipe." His tone was urgent. "We've got to get the enterprise back on track or more people will have no work. We are the major employer in the area. In fact, we're nearly the only employer of any note.

There's nothing else for these folk to do. Do ye know what the statistics are for unemployed country people and suicide?"

"Hey! Hold on. You're not going to lay a guilt trip on me for people I've never met, nor am likely to meet." She flung the biscuit back on the plate.

"What can I say to persuade ye?" His hands stiffened on the table as he glared at her. His voice seemed to bounce off the mezzanine overhang above them.

"Don't raise your voice at me. It will not help your cause. What's in it for me? What did the other women get from sautéing chicken livers day in and day out? Were they paid as workers or were they partners in the enterprise?"

"They are the enterprise. Simone's Pâté is operated by the incumbent recipe holder. It's for ye to set yer own rates. The other women did quite well financially. They made sure their workers were rewarded too. They regarded their special gift as a legacy borrowed from the family line. It only belonged to them for their term. They passed it to their daughters with the same sense of holding true to Simone's vision."

"Hang on, if there were others working with her, how come they don't know how to make it?"

"Ye would know better than I. If it were easy, we'd be making it by now. The secret has to do with the liquor, I believe, and the finishing of the product. Those are the things the *Simone* does away from the workers. Only she knows how to do those things."

"You call her 'the *Simone*?"

"Aye, it denotes her as the secret recipe holder who can trace her line directly to the Comtesse. She has total control of the pâté business."

"I don't see how it might work for me. I've never run a business. I wouldn't know the first place to start."

"McKells is a large enterprise. Part of it is dedicated to Simone's Pâté—human resources, payroll, accounting, marketing. The *Simone* makes the decisions, and we give her the support."

Cat would admit using her skills to make money was an inducement. She and Gran could move beyond their basic existence. She'd love to be in a position to do more for Gran. There were no guarantees here though. She had a life to live. Did she want to spend it chained to a sauté pan? Nevertheless, the thought of financial independence was seriously enticing.

She studied his face. He seemed genuine. She shouldn't immediately lump him in with the men in her life who hadn't inspired her with confidence. "I've got to go." She dragged herself to her feet.

Lachie stood too. He towered over her. "Can I ask ye to think about it, lass?" He raised one finger and tilted her chin.

She took in the serious electric blue orbs looking back at her. A new frisson passed through her body. He was mesmerizing. "I thought Scots had brown eyes," she said.

He appeared startled by the non-sequitur. "Some of us do, lass.

When there's this colored hair atop his head," he tugged at a tuft of it, "he's far more likely to have the blue."

"Right." She stepped back from the sizzle frying her senses. "I will think about what you've said. I'll go talk to my grandmother after work tomorrow to see what she knows."

"Ye have a grandmother? Is she yer mother's mother?" he asked.

"Yes."

"She taught yer mother to make the pâté?" Lachie demanded.

"You're getting pushy again."

"I can't help it, lass. This is important to me. Where is yer grandmother? Can we go and see her now?"

"She's in a care facility. I'll go to see her tomorrow, I said."

"Ye can't go sooner?"

"There you go running my life again. Tonight, I make pâté. To-morrow, I work. In between, I try to sleep. Tomorrow, after a day in the café, I will go to visit my grandmother."

"I'm sorry. Again, this is urgent."

"I know. I'll be in touch. Where are you staying?" she asked.

He pointed to the premier hotel looming fifty stories above their heads.

"Can I drive ye to yer grandmother? I'd like to meet her. I suspect she might be a descendant from Simone, even if we don't know the connection yet."

She narrowed her gaze on him. Being driven to the nursing home would be far preferable, after a day on her feet, to fighting with peak hour trams. It was taking a leap of faith, putting her trust in this man.

"All right. I'll meet you in the forecourt next to the bell captain's desk at five-fifteen tomorrow."

"I'll be there, *mo leannan*."

2

Chapter Two

Lachie hadn't known what to expect of Catriona. Elspeth and Alethea returned to Kellburgh from their holiday in Australia full of excitement because they'd found Simone's Pâté in Melbourne. They couldn't have known how his heart and mind would react to the lass when he first caught sight of her.

Even though he'd previously been married, he'd never found this instant attraction, this kindred type of feeling he was experiencing with Catriona. He tried to remember he hadn't flown around the world to find a love interest. He was here to do a job and he'd use every tool at his disposal to do it, short of kidnapping her and bundling her onto a plane. It seemed, though, his logic was at war with his emotions.

Thinking about her made his heart beat faster. She was a dream, a pint-sized dream. Her fair skin appeared even fairer against the deep black of her hair. Her lips were a natural red and full, offering an invitation to be kissed. Her lips, more than anything, were what drew the endearment from him when they'd parted last night. Thank goodness she didn't appear to understand Gaelic, or she may not be coming toward him now. She'd be running for the hills if she knew he'd already called her his sweetheart.

She strode across the forecourt. For such a wee thing, she certainly displayed an attitude.

A bellboy passed him the keys to the luxury rental car parked in front of him. Lachie nodded his thanks and held the door for his guest.

"Ye'll have to direct me to where we're going," he said, by way of greeting.

"I'll plug the address into the mapping system. I catch the trams. I don't know the car route." She set her actions to her words and the system displayed the direction as they emerged into Collins Street traffic.

Silence reigned in the vehicle until they escaped from the central business district. "Do ye want to tell me, lass, why ye have such an aversion to my countrymen?"

"Hmm. It's not my story to tell. It relates mostly to my great-grandmother and her expulsion from her Scottish family because she fell in love with an Englishman. I don't know a lot more of the details. Gran might, if her memory is working today. The dislike was bred into me, if you like."

"Ye canna let the sins of the past color the person y'are today."

"My mother thought along those lines, too. She married a Scot. Big mistake. He was as reprehensible as the worst stories my great-grandmother ever told me. He was all lovey-dovey until my mum became pregnant. Then, he tells her he's not ready to be a father and hightails it. Not ready? He should have kept his dick in his pants."

Lachie roared with laughter. "Ye sure say what ye mean, lass."

"You know now why I don't have a lot of love for the beast who is the Scots male."

"I'll have to work on changing yer mind then." He frowned at her. She offered a cheeky smile and it made him chuckle. She had no idea how serious he was in his intention. He wanted her, and not only for her pâté.

"You can try. I wouldn't bank your life savings on it," she said.

"Does yer grandmother feel the same way?"

"You'll find out."

"What's her name?" Lachie cocked his head.

"Isla Jenkins."

"For a family who doesn't like the Scots, ye seem to have a few Scots first names."

"Mmm. Alongside the dislike of the men, there was always a bit of sentimentality and nostalgia for Scotland, itself. The land, the highlands, the lochs, even the weather. It was a contradiction. We lived with it," she shrugged. "Oh, I know where we are now. Turn on the next street. Don't follow the nav. This street is not a through road anymore. The nav hasn't caught up yet."

Lachie piloted the car at her direction and parked halfway along the driveway to the facility.

"We have to sign in at the front desk. I doubt they'll ask you for ID or anything because you're with me," she said.

Catriona sailed through the corridors of the home, greeting carers and residents as she went. Lachie followed behind.

She walked into a bright, airy room where a small woman sat as though deep in thought, looking through the window. Cat grasped his hand. The unexpectedness of it startled him. He returned the grip, enjoying the sensations hurtling through him.

"Hello Gran."

The woman rotated her head to face them. "Hello, Catty dear. Who do you have with you? Are you the new doctor?"

Catriona's grip loosened and her shoulders relaxed as a sigh escaped her lips. "No, ma'am. I'm a visitor," Lachie said.

"He's a visitor from Scotland, Gran. His name is Lachie McKell."

"McGill!" The elderly woman seemed to inflate to twice her size. She imitated spitting at his feet.

"Gran!" Cat admonished, glancing at Lachie. An "I told you so" smile lurked on her lips.

"You'd bring a McGill here? What were you thinking? After what they put my beloved mother through? Why is he here?"

"It's to do with the recipe for the pâté. He's a McKell, Gran, not a McGill."

"Don't you tell them about the pâté, dear." The woman's voice lowered into what would have been a conspiratorial growl if Lachie hadn't already been standing there in full view. "My mumma's life was nearly ruined because of the damned pâté."

"Are ye saying it's Simone's recipe, Mrs. Jenkins?" Lachie interjected.

The look speared at him could have sliced him in two. "Is there another pâté recipe you would travel to the other side of the world to find, young man?"

Lachie almost grinned at the address. At nearly thirty-two he didn't think of himself as a young man. "Mrs. Jenkins, can I tell ye my history and yers too? Do ye know Simone's story?"

"Some. My mother wasn't too keen on talking about the old days. Though she did become wistful for the place she'd left behind, along with one or two of the people."

"Would ye like to hear?"

Isla's sneer was not encouraging. "If you must."

Lachie dragged a spare chair close to the woman. He let his hands fall loosely between his knees and leaned toward her. "Right then. We call it *The Salignac Legacy*. It starts with, 'once upon a time, around two hundred years and some ago...'?"

The sneer softened into a severe moue. It was a start. Lachie told Isla the same history he'd recounted to Catriona the previous evening.

As he finished, Isla stared him down. "It serves them right. If they wanted to hold the recipe, they should've treated the recipe holder better, not thrown her out because she fell in love! Salignac legacy, bedamned. I'm tired." Isla picked at the rug covering her knees. She looked around the room before coming back to him. "Who are you?"

"I'm Laochailan. Most people call me Lachie."

"I don't know any Laochailan, or Lachie, or whatever. Who is he, Jeanette? Is he the new doctor?"

"No, darling, he's not the new doctor. He's a friend."

Who the hell is Jeanette? What's going on? Lachie swung his gaze to Catriona for some clue. "Would you like us to go since you're tired?" Cat asked.

"Yes, please. Jeanette, can you bring me some more chocolate pineapple lumps?" The woman's voice became frail, almost querulous.

"I can. Tomorrow?"

"Uh-huh."

"Okay." Catriona bent, gave her grandmother an awkward hug, and kissed her forehead. "Love you, Gran!" She grasped Lachie's arm, dragging him from the room.

"What happened?"

"Gran has a form of dementia. Today was a good day. She was wonderfully lucid. She was able to put you in your place, young man."

"Hah!" Lachie laughed. "She did. Who is Jeanette?"

"Jeanette was my mother. She died when I was eighteen. She's been gone more than seven years. I don't think I'm much like my mum, though I do think Gran recognizes an emotional connection and links it to her daughter," she said.

"And what the heck are chocolate pineapple lumps?" "Oh, they're wonderful." The grin bloomed on her face again. "They're chewy little squares of pineapple-flavored nougat covered in dark chocolate. Some days they're the only thing the carers can get Gran to eat." Her grin settled into a worried frown.

"Does she have to be in care?"

"I could handle her at home, but I work. I can't leave her on her own. She wanders off and becomes confused, or she leaves the stove on and forgets it." She waved a farewell to the desk staff.

"Why not hire a daytime carer?"

"Oh yeah, money grows on trees in Scotland, does it?" she smirked.

"But the facility must cost ye a fortune?" he persisted.

"It's mostly means-tested and paid from Gran's pension. I can afford the extras she needs. Home care is too expensive."

Lachie clicked the car remote. A small beep sounded, then he opened the door for her. His mind was mulling over what she said. He reversed from the parking spot and drove past the straggly roses flanking the driveway.

"What if ye lived where there was someone on hand around the clock and ye didn't have to pay for it?"

"Where would I find this Nirvana?"

"With me, in Scotland; I can make it happen," Lachie said.

"I'd have to sell my soul or the secret my great-grandmother, my grandmother, and my mother made me swear to protect?"

"Ye're being a bit melodramatic, aren't ye?"

"If you think so, you don't understand your own family's history," she snapped.

"The damned recipe is my family's history."

"Hmm, are we related? You and I?" she asked.

"We would definitely be related, back in the mists of time. We'd have to go back six generations, at least, to find a common ancestor."

"Not kissing cousins then?"

His groin tightened in response to her words. He'd like to be much more than cousins of the kissing variety. "This means ye must come back to Scotland with me. Ye know it, don't ye? The recipe belongs with my family," Lachie insisted.

"You heard what Gran said. If the family was all-fired keen on keeping the recipe, they should have safe-guarded the recipe holder. Clearly my great-grandmother, Rhona, was not worth protecting when she fell in love with a wonderful Englishman who made her happy. She was forced to leave her home country to get away from her father's vindictiveness and his trying to force her to marry one of her slimy cousins."

"I thought ye didn't know her history," Lachie mused.

"I knew her history. I didn't know how it might connect to the pâté or to the McKells. Listening to Gran this afternoon, I put the pieces in place."

"Why don't we ask yer grandmother if she would like a trip to Scotland?"

"She's seventy with dementia. She can't make her own decisions."

"She was bright enough when we spoke to her. Why not let her have her own say? Or is this a control thing for ye?" Lachie flicked his gaze off the road and aimed it at her for a millisecond.

"Listen, buster, you're the only one who's the control freak around here."

"I wouldn't say I'm controlling. What I would say is I have concern for the people around me, especially people who are losing their livelihoods when there's the slimmest possibility I might be able to do something. We can go back to yer grandmother tomorrow and ask her. Or I can go on my own when ye're at work," he suggested.

"You wouldn't dare. You'd lose any smidgen of a chance for my co-operation if you were so underhanded. You would upset and confuse her. You saw how she was about the Scots today. Don't. You. Dare!" She glared at him.

"All right, we'll go together. Same time, same place?"

"Okay."

To Lachie it sounded like a begrudging acceptance, but it was an acceptance. He relaxed his tight grip on the steering wheel.

"Lass, what ye need to know about me is that being responsible for my community and the folk within it is who I am. That goes for ye as well, now. There's a link between us. If ye need anything, anytime, come to me first."

His speech drew a sharp glance from her. "I mean it," he said.

"I've looked after myself for a long time." She turned her head away from him.

"Because ye've had no choice. Ye have the McKell now and ye can count on me." She was a fighter, aye, but even fighters needed someone at their back.

She reached out one hand and touched his arm, sending a jolt of energy into his soul. "Thanks, Lachie." Her voice was quiet. She dropped her hand and returned her gaze to the world beyond the windscreen.

A few minutes later, he drove the car into the turning circle of the hotel's forecourt and levered himself from the vehicle. A bellboy opened Catriona's door.

"The tag is on the keys," he said to the bellboy.

"Thank you, sir."

Lachie placed a hand at Catriona's waist and another frisson passed through him. This was not a connection he was used to, but where this woman was concerned, it was becoming a familiar sensation. Was it because he'd been celibate for years, or because hers was a new fresh face, with an attitude which challenged him on every level? If he could, he'd pick her up and hold her close, safe, quiet, his.

"Would ye like to join me for dinner?" he asked, not willing to let her go.

"I'm dressed in work clothes, not fit for fine dining."

"There's a Japanese restaurant here I went to on my first night in Melbourne. The food was good and the place was packed with people straight from work. Are ye prepared to give it a go?"

"Are you going to nag me all night about chicken livers?"

He chuckled. "No chicken livers. Lovely food and charming company."

"Yeah, right. Okay, lead on. I wouldn't mind a good meal and someone else to do the dishes."

"What a delightful acceptance, *mo gràidh*." He gave a small bow and was rewarded with a hearty gurgle of laughter.

Oh Lord. If she kept that up, he'd be regretting not inviting her to enjoy room service in his suite.

3

Chapter Three

Catriona sped across to the bank of elevators at Lachie's hotel. She hugged her arms around her waist and waited until the lift doors opened. Mentally thanking the universe for an empty compartment, she used the keycard the receptionist gave her at Lachie's request, and the lift rode upwards. She was grateful for this minute to herself.

The lift doors opened on the top level and she heaved a belly-deep sigh to set aside her fear and stiffened her spine. She needed Lachie's help, but she didn't want to give him the impression she was a needy person. Usually, she was quite capable of handling things on her own.

Glancing over the railing barricading the corridor from the central light well festooned with sails of fabric designed to soften noise, she found a dizzying drop to the atrium level fifteen floors below.

Pulling back, she scoured the door numbers and rang the bell for the suite in the center of the far corridor from the lifts. Lachie opened it immediately, dressed in a pristine, hand-stitched business suit. She gulped. This was not the approachable man with whom she'd enjoyed dinner the previous evening.

"Catriona, come in. We were talking about ye," he said.

She swung her head around to find another man also dressed in a suit, though not of the same quality as Lachie's.

"This is James Gallien, he's McKell's agent here in Australia. Catriona? Are ye all right, lass? Ye're deathly pale. Come and sit. James, grab us a whisky, would ye?" Lachie said.

He led her to a sofa away from the large table with papers spread across it and sat beside her. "Yer hands are frozen. What's happened? Is it yer grandmother?"

She shook her head and tried to speak, but no sound came out. She threw herself against Lachie's chest. "I don't know what to do." *So much for not wanting to be needy. A safe harbor and she was a watering pot!*

Lachie held her head close and smoothed his hand the length of her hair. "Come on. It's okay. Whatever it is, we can probably fix it. So long as Isla is all right."

She nodded against his lapel.

"Here, drink this." He held a cut crystal glass to her lips. The whisky was smooth and potent, and burned her throat. Tasting whisky was part of her daily routine and she welcomed the familiar warmth. She slumped against the seat.

"Now tell me."

She cast a sideways glance at the other man who retreated to the table.

"James is okay unless ye want to speak to me on an entirely private matter?"

She searched Lachie's face and found concern there, and something else…it made her feel safe and protected.

"I went in to work this morning and told my boss, Charles, I'd be taking some time off. I told him I wanted to visit family in Scotland. He flew into a rage. In the five years I've worked there, I have never seen such a reaction from him.

"He screamed at me and said it was to do with his pâté. The bloody Scot was going to steal it from him. I told him I wanted to meet my mother's family and I would take Isla with me. He kept screaming and told me I wasn't welcome there any longer. He accused me of industrial espionage, for God's sake! He said he would take out an injunction against me leaving the country, and another one to prevent me from making pâté from his recipe anywhere in the world. It wasn't his recipe, I reminded him. He said because I'd made it when I was an employee and sold it from his shop, it was his. I left. I didn't know where to turn, so I came to you."

Lachie tugged her into his arms and went back to stroking her hair. Catriona could have cried. The warm cloak of security was something she'd missed since Isla went into care. Behind it, she sensed she'd be happy to spend forever with this man, protected this way, feeling cherished.

The thought struck her, and she pulled away.

"Better?"

She bobbed her chin.

"James, can ye call for some coffee and pastries please? Black coffee, no sugar, *m'eudail?*" He waited for her nod. "Good. Up ye come. Go into the bathroom and freshen up. What's the name of this eejit who thinks he can intimidate a fine young Scotswoman?"

"Charles Sopworthy. And I'm not a Scot."

"Ach lass, of course y'are. Off ye go."

The ensuite bathroom was huge, and she sat on the edge of the bath to calm her thoughts. After a few minutes, she used the facilities and washed her hands. Dragging a towel over her face, she examined herself in the mirror. Her reflection was wan and ghostly. A trick of the artificial light? She tried to bring color into her cheeks by massaging them with the palms of her hands and ploughed her teeth across her lips for a similar effect. There was a comb lying on the benchtop and she used it to straighten her hair as best she was able. She pulled away any remaining strands of her hair from the comb, rinsed it, and returned it to where she'd found it.

When she came back to the outer room, the table was cleared of paper and set with pastries and aromatic coffee. The man, James Gallien, was nowhere in sight.

Lachie strode across the room and hugged her close. She leaned into his chest and put her arms around him as far as they would go. Only her fingertips met at his spine. Want, need, gratitude, and desire flowed through her—all mixed up and scrambling for ascendancy. Lachie's arms held her in place with his cheek resting on her head.

"Ah *mo cridhe,* we'll work it out." One massive hand shifted over her shoulders.

She tilted her head to glance up at his face. He returned her stare and the air changed. Her sights shifted to his lips and she fixated on them as they edged toward hers. Her stomach reacted as though it were practicing a Riverdance routine, bouncy with lots of high kicks. Those lips moved closer until they touched hers with the slightest pressure and moved away. She tracked their retreat and raised herself onto her toes to follow them.

His arms around her tightened and their mouths crashed together. This was it. This was what she wanted, needed. This was her life force writ large. She never wanted the kiss to end, and it seemed like it never would. His mouth lifted only to find a different angle and the fierce onslaught continued.

Her pelvis flexed against him and found his manhood rock hard and ready. She lifted one hand to rake through his silky hair and keep his face within reach. Her tongue rasped across his teeth. Lachie's palms cupped her buttocks and held her closer still. A groan escaped from deep in her throat and reverberated between them.

The pressure of his mouth lessened. His hands left her backside and she slipped to her feet. He trailed his fingers along her spine and around to cup her face. The fierce kiss of possession morphed into a series of butterflies across her cheeks, her eyes, her forehead. He dropped his hands to her shoulders and held her steady.

His pupils were huge, as though he'd suffered a shock. He leaned down to her and kissed her forehead with care, then stood back and took one of her hands, leading her to the table.

"Ye didn't come her to be assaulted, *mo ghràdh.* Have something to eat."

She followed his directions in a daze and sat down. He poured a demitasse of strong coffee and placed a Danish pastry on the plate at her side, repeating the process for himself.

The fragrance of the coffee cleared her senses. She took a sip, willing her mind away from his amazing kiss. "Oh my. If you're used to this coffee quality, I'm not sure how you coped with the stuff in the food court the other day."

Lachie grinned. "I didn't taste it. My thoughts were on ye."

"Or was it my chicken livers?"

One side of his mouth tipped up in wry acceptance. "Those too. We're not going to discuss what happened here?"

She placed a half-eaten section of pastry back on her plate. "Um. I won't deny it…I mean, I could have…I mean…hell's bells. I don't know what I mean. I liked it and I would do it again…it's complicated."

Lachie's smile grew wider with each of her attempts at an explanation.

"What of you then?" She raised her brows. "A bit of fun on the side for your trip Down Under?"

"I don't think that's it, lass. I think a wee kiss has been coming since the moment I went into the poncy café where ye work. To be honest, I didn't think I'd ever have a chance to experience it. Ye are so fierce." He goosed his head backward, projecting faux fear.

"So, there's a chance it'll happen again?" She lifted her eyebrows.

"Oh, aye. If I have any say in the matter. It's up to ye, now." The look in his eyes sent shivers of delight rocketing through her body.

"Good, I'll let you know." She grinned at him.

"Minx. I'm glad yer spirit is back." He adjusted his body on the chair. "Tell me about this arse who upset yer morning. James tells me yer man is a sycophant. He's got enough wealth, but he plays around in his café because it's where the politicians come to get away from the parliamentary buildings. He likes to be in the know, to see and be seen."

"Yes, though to give him his due, he works hard too. He does a lot of the kitchen work and he pays his staff fairly." She picked up the discarded pastry and distractedly tore small chunks from it. Lachie's gaze followed her movements.

"How did he get yer pâté?"

"I took it as a contribution to one of the staff evenings we have occasionally." She dropped the confection back on the plate and dusted her fingers with a napkin. "He fell in love with it and said he needed it in the shop. I agreed to make a few pots to see how they went. He used small portions as an *amuse bouche* for those who ordered a meal at lunch time—not the coffee and run crowd. It was an immediate hit, so he wanted more," she said, her head moving slowly from side to side. "And so it began," she shrugged.

"I made it as terrine-type loaves. It could be sliced to serve at the table or to take away. No matter how much I made, it was outstripped by the demand. Gran was at home then, and she gave me a hand. When she went into care, I cut right back. There were too many competing interests." Cat swallowed against the memories of those happier days with Gran in the kitchen.

"Anyway, Charles suggested I should give him the recipe to make it. He would help, he said. It was a bit tricky for a while. How do you keep a secret recipe secret if you hand it off to whoever asks?" She creased her forehead into a frown.

"What did ye do?"

The concern in Lachie's eyes teased her with the idea she could hand all her troubles over to him, but she was made of sterner stuff, she hoped. She shrugged one shoulder. "I told him there was no recipe. I made it by touch. I might teach someone else in a hands-on way. It's the way I was taught. From the first time I helped in the kitchen, my great-grandmother, my grandmother, and my mother made sure I understood this was a secret to be passed on to my daughter. Over time, Charles has continued to pressure me into teaching him how to make it. I'm positive he's spent hours trying to work it out."

"What made ye tell him ye were going to Scotland?" He leaned his elbows on the table and linked his hands.

"After the visit to Gran yesterday and working through the connections with the family history and how everything went right back to your Simone, I figured there must have been a reason why your great-aunts stumbled upon the exact café where I was selling chicken livers. It had to be more than coincidence. My women forebears were each a bit fey. They didn't believe in coincidences. Everything happened for a reason—even the bad stuff." She bit the inside of her bottom lip. "Meeting your aunts, and now you, I figured I should go to Scotland and check out the people there to find out...I don't know. It's difficult to articulate. I need certainty I'd not be defiling my legacy if I helped you, I guess. I figured a couple of weeks in Scotland would be enough, and I'd make an informed decision from there," she said.

"Aye, except I'd prefer ye to stay much longer." He flicked his eyebrows.

"Don't get too enthusiastic. My plan was to come home, and things would continue the way as always—same job, same routines, life would go on. It changed this morning."

"Ye're not going to Scotland now?"

"I don't know if I can. I asked Charles for some holiday leave and he asked what my plans were. When I told him I was going to Scotland, he lost it. He has the contacts and the money to make things uncomfortable for me. I'd get to immigration at the international airport and get hauled off because of some damned injunction. I can't risk going to jail for illegal fleeing of the country or whatever they might want to call it, because there's Gran to consider.

"And if he stops me from cooking my chicken livers, if I can't make my pâté anywhere in the world, I may as well give in now. Somehow, don't expect me to explain this, somehow the pâté defines who I am. I have a responsibility in this life. Without this, without me, the world would be a wee bit poorer." She arched her back so her head rested against the chair back and looked down her nose at him.

"We'll work it out, *mo laochain*. I've tasked James with finding someone who can help us to fight this."

"What are these Gaelic words you use. They are Gaelic, yes?" Lachie's grin peeked out and his eyes lit up. "Ye'll learn them all. *Mo laochain* is my little hero in English, and it's sure how I see ye today. Fighting yer battles and not backing away."

"And what are the others? Mocha and modal?"

"Not quite the pronunciation. I'll tell ye more when the time is right." He leaned forward and pulled her to him. He kissed her forehead, sending trembles of desire through her body.

She closed her eyes to savor the moment. When she opened them, she looked directly at him. "Lachie, I don't have the money to fight battles. If the court orders me to hand him the recipe, what do I do? Nothing is written anywhere, there is no provenance. How do I prove the recipe was mine before I went to work in his crappy café?"

"Why don't ye have money?" He seemed incapable of thinking any descendent of his precious Simone would not be wealthy.

"Our family has never had big money. We've enough to have a comfortable lifestyle. We don't want for anything. There is not enough, though, to fight legal warfare. The extra I earn these days goes to Gran's care and I'm okay with that. She is all I have in the world."

"Then the McKells will fight the battle for ye."

"No, then I'd be in debt to you. I'd be exchanging one prison for another."

Lachie lurched backward in his seat as though he'd been struck. "Is that what ye think, Catriona? I would force ye into doing something ye didn't want to do because of money?"

She surveyed the harsh angles of his face and realized too late she'd hurt him. Her shoulders slumped. "To be honest, I've known you less than three days. I don't know what you would do."

Lachie rose from his chair, stalked to the far end of the room at least fifteen meters away, and raked his hands through his hair in a manner that was becoming familiar to her. She bit into her bottom lip to stop its quivering. She was an emotional wreck this morning.

"Right!" He stormed back toward her, his face set. "Give me yer contact details. I'll pass them on to James and he'll be in touch with ye. He will handle the accounting. By the time we've finished, it will be yer boss who is in debt to ye, and ye can repay James. Will those arrangements suit ye? Does it keep the money," he almost spat the word, "sufficiently dealt with so ye do not feel forced to care for my people?"

"Lachie, it's not—"

"Enough. Talk to James. Did ye have a jacket with ye?" She waved her head in silence.

"I think it's best if ye go to yer grandmother on yer own today. Don't forget her sweets."

Catriona stood as tall as her petite frame would allow and firmed her lips. "It's a wrap. All men are arseholes." She steamed to the door through which she'd entered and closed it firmly behind her.

4

Chapter Four

Cat hadn't left her contact details, and without them, there was nowhere for Lachie to look for her now she wasn't working at the café. Without a job, was she able to support herself?

The woman was going to turn him gray before his thirty-third birthday. As if a McKell would hold someone to ransom in the way she'd implied. It would be best if he stayed away, at least until his blood stopped boiling.

He rang James. "I want a damned injunction or whatever is possible against this Charles Sopworthy to prevent him from seeking any injunctions against Miss Cameron. Find out what ye can about this horse's arse. If he's coming after the pâté recipe, we need to be ready for him.

"Oh, and James, will ye search out contact details for Miss Cameron, please. Let me have what ye can later today."

Bluidy woman. She was perfect in his arms—tiny, but she fit against him in all the best places. Her kiss rocked him to his soul, and teased of a happy ever after. He'd never thought about a kiss in such a way. She was the one. The one he must have been waiting for.

And she went and said that.

Yes, they'd only known each other for three days, but surely she knew the kind of man he was. He was no manipulative *blaigeard*, even if she thought of him as a bastard right now. She'd find out for herself.

He'd take her to Scotland to make her "informed decision". He'd make sure to get her away from Sopworthy. If the man were the sycophant James suggested, the *blaigeard* could kiss the McKell's butt and see how he liked it.

Lachie was too hyped to sit and work. He wanted to go talk to Isla. Maybe she'd throw a clearer light on the family fortunes, perhaps persuade the lass to accept his help. But no, the pint-sized shrew nixed the idea of him visiting her grandmother on his own.

He'd be sure to be there when she arrived, though.

Lachie spent the next half hour scouring the nearby convenience stores for pineapple-flavored sweets without success. He went back to his room and rang reception.

His call was answered by the same receptionist as earlier. When he explained what he was looking for, Moana gave a squeak of delight. "I know exactly what they are, sir. They're very popular."

"Where can I buy them?"

"I get mine at the supermarket at the Flinders Street end of Elizabeth Street."

Lachie was confused, not being familiar with the streets of Melbourne's central business district.

"Is it in walking distance?"

"Not really, sir. You can take a tram."

"Oh." Lachie's uncertainty must have telegraphed itself to the receptionist.

"Sir, I bought a couple packets this morning for my kids. If you trust me not to have tampered with them, you can have them. I'll pick up some more on my way home later."

"I wouldn't want to put ye to such an inconvenience."

"It's no problem. I pass by there every afternoon."

"Well, thank ye Moana. May I collect them in a couple of hours?'

"Of course, sir."

With a strategy in place, Lachie sat at the table, trying to focus on the work in front of him. He hadn't redoubled his family fortunes by letting distractions like feisty women get in his way. If he couldn't rekindle the pâté production, he must find alternatives.

The morning passed quickly. He left the table satisfied there might be a market in Australia and New Zealand for their whisky. There'd be stiff competition from the Scottish brands already in place, along with some from the Americans. "Whiskey", they called it, like the Irish. They couldn't even spell the word.

Lachie checked the time. If he left now, he should be at the care facility ahead of Cat. Far better to be early than go later when he might miss her entirely.

He gathered his wallet, shrugged into his jacket, and left the suite.

At the receptionist's desk, Moana smiled broadly as she handed him a paper bag with two packets of the sweets in it.

"I hope this will cover what I owe ye." Lachie placed a twenty dollar note on the counter.

"I'll get you some change, sir."

"No, don't bother. The extra is an apology for the inconvenience I've caused."

"You're very generous. Thank you, sir. I hope you enjoy them."

Lachie nodded, then made his way down the escalator to the hotel's forecourt in time for his rental car to be driven to the door by a bellboy. Tapping through the car's controls, he was relieved to find the address for Isla's care facility still in the navigation system, otherwise he would have been lost. His plan was to be waiting when Catriona got there to visit her grandmother. The biggest problem would be if Cat had already come and gone.

He slid the car into a parking spot near where he'd been the previous day. Grabbing the bag of sweets, he climbed from the vehicle, and engaged the lock using the remote. A small figure walked into the driveway from a street at right angles to the one he'd driven in on. Luck was on his side; he'd arrived in the nick of time. She was earlier than he expected.

She stopped when she saw him. "What are you doing here? I told you not to go near my grandmother without me."

"I've held to yer wishes, lass. I arrived moments ago myself. I was going to wait for ye."

"How did you know when I'd be here?"

Raking one hand across his forehead, he growled, "I didn't. I was prepared to wait on yon wee seat in the shade till ye came. All right?"

"If I didn't come?" The wee nymph tilted her head to the side.

"Ye respect yer grandmother's routines. I figured ye'd be by during the afternoon."

"You haven't explained why you're here." He wasn't too keen on the suspicious look in her eyes.

"I want to talk to yer grandmother."

"She may not be lucid today. You do understand?" Cat firmed her mouth.

"Let's find out, shall we?" He swept his hand toward the door of the center.

As she had yesterday, she led him to Isla's room. It gave him a sense of déjà vu to see the woman sitting in the same position as they'd found her the day before.

"Hello Gran," Catriona knelt on the floor in front of Isla. "How are you?"

The woman showed no reaction to the question, instead staring blankly at Catriona and asking, "Chocolate?"

"No Gran, I—" Lachie thrust the bag into her hand.

She peeked inside then glanced at him. Her brow was lightly furrowed, but her lips broadened into a small smile. "Here we are Gran, Lachie remembered."

Lachie let go of the breath he'd been holding.

"Who?" Isla asked as she caught hold of the small sack Cat passed to her. She smiled and sighed when she saw the contents.

"Lachie McKell. You met him yesterday."

Isla rotated her gaze to the big man. "Don't be a dill, Jeanette. This is Angus. How are you, Angus? I thought you'd be older by now." She dipped her hand into the bag and pulled out one lot of sweets.

Catriona retrieved the packet from her, opened it, and handed it back. Isla took one, then offered the pack to Catriona, then Lachie.

"Angus who, Gran?" Cat asked.

"Angus McKell, my dear. You should know. You brought him here." She tucked the bag beside her.

"Where did you meet Angus?" Cat asked.

"At Kellburgh."

"Ye've been to Kellburgh, Isla?" There'd been no mention of this previously. Lachie raised his brows and thrust forward his bottom lip. "Huh, I'd forgotten ye'd visited us." He popped the sweet he'd been holding into his mouth and bit into it, releasing an intriguing blend of pineapple and dark chocolate flavors.

"It was a long time ago and you were young." Isla shrugged.

"When did ye come to Kellburgh?" Lachie asked.

"I was fifteen, I think." She shrugged again. "It was when my miserable grandfather died. My mother wanted to farewell him, make sure he was dead more like, and to visit some of her family again. Her brother wouldn't let her near any of the family. Told her she was a disgrace. We only met you because you came to the house with your father shortly after we arrived."

"My father, Donald?" Lachie drew the visitor's chair close to Isla and leaned toward her.

"He's the one," Isla said.

"Who was yer mother's brother?"

"Dougal McGill." She mimicked spitting on the floor again like she'd done yesterday.

"Why wouldn't Dougal let the family see yer mother? What was her name?"

"She was Rhona. 'Rhona,' he said, 'there's no use coming back now making trouble. You made your bed with your fancy Sassenach.

There's no more money and no more family for you here. Go back to where you've come from.'"

Isla's eyes widened, her tone urgent as she said, "My mother tried to explain I was the next *Simone*. Every recipe holder was called *Simone* apparently. Dougal said he didn't believe in such nonsense. There were enough bloody *Simones* in the world, they didn't need an English one."

"I'm sorry yer uncle said such a thing to ye, Mrs. Jenkins." Lachie rested his hand on her tremulous one. "Do ye know if yer mother received an inheritance when she left Kellburgh?"

"She did. She looked after it well. There's not as much as there used to be because we bought the house. There's a tidy sum left for Catriona when she turns twenty-one."

Mouth agape, Cat gasped. "But I am twenty-one, Gran. I'm nearly twenty-six in fact. I don't know of any money."

Isla narrowed her gaze at Catriona. She screwed up her face and closed her eyes. "Jeanette, we put the money aside when you were first diagnosed. We said if neither of us was around when Catty grew up, at least she'd have something to stand by her. We're still here so she's okay, right?"

"Of course. Where did we put the money, do you remember?" Cat asked.

"Oh, I don't know," Isla huffed, opening her eyes again. "I'm getting old. The paperwork is in the tub in the hatbox of my wardrobe." She sat back in her seat and helped herself to another chocolate. "How is your father these days, Angus?"

"I'm afraid Donald McKell passed away many years ago now."

"Is the miserable Dougal around?"

"No, I'm sorry to tell ye he passed away too. He had one son, Donnell. Everyone thought there were no more *Simones* from his branch of the family. Now, we've found ye."

"There are two *Simones* in front of you, I'd like you to know," she snapped. She stiffened her spine as much as she was able while seated in her chair, then she slumped. "I'd like to go to Scotland again. I'll take Jeanette and Catriona. The world can see who we are."

"Would ye really like to go to Scotland? To Kellburgh? Would ye like to go by air or by ship?" Lachie prompted.

"Oh, by plane. There's not much of my life left. I'm not going to waste it sitting on a ship."

He caught Catriona's warning glance but ignored it. "We'll manage it when we can. Are ye all right to stay here in the meantime?"

"Oh yes, they're good to me here. Catriona comes every day."

"Gran?"

"Yes dear?"

"Is there anything you need me to bring tomorrow?"

"I don't suppose you might bring some more of these? You can bring this young man again too. He's a bit of a giant and takes up lots of room, but he's pleasant enough. Lachie, did you say?"

"Aye," he said.

"Good. I think I'll have a nap until they bring dinner. You young people look after each other."

"I love you, Gran." Cat dropped a kiss on her grandmother's cheek.

"And I love you too, Catty love."

Lachie patted Isla's hand and stood. He replaced the chair he'd used against the wall and followed Cat's exit from the room.

As they emerged into the open air, Lachie put his hand on her arm.

"Can I give ye a lift home, lass?"

Her gaze studied him, as if measuring him with her eyes. She pursed her lips and squinted her eyes.

"Back to your hotel will be fine. Thank you," she said.

He held the door, waited until she was seated, and moved to the driver's side of the car.

"I'd rather take ye straight home. There've been a few shocks for ye today."

"I can look after myself."

"Aye, I can see, but the car is right here. Does yer grandmother's memory always flit around?" he asked, directing the car along the driveway.

"Not always. Some days it seems like she has no memory. I didn't know she'd ever been to Scotland. This Dougal character, what do you know of him?"

"Not a lot to be honest, though I know the McGills by reputation. I'll ask my uncle if he knows anything."

"You were patient with Gran. Thank you for being careful."

"Not at all, lass. I followed yer lead from yesterday not to correct yer grandmother when she called me by my father's name."

"Good. I've tried correcting her in the past. It upsets her. She thinks I'm trying to confuse her."

The phone in the car rang.

"McKell."

"James Gallien here. I've hired a solicitor. We have a barrister on standby if we need to go to court. Sopworthy is not happy. I got the impression he thought Miss Cameron was alone in the world and fair game. He was taken aback at the news she has your full support. I don't think it will stop him entirely though. He seems to think he has a claim on the recipe. He keeps saying she developed it while she was in his employ and he owns the intellectual property rights."

"I know it's not true. Anything else James?" Lachie's hands tensed on the steering wheel.

"Yes, sir, Miss Cameron's home address is in Kew. Number nine, McCoullough Street."

"Thank ye, James. Good work. Keep me updated on any further developments with Sopworthy please."

"You asked him to find my address?" Catriona demanded when Lachie ended the call.

"Ye didn't leave yer contact details. I can't help ye fight if I don't know where to find ye. When ye left this morning, I knew ye wouldn't come back willingly." He dragged a finger along the crease between his chin and his bottom lip. "Are ye going to direct me to yer home, or shall I stop the car to enter the address into the navigation system?"

"Oh, for goodness sake. You're past it already. Go to your hotel. I'll tram it back just like I always do."

"Next right then?" He swung into the right lane and turned the corner. "Next?"

"Grr! Third street on your left, halfway along."

"Not so hard, was it?" he asked, pulling the car into a space outside a neatly kept federation-style bungalow.

"Thanks for the lift."

"Invite me in."

She speared a glance at him and sighed. "Lachie, would you like to come in? For a coffee perhaps, or something stronger?"

"Thank ye, lass. I'd be delighted." Ignoring the *grr* wrestling its way from deep in her throat, he circled the car and opened her door, then placed his hand on the small of her back as they walked up her driveway.

He held in the quiet smile of satisfaction at being able to touch her again. If three days were not long enough for her to judge his character with any accuracy, he'd have to make sure she got plenty more time to do so.

5

Chapter Five

There he was touching her again. She couldn't think straight. Cat scrabbled in her handbag to find her keys.

"How long have ye lived here?" Lachie asked, as she directed him into the living room.

"It must be fourteen years now. Little Gran had passed on. Gran was living alone in her house. Mum and I were living in South Yarra. We sold both houses to buy this one. Mum said it was to look after Gran when she got older. Gran said it was to help Mum look after me when she was working. Either way, there are a lot of great memories here for me. Some not so good ones, too, I'll admit." She bit her tongue to stop herself from rattling on. "Would you like coffee?"

"Do ye have a whisky?" Lachie asked.

"I have a scotch. It's nothing like the one you gave me this morning."

"Ah, that was McKells."

"I've never seen it in shops here. I've tried a number of Scottish whiskies trying to find the perfect one for my cooking."

"It's one of the reasons James was with me this morning. We're working on a marketing strategy to introduce our label here. Since I believed I was here on a wild goose chase to locate a phantom *Simone* Elspeth and Alethea believed was lurking in this part of the world, I set up business meetings to make sure it wasn't a wasted trip. I'm not sure which was the bonus—finding ye or having James's help in navigating Australian import laws."

"Ice?" she asked.

"Noooo, thank ye."

She handed him a glass with a finger of scotch and poured one for herself.

"Ye looked shocked when yer Gran spoke of yer legacy today."

"Mmm, I've never heard of it. I'm not holding my breath. We've been strapped money-wise since my mum got sick. A fortune is relative, isn't it? To a homeless person, five bucks means he or she might be able to eat. For me, now, a fortune would be having enough to be able to fend off whatever Charles has planned."

"Yer whisky isn't too bad," Lachie said.

"Huh. Damned with faint praise?"

The wry smile spreading across his face turned her legs to water. She shouldn't be feeling this reaction to him after basically telling him to take a hike this morning.

"Would you like to stay for dinner?" *Why did I go and blurt an invitation?*

"Yer offer surprises me, lass. Yes, I think I would, if ye don't mind." He nestled further back, the sofa squishing around him as his bulk settled.

"You're not even going to ask what's on offer?"

"Nay lass. If ye can make Simone's Pâté, I don't fear whatever ye put on the plate, so long as it's not haggis."

"You don't like haggis? Almost high treason for a Scot, is it not?"

"Aye. If ye repeat it, I'll deny it. Let's be clear."

She choked on a laugh. "You know, I might be able to get to like you—even though you're male and a Scot."

"Well, thank ye, Catriona."

"...If you call me Cat. I won't be offering you haggis. I have a couple steaks we can grill on the barbie. What would you like on the side?"

She waited. *Lordy, lordy! The things this man can do to a woman's insides with just a look.*

"Food, Scot. Not what your raised eyebrows are suggesting." She twisted her mouth.

Lachie flicked his brows upward. "Now why did ye have to go and spoil my fantasies? Food, eh?"

"Uh-huh. Would you prefer cooked vegetables or salad?"

"I think I'd kill for some over-done cabbage."

"You sound serious." She tilted her head to one side.

"I am. Our cook was no Simone. She kept us well fed, though, with over-boiled cabbage a staple of nearly every meal." He chuckled loudly. "I love the stuff, but fancy restaurants don't seem to serve the humble cabbage at all."

"I'm sure they will when someone declares it to be a superfood or some other such nonsense. I do have some cabbage; I use it for coleslaw. I can probably manage to boil some for you. Come into the kitchen. You can tell me what else you'd like."

"I can tell ye from here, lass," he said, with a twinkle in his eye. Butterflies danced in her chest. She shook her head with a smile.

"I've warned you once. Let's keep it at food, shall we?"

"If ye insist. For now."

A zip of energy spread from her stomach to her throat and cascaded through her body. She bit her bottom lip to stop a smile from bursting loose. There was no way she even wanted to stop the burgeoning zing of happiness. The bulk of him dwarfed her in the kitchen, his presence embracing rather than threatening in any way.

"The barbecue is on the patio." She jerked her head toward the door. "You can get it started while I do the veggies." She grinned at the puzzled look he threw her. "It's automatic, but call me if it's too much for you to handle."

He dipped his chin to one shoulder, a wry smile breaking free as he held her gaze. "Ah, lass, ye're a sad trial sometimes. Ye canna impugn a man's character in such a way and expect to get away with it."

She giggled past the punch of delight rocketing through her. "No? You can tell me more when we've eaten. Off you go."

Lachie shook his head as he crossed the kitchen in the direction she'd indicated and strolled out the door.

Cat retrieved the vegetables, including the much sought-after cabbage, then rummaged around in the cupboards looking for inspiration for a quick dessert. She grasped a can of tinned peach halves. Brilliant! Some toasted muesli, butter, and cinnamon—she'd have a classy finish to the meal in no time at all. Stuffed peaches with vanilla ice cream.

When Lachie strolled back into the kitchen, she handed him a bottle of South Australian Cabernet Sauvignon. "Do you drink wine? Or only whisky?"

"A Coonawarra red? I'll drink one of those any day of the week. Where do ye keep yer bottle opener?"

She indicated the second drawer with a wave of her hand and continued to scrub potatoes. A couple of minutes in the microwave, then a few minutes in a hot oven, and she'd have crisp baked potatoes before the meat was cooked.

Lachie poured two glasses of wine. He sat at the kitchen table watching her work, his face a study in contentment.

With the vegetables prepared, she took a seat opposite her guest and surveyed him as she sipped her wine. "What family do you have? Are you married? Brothers, sisters?"

A shadow passed across his face, then disappeared. "I'm not married. I have two younger sisters."

"Your sisters aren't *Simones*?"

"They're McKells. The *Simones* only come from the matriarchal line, so, unless they married a McKell, a *Simone* is not going to bear the name."

"Of course. Do all the *Simones* have 'de Salignac' as part of their names?"

"I've never checked. The last *Simone* did, her daughter too."

"Hmm. We'd better get the steaks on or your cabbage will be black rather than overdone." She stood and moved to collect the meat.

"I'll cook it, lass. Medium rare for ye?"

"Straight medium, please. Not too rare, not well done."

The grin peeked out again. "A straight down the middle lass, eh?"

"Maybe. What will yours be? Blue?"

"Aye, enough heat to take the chill off." He chuckled, took the tray of meat and a spare plate from her, and went out.

She presented the array of vegetables in bowls on the kitchen table as she pondered his hesitation when she'd asked if he was married. Divorced, maybe? Or love gone wrong? Or never found the right woman?

She was puzzling over it when he walked back inside a few minutes later with the steaks. "Tell me about your wife," she said, narrowing her gaze at him.

"I told ye I wasn't married," he said. He leaned forward and placed the plate on the table with a care that radiated leashed tension.

"But you were?"

"Aye," he said, "for a short time." His fingers folded into his palms at his sides. "She died in a car accident nearly a year ago, along with the baby."

"Oh, Lachie, I'm truly sorry for you." She bounded across to him and placed a hand over his heart. He gave it a small squeeze.

"Thank you, lass, it's water under the bridge now." He heaved a breath, relaxing his shoulders. "Shall we sit?"

Cat took her seat while he topped off their wine, then seated himself. The shuffle of passing bowls caused their hands to meet often, and each time she felt a zap. The third or fourth time it happened, he caught her eye. His familiar grin was in evidence and lightened the mood affected by the mention of his wife.

"More static electricity," he said. "We'd better start wearing rubber gloves."

The thought brought a smile to Cat's face.

The meal passed with him offering anecdotes of running a distillery. They tried to outdo each other with one-liners about whisky and whisky drinkers.

"Are you a glass half full or a glass half empty, Scot?" she asked. "I'm happy with either if it's whisky in the glass," he responded. "What's the difference between vodka and whisky?"

She considered whether she should answer in terms of flavor, ingredients, or aging, but he jumped in before there was time for her to respond.

"If ye don't know the difference between whisky and vodka, ye should stay away from our whisky." He smirked. Laughter echoed around the room.

"Ah lass, ye made the best meal I've enjoyed in a long time."

The bubble in her chest wasn't pride exactly, more a warm glow because he appreciated the effort she'd made. "I have stuffed peaches with ice cream for dessert."

"Ach, aye? I can make room for more goodness."

Standing, he cleared their plates, then took his seat again while she pulled the peaches from the oven.

"Ye've not taken this from the freezer. When did ye have time to prepare it?"

"Secrets. The ice cream is ready-made though." Dessert passed in near silence.

"I'll make coffee and bring it to the lounge room."

A few minutes later, hot drinks in hand, she found Lachie perusing the family photos on the mantelpiece above the fireplace and along the walls.

"On the surface, ye women look quite different, but there's something around the eyes."

"It seems we threw back to our fathers, though people have mistaken Rhona's photo for me. She was my great-grandmother," she said, drawing a finger along the ledge.

"This one must be Rhona, then? Was Rhona her full name or was she Catriona too?" He took a mug of coffee from her.

"I don't know." The question surprised her. "Why do you ask?"

"Long before Simone joined the family, the eldest daughter of each McKells generation was named Catriona. It's fallen away in the last few generations. The first born of my twin sisters has a variation of it," Lachie said.

"I'll ask Gran, she'll know."

"This Rhona, was she the one who was thrown out of the family?"

"Uh-huh."

"She looks like she was a bonnie lass," he offered.

"She was. I loved her to bits." She adjusted the frame on the shelf.

"She fell in love with someone her parents didn't approve?"

"Her father arranged for her to marry a cousin to keep her close. Now I can fill in the blanks, he probably wanted to hold onto her knowledge and power. She fell in love with an Englishman she met at a market stall in the village; love at first sight. Her father flew into a rage and told her to choose between her family and the Sassenach. I knew this, though I didn't know the relationship to the pâté or to the McKells," she said.

He grinned. "If it was the village square in Kellburgh, it has a lot to answer for. My parents met there too." His forehead drew into a frown. "But ye say ye didn't know about the legacy yer mother saved for ye?"

"I didn't. I'm not convinced there's anything in it. I'll go through Gran's box for her sake. It seemed to be important to her I find it. In fact, with your height, you can help me to get the box. Come on," she said, placing her mug on the coffee table and taking his hand.

She led him along the corridor which split the house in two. Her grandmother's room was the first on the right. The room was waiting for Isla if ever she should return. Cat opened the wardrobe door, emitting a fragrance of cedar and lavender. She looked into the shelf her grandmother always referred to as the hatbox.

"Oh, there are two boxes. Get them both please."

He withdrew a large plastic tub and a smaller shoebox. He placed them both on the double bed.

Flicking open the lid of the larger box, Cat stopped. Staring at her was a life-sized photograph of her with her mother, their faces in profile, laughing at each other. Her mother appeared happy, brimming with life.

A hand flew to her mouth, and tears spurted from her eyes. "Mumma!"

She was dragged into Lachie's firm embrace. "Wheesht there, lassie." His hand rubbed up and down her spine.

Resting her head and hand against his chest, sensations lit her body. Her heart was mourning her mother. The rest of her was on high alert, wanting, needing more of this man.

His body wrapped around her, arching her closer. Everything stopped. His face lowered to hers like she'd pulled him by a string. She strained onto her toes to meet him, her mind wholly on him now.

A strident ring emanating from his trouser pocket sent them springing back from each other. Retrieving the phone, he answered with an abrupt, "Aye?"

Cat was able to hear the voice on the other end as though the phone was on speaker.

"It's James Gallien, sir. It's on. Sopworthy has sought an injunction against Miss Cameron leaving the country and against her making the pâté for sale anywhere in the world. Our team has countered, asking for mediation. If it works, we may be able to head off a court battle. We'll need your input on this, sir."

"Where are ye now?"

"In my office, sir."

"I'll come to ye. I'll be there in ten or fifteen minutes." He flicked the button to finish the call. "I have to go deal with this."

"Uh-huh." Cat grasped her hands behind her back feeling like she'd been caught with her hand in the lolly jar. She tilted her chin, willing it not to wobble. Damn Charles Sopworthy. Was he seriously going to destroy her?

Lachie's eyes burned into hers, dark and shadowy. "Shite!" He hauled her back into his arms, slamming his mouth on top of hers almost lifting her off her feet.

She clung to him for dear life, giving back as good as she got. The kiss lasted moments but it lightened her heart. She was not alone in this.

He let her slide back onto her soles and held her steady. "Ah lass, I'm thinking I should have asked first."

"Probably. I'm sure you'll remember next time." She twitched one eyebrow.

A broad grin lit his face. "Aye, I will." He pulled her into a tight hug, released her, then walked out the door.

6

Chapter Six

Lachie strode into the lobby of the building where James kept his offices. He was unconcerned the hour was one where normal people were already gone for the day. James's work revolved around international clients, and his hours reflected those constraints.

Riding the lift to the forty-fourth floor, Lachie exhaled in a huge calming sigh. The trip to Australia was intended to be quick, not one wrapped around by legal issues associated with the pâté. He'd certainly not considered he'd fall for the lass his aunts sent him to find.

Such a lass she was. He'd had his share of women over the years, even married one. None rocked him to his core as she did. The scene he'd just left? If the phone hadn't rung, things might have been different. The way her body aligned with his in all the right places, the intoxication of her mouth, the proximity of the bed…it was too soon. He needed her help. To get it, he must keep his hormones on a short leash until the extraneous matters were handled.

Stepping from the lift, he found James waiting. "What do we have?"

"Charles Sopworthy is claiming the girl developed the pâté recipe when she was working for him. She provided the basic recipe, he says, but he has provided the research and development to get it to the point where it is a much-desired product line in his shop. Sopworthy wants recompense and to make sure the girl is prevented from leaving the country until these matters are settled. He is also demanding

47

she not be able to produce the product for anybody else, anywhere in the world."

"The girl has a name."

"Apologies, sir. Miss Cameron, I mean."

Lachie nodded, staring at the sheet of paper James handed him.

"Shite! How do we fight his ultimatums? Miss Cameron's recipe has been in the family since the early eighteen hundreds."

"Can you prove it? Is there a two-hundred-year-old paper somewhere with the information written on it?"

"My understanding is the women decided if it wasn't written anywhere, there was no chance for it to be stolen."

"Ah, we might have a problem then."

"Shite! Shite, shite, shite." Lachie let loose a heavy sigh. "But he can't prevent her from traveling, surely?"

"His claim is she intends to travel to Scotland expressly to start your pâté manufacture again. She said she wanted to visit her family, but Sopworthy didn't buy it. He knows who you are, sir."

"How the hell would he know me?"

"He follows the business pages, domestic and international. There was quite a splash when your wife died—about how she ran the pâté side of the business, sir. There's been a fair bit of commentary, then and since, on what it would mean for McKells, and how Simone's Pâté isn't the same premium standard it once was. I think Sopworthy was planning to waltz into the vacuum with Miss Cameron's product."

"But she would never tell him how she made it, because it's secret!" Lachie heard the level of his own voice rising. He strove to calm himself. Good decisions were not made under stress. "Right then. What's next?"

"Our legal team expect to be able to get an out-of-sessions order for mediation. If they can do it, we might be in mediation tomorrow or Friday. Would your girl be ready?"

"Miss Cameron is not my girl, James." *At least, not yet.* "She's an intelligent woman and she knows the provenance of the recipe. She's angry Sopworthy is implying she stole the recipe from him. Aye, she'll be fine. When ye have some details around the hearing, let me know. I'll talk to her." He turned to leave and pivoted back. "What does mediation mean in this country? Is it binding?"

"Well, no. It's the first step in the process. A mediator is appointed. He or she tries to get both sides of the dispute to consider the other's point of view. Sometimes, it's enough for one party to walk away. I don't think that's likely here, sir, unless Miss Cameron agrees to give him the recipe and not to make it commercially available elsewhere."

"Not going to happen," Lachie growled.

"If mediation fails, there are two courses of action. One is arbitration, where the arbitrator determines the facts of the case, without it going to court. My understanding is their decision is binding, though they're limited in what they can demand. The alternative is a court process which may be a drawn-out and expensive battle. My fear is Sopworthy will take that route. If we can show he has been uncooperative in the earlier stages, it will play well for us in the court room. There are no guarantees."

"Shifty little buggar."

"Yes, sir." James grinned.

"Can we go straight to court?"

"If we tried, it's more likely the magistrate will send us back to mediation or arbitration before hearing it in court. It's better, I think, sir, to show we have tried every option prior to taking it to the magistrate's court. It should provide a smoother path. The legal team may be able to book a court date in case mediation fails. I can't be sure. The process will not be quick, sir."

"I do have a business to run, James, back in Scotland." Lachie ran one hand through his red mane.

"Yes, sir. Would you feel comfortable leaving us to work with Miss Cameron?"

Lachie hesitated, weighing the options. "I have no doubt yer team can handle whatever comes, but Miss Cameron has no family around her. I'll stay at least until I can arrange for one of my sisters to come. Iona is our marketing manager. She understands both the history of the pâté and the impact its loss is having on our bottom line. I think she and Catriona would like each other."

"Yes, sir."

Lachie folded the piece of paper James gave him earlier and slipped it into his inside jacket pocket.

~ * ~

"Come on, Iny. Ye'll like her. She's sweet and feisty, and she only has the support of her grandmother, who has dementia." His phone call to his sister, Iona, was not going well.

"Great. What sort of mad house are ye inviting me into, Lachie? It's not like ye to care this much beyond the business. Are ye interested in her?"

"Umm…"

"If ye are, it better be because of who she is, not because she's a *Simone*. That sort of thinking already dragged ye through hell once. Next time ye decide to take a wife, make sure it's for the right reasons, not for the sake of the business, right? Ah hell. I have to come to Australia now, to make sure ye're not digging yerself into some hole."

"Thanks for the vote of confidence there."

"No need to sound pissed off. Ye know I love ye. Us, yer family, we love ye because ye're our brother. If ye were as tough with needy women as y'are in business, we wouldn't worry for ye so much. Sometimes, ye're too soft. Women, like the one ye married, use ye for who ye are. They land ye with a bairn who's not yers, and yet ye look after them."

Lachie could almost see the frustration on his sister's face.

She heaved a heavy sigh. "Okay, tell me more. Let me know what I'm in for."

It was the cue he needed. His sister might think he was a soft touch, but she was too. He recounted the history of Cat's family, along with their links to the McKells and the pâté.

"When Rhona came to Australia, she continued the pâté tradition. Rhona taught Isla, Isla taught her daughter, Jeanette. Together, they taught Catriona."

"Hang on, ye said there was only the grandmother. Where's the mother?"

"She passed away with cancer seven years ago. Then Isla developed signs of dementia. Cat's had it pretty rough for a while now."

"Cat, huh? Ye do care for her."

"I'll ignore that. She made some pâté to take to a work function. The boss liked it and asked her to make some for the café. It's been a pretty significant hit there by all accounts. There's where the trouble starts. Because she was making it to sell in his shop exclusively, the owner is claiming he has rights to the recipe. He's taken an injunction to stop her leaving the country or from producing the pâté for sale anywhere in the world."

"Was she planning to leave the country?"

"I'd told her about our workers. She agreed to visit Kellburgh to meet them for herself. She doesn't trust Scots much. She was raised on horror stories of Dallin and Dougal. Her own father, a Cameron, left before she was born."

"That's one hell of a generalization, to lump every Scot into one basket!"

"It's what people do, don't we? Look at the way the Scots have regarded the English, or how Americans see Muslims as terrorists."

"I suppose…"

"James Gallien reckons this Sopworthy character knows McKells. He knows who I am. It's why he's trying to play hard ball. James thinks Sopworthy might have recognized me straight off when I went into the café to find Cat." Lachie tapped the fingers of one hand on the side of his leg.

"A strategic error, then," Iona mused.

"Why on earth should I anticipate anyone in Melbourne would recognize me?"

"It does seem a bit far-fetched. What do ye want me to do?"

"Be her support. Ye know our business and ye know the pâté," Lachie said.

"I won't play matchmaker. Ye'll appreciate I'm more likely to tell her to stay away from ye."

"That's not the important thing here. What is important is getting the recipe back to Kellburgh."

"It's a pity she can't give you the recipe, or me, for that matter."

"Aye, but it's not the way the legacy works, is it? The *Simone* must be a direct female descendant through the female lines from Simone de Salignac. It doesn't matter who the father is, so long as the *Simone* is the daughter of a daughter of a daughter right the way back to de Salignac herself."

"We've all the trappings of a secret society cult." Iona's laugh gurgled across the line.

"It is something similar. If we lose Catriona's recipe, we're done. She's the last."

"All right, I'll come. Ye can arrange accommodation for me?"

"I have a suite with two bedrooms. Ye can stay here," Lachie said.

"Fine. It won't matter when I arrive. I'll be there by Sunday."

7

———————

Chapter Seven

On Friday morning, Cat answered the knock on her door to find Lachie waiting. There was tension in his muscled body and determination in his eyes. She wanted to drag him into the house to continue with the interrupted kiss. There was a primal need in her that responded to this man as it did to no other. She wanted to find a way to explore it further. She blinked, finally tuning into his words.

"I thought we might drive in together," he said.

She chuckled. "You could have walked around the corner from your hotel. You'd have been there in three minutes."

"Aye, but I wouldn't have the pleasure of yer company. Ye look different. I like the business suit." He flicked his eyebrows.

His accompanying half-smile tightened her chest as though she was out of breath. "I needed something to boost my confidence," she said. "When you told me the mediation attempt was going to happen, I searched my wardrobe."

"And, let me guess, ye didn't have a thing to wear." His eyes glowed with laughter.

"Don't be sarcastic, Lachie. It doesn't suit you." She rolled her eyes and giggled. "Really, my clothes are suitable for working in the café, which also means okay for going to the movies or casual stuff. There was nothing there remotely suitable for a serious business discussion. I needed new shoes, handbag, everything. I haven't been shopping for myself in ages. I enjoyed it." Although the spending spree stretched her finances, it was worth it. Today might be a turning point in her life. She wanted to feel in control.

"The dentist would be more fun than clothes shopping." Lachie grimaced.

"It's lucky I didn't invite you then. And just for the record, my dentist is wonderful, and I never mind going to see her. I'm ready to go."

He led the way to the car, holding the door for her to get in. "Do ye know what ye're going to say?"

"I went onto a website to look for advice on what I needed to prepare. I found it straight forward. It said to think about the outcome I wanted. I want Charles to acknowledge the recipe is mine and he has no claim to it. The other advice was to prepare my story and stick to the facts. I emailed my statement to James last night, as requested. We can only wait to see how it goes."

"Have ye considered what ye will do if Sopworthy gets his way?"

"In the end, they can't get inside my head where the knowledge is. It's not something I can write easily. Every day is different. Every batch has a slightly different outcome. The recipe on its own doesn't take account of the preparation. You can't record those bits and pieces."

"The difficulty will be convincing others. Be prepared for the opposition to be nasty."

"I wouldn't have thought it a week ago. Charles's tantrum on Monday changed everything."

"Where would be the best place to park?"

"Back at your hotel. The venue is five hundred meters max from there, and parking is at a premium around the top end of Collins Street."

"Ye're the boss."

They walked through Collins Place to the Exhibition Street corner and waited at the lights to cross the street. She saw Charles flanked by two serious-looking men, turning into the building she and Lachie had as their destination.

"There's Charles," she said.

"Catriona? Ye've gone pale. Ye're shaking like a leaf. Do ye want to go sit inside for a while? We have time. I'll ring our people, they can meet us here." Lachie pulled out his phone. "Good morning, James. Catriona and I will catch up with ye in Collins Place for coffee ahead of the meeting. Yes, we saw him arrive. Thanks." He flicked the phone into his pocket. "Can I leave ye, lass, while I order the coffee?" She gripped her hands in her lap and nodded.

When he returned, he took one of her hands in his and held her gaze. "Ye're a mighty warrior, lass. Don't let this piece of shite intimidate ye. Stand tall. Ye've the mighty army of yer Scottish ancestry behind ye."

The imagery his words evoked straightened her spine. "Thanks Lachie." She chuckled, squeezing his hand. "Standing tall is a bit of a stretch when you're my height."

Lachie grinned and settled in his chair, keeping hold of her hand.

James arrived moments later with another spare-looking man in tow.

"Good morning, sir. Miss Cameron, this is Phillip Walker. He'll speak for you when you can't. Sopworthy has Troy Baxter with him, sir. Troy Baxter! For a mediation hearing."

"Who is Troy Baxter?" Lachie asked.

"He's likely Melbourne's top senior counsel, no offence to Phillip here."

"No offence taken. Miss Cameron, may I have a word, please?" Phillip nodded seriously.

"Lass, are ye okay to talk to Phillip?" Lachie asked.

"Certainly."

"James and I will be close by. Ah, the coffee." Lachie acknowledged the waiter who arrived with a tray of mugs each labelled with a well-known coffee brand. "I wasn't sure what yer preferences were gentlemen. They're long black all round. Ye can add milk at the counter."

Lachie lifted a cup for himself and took it to a table several meters away where James joined him.

Phillip sipped the hot drink in front of him, grimaced, and set it aside. Cat sat beside him with her hands around the mug.

"I read your piece, Miss Cameron. Do you have any questions on how today will run?"

"I'm a total novice. I don't even know what questions to ask you. Please, call me Catriona or Cat."

He inclined his head. "I will. You should call me Phillip, except when we're in mediation. We use surnames in the formal setting. Now," he leaned forward, "when we get into the meeting room, you will each be asked to state your case or the story in your own terms. The other team will try to cast their story in as convincing light as they can. They might not offer the whole truth. It's a ruse to get you to react, but you won't. You will hold your nerve. You can make notes of any errors you find and we can address them later. Sit straight. Look interested. Show no fear."

He punctuated the words by patting the table with a clenched fist.

"If the mediator asks who would like to go first, stay silent. We want to hear the other side ahead of you putting your case, if possible. If the other side offers 'ladies first', your response will be, 'oh no, age before beauty', or some other diversion." He tapped an index finger on his bottom lip. "Remember, they're trying to psych you out. Think like boxers at a weigh in. They're each trying to do psychological damage to the other prior to getting into the ring. Do you understand what I'm saying? Is Mr. Sopworthy the only one who knows you?"

"I believe so. He was my employer."

"Then be prepared for him to use it to his advantage." Phillip crossed his arms on the small table. "He'll aim to put you into an inferior position. He'll comment on your clothes, your shoes, even your makeup; anything to cause you to doubt yourself. You have the upper hand here. You are the one in the right. You have the McKell on your side and that's saying a lot. And, you have me."

It was the first time she saw any crack in the serious face in front of her. She relaxed, exhaling. "Of course, thank you."

"Fifteen minutes to show time. Let's go."

When they arrived at the venue, a bureau staff member showed them into a sizable anteroom and addressed Cat. "This is your room for the day, Miss Cameron. When you're ready, you can use this door to go into the meeting room. Your session is due to commence in five minutes."

"Thank you."

The woman nodded her response and left the room.

"Sit quietly. Read your statement, Catriona. Don't allow yourself to be rushed."

She smiled her thanks at Phillip and took a chair against the only window in the room. Reading the document and rehearsing the nuances of the presentation in her head, she moved one hand to her midriff to calm the horde of malevolent insects buzzing around in there.

When she'd finished reading it through, she stood, letting her hand drop to her side. She smiled at the men in turn. "All righty. This should be fun."

He led the way into the mediation room, followed by Catriona. Lachie held a hand at her back, his fingers stiff with tension. It would be easy to fall back on his strength, but this was her fight.

Conversation in the room came to an abrupt halt when they entered.

Charles's voice broke the silence. "Looky, looky. What do we have here? Little Miss Priss, all dressed up. Don't think fancy clothes will get you far, girlie."

Her gaze shot to meet Phillip's. He winked. She giggled and took her seat. The smile was still on her face when the mediator walked in.

The middle-aged woman wore a floral skirt and pastel pink blouse, and exuded calm. "Good morning, everyone. My name is Gabrielle Simpson. My goal today is to help you come to an agreement around the outcome of this dispute. If we can manage it, you won't have to take any further action."

"It's a waste of time," Charles' voice growled from the other side of the table.

"We'll see. Now, let's go around the table. Please introduce yourselves and your role in these proceedings."

With the introductions completed, Gabrielle asked Cat if she would like to present her case. Cat demurred. "I'm okay, thanks. Mr. Sopworthy likes to have the first poke. I'll cede to him." She spoke with a smile and gestured with a flowing raised palm to the group opposite.

Sopworthy's face bloomed bright red, and his eyes blazed with anger.

Gabrielle said, "You have the floor Mr. Sopworthy, proceed."

"You're going to let her get away with what she said?" he demanded.

"Please don't raise your voice. I have no idea what you mean, Mr. Sopworthy. Would you like to explain?"

"No, I would not."

"Then please continue with your statement," the mediator ordered.

Charles stated he hired Catriona five years ago. She was a lost soul whose mother died, plus she was caring for her elderly grandmother. He took her under his wing, teaching her how to make everything from eclairs to baklava. He also taught her how to make pâté.

He continued to work with her, he said, to develop the flavor to the point where it was now in high demand in the café. She told him she wanted to go to Scotland to visit her family. He feared the McKells would exploit her, beguiling her into producing his pâté to fill their line. He was aware the sales of McKell's Simone's Pâté had fallen dramatically in the last year. In the end, he wanted what was best for dear Catriona—for her to stay in Melbourne and continue to work with him.

Gabrielle nodded. "Thank you, Mr. Sopworthy. Miss Cameron, are you ready to continue?"

"Yes, thank you, Ms. Simpson. May I address Mr. Sopworthy's statements first, please? It is true he taught me to make eclairs and baklava. It is also true I was a bit lost at the time he hired me. I have no qualifications because I was caring for my mother for the last two years of her life at a time when other young women were heading to TAFE or university."

She drew a breath against the stab of pain caused by her mother's memory. "I appreciate Mr. Sopworthy was prepared to hire me despite it. What is not true is he taught me to make pâté. My mother, my grandmother, and my great-grandmother, when she was alive, taught me. Let me explain."

"Please do."

Cat shuffled in her seat. "All my life, I have watched my great-grandmother, my grandmother, and my mother make this pâté. They handled the ingredients with care. As soon as I was old enough, they allowed me to help. First by learning to operate the food mill my great-grandmother bought to replace the ancient sieve she'd brought with her from Scotland. Later I would sauté the livers under guidance, and finally I was instructed in how to handle the sharp knife required to trim the livers. They told me theirs was a secret recipe passed only to daughters in the family, and that I should never share it with anyone who was not my daughter. I never have."

Her teeth dug into her bottom lip, and she raised her chin. "About three years ago, I made a batch to take to a staff function Mr. Sopworthy arranged. He enjoyed it greatly and invited me to make some for the café. I did. It became a hit, with customers coming in regularly to request it. I made it at home in my own kitchen to take into work. I have never made it in the café's kitchen. I have never deviated from the recipe my forebears handed to me in trust."

She laid one hand flat on the tabletop, then brought it back to rest in her lap.

"When I met Mr. McKell earlier this week," she cast an open palm to where Lachie sat, "I became aware of a family I didn't know beyond my grandmother's stories. Those stories were not complimentary to my Scottish forebears. Until I met Mr. McKell, I also didn't understand the recipe predated my great-grandmother. He informed me the original recipe was devised by my ancestor, Comtesse Simone de Salignac, who decreed the lineage for the product. My mother told me the rightful recipe holder would be determined by having de Salignac as part of their name. I have, just as my mother, grandmother, and great-grandmother did. It's a provenance if you like." She smiled.

"I met Mr. McKell's great-aunts when they were visiting

Melbourne and came into the café." Cat glanced at Lachie, drawing on his strength. "They recognized the flavor as Simone's. Their discovery is what brought Mr. McKell to Australia. When he explained I have a whole family who would like to meet me, I was hesitant at first. But my grandmother is my last living relative in Australia, and she has dementia. The excitement of having many more relatives persuaded me it couldn't hurt to travel to Scotland to meet them. When I conveyed my decision to Mr. Sopworthy, he flew into a rage, dismissed me from my job at the café, got one injunction to prevent me from leaving the country and, worse still, another to stop me from making the product that is the gift of my ancestors. Thank you."

"Mr. Sopworthy, what do you say?"

"It's a concoction of lies," he snarled. "I know the girl is a good cook. Now, I've found she is an effective spinner of tall tales, too. To think I've trusted her all these years."

"Your comments are not helpful, Mr. Sopworthy. What do you have to say to the argument Miss Cameron's recipe predated her employ with you?"

"It's a fabrication! I taught her how to make it. It's my recipe," Sopworthy said.

"Madam, if I may?" Phillip interjected.

"Yes, Mr. Walker."

"If Mr. Sopworthy devised the recipe and taught it to Miss Cameron, why can he not produce the pâté himself? It would surely pre-empt Miss Cameron selling an exclusive product elsewhere."

"Of course, it's possible, but why keep a dog and do your own barking? Or bitch, in this case," Charles snapped.

"Mr. Sopworthy, if you continue with these statements, I'll terminate these proceedings."

"Suits me. Let's take it to court." He stood and stormed from the room.

"I apologize for my client, Miss Simpson. Thank you for your time. It appears we'll be escalating this to the magistrate's court." Troy Baxter's urbane tone was condescending.

"Mr. Baxter, my report will reflect your client was not cooperative. The magistrate's court will take a dim view of your client jettisoning mediation and foregoing arbitration too."

"I'm not a fool, madam. We feel we have a compelling case. In my client's view, taking it straight to the courts will be the most expeditious channel to have the matter resolved."

"Very well, Mr. Baxter. You've been warned. Good day."

Sopworthy's supporters shuffled from the room. Gabrielle continued, "I'm sorry the mediation was not productive for you, Miss Cameron. If the matter goes to court, which appears likely, you're going to have to provide proof this was a long-held secret recipe. Can you? Is it recorded anywhere? Are there photos? Any exchanges between you and your forebears? I'd advise you to muster as much concrete evidence as you can."

"Thank you. I don't know. I'll search my grandmother's things to find what I can."

"Do it. Anything further, Mr. Walker?"

"Thank you, madam. We have nothing further other than to thank you for your time today. It is appreciated."

"We'll take this back to my suite." Lachie spoke for the first time since they'd entered the mediation meeting room. Cat was aware of him throughout the proceedings as though he wrapped some invisible cloak of energy around her. To be honest, she'd surprised herself with her composed presentation. She'd expected to be a bundle of nerves. The quiet calm exuded by Phillip and by Lachie rubbed off on her.

She was in the right here. If Charles wanted to take it to court, so be it. She could, and would, win this battle.

8

Chapter Eight

Lachie was more than a little frustrated with the outcome of the morning's work. Cat's calm confidence, a warrior queen holding herself in check, had been the single positive. She was less serene now. He rubbed her back to soothe her. At least it was the explanation he gave himself. Really, he'd take any excuse to touch her. The private smile she sent him was hot. She knew what he was doing, it seemed. He loved her for it. He hoped she'd be able to sustain her strength through the next battle of the war.

He stepped away from Catriona to address the lawyer. "What do we do now, Phillip? Do we need James to take notes?"

The spare man folded himself into an armchair and steepled his fingers under his chin. "I think James can relax for a while. As far as what comes next, we have two options. The first is we sit back and wait for them to file a complaint in the magistrates' court, then respond to their summons. It will be what they're expecting us to do. I don't think they'll be in any hurry. Miss Cameron can't work until the matter is resolved. Any potential employer would contact Sopworthy for a reference, and he would not be complimentary. It's pointless for her even to try to find a job. Sopworthy is aware she's caring for her grandmother and will need cash. The longer the matter drags out, the sooner she is likely to cave in to their demands and surrender the recipe—hypothetically, Catriona."

"The second option?"

"We file a complaint against Sopworthy for undue pressure, attempting to apply a restraint of trade on Miss Cameron. We become the complainant, Sopworthy the defendant. We set the agenda. We apply for a court date, and we move forward at the pace we set." Phillip shrugged.

"Taking charge ourselves sounds like the better course. When can we get started?" Lachie asked.

"It's not a smooth ride. The mediator was correct. We must have proof, or some supporting evidence." He glanced at Cat. "Catriona is in the right here. But we can't be the complainant if there is nothing to complain about. As soon as we have a strong case we can defend, with substantiation, we can advance the process."

"Did ye find anything in yer grandmother's box, lass?" Lachie turned his attention to her.

"I haven't looked. I've walked past Gran's room a dozen times but..." She divested herself of her suit jacket as she spoke, revealing the blouse molded to her body.

Lachie cleared his throat, dragging himself back into his sharp business mode. "I can give ye a hand. If we find anything, we can try it on yer grandmother this afternoon."

"Um, it might work. But if I call time, you have to respect my decision."

"I get it is an emotional roller coaster for ye. Ye must set yer feelings aside. This is business. This man wants to paint ye into the corner, to label ye a thief and a saboteur. Ye must have the strength to fight back," he said.

"I'm not going to rush this. It would be as bad as dancing to their tune in the way Phillip has outlined."

"Shite. What don't ye understand here?"

"Lachie, have you ordered refreshment? It seems to be taking a long time to get here. I'm absolutely parched," Phillip said.

Flinging a furious glance at the senior counsel, Lachie stomped away to pick up the telephone handset while keeping an ear to what was being said around him.

"You did well in there this morning, Catriona. Your voice was calm and measured, and your giggle right at the beginning put Sopworthy off a bit."

"Thanks to you. If you hadn't primed me, I would have taken his jibes to heart. Because he followed the script you anticipated, almost word for word, it made me laugh."

"Hmm. What was the 'poke' comment about?"

She frowned. "About a year ago, a new girl started in the café in the afternoons. Charles said it was so those who started early were able to get off at a reasonable time. She was a lovely kid, with a well-rounded figure and, I must admit, was sexy without needing to flaunt it. I'd been in the alley and came back through the kitchen door. Charles and the chef at the time were standing together looking at the girl as she was working, making smutty comments about her hips, her breasts, et cetera. I don't need to tell you guys the way men talk about women." She cast a glance to the ceiling.

"I would hope, Catriona, the men in this room would not conduct themselves in such a manner." Phillip looked affronted.

"Right, you're angels. Sorry, I shouldn't be sarcastic. I don't know any of you well enough to jump to conclusions. Anyway, the shitty little chef flexed his pelvis, declaring he wouldn't mind giving her a good poke. Charles responded the chef could do what he liked after he'd had the first go."

"And then?"

"I went in and, in my best 'grandmother being superior' voice, informed them I noted their conversation in relation to a child under sixteen. If I heard anyone poked the girl, or indeed any staff member, I'd be the first witness for the police. Charles swore at me and said it was just fun. What bothered me is the girl this one replaced left the previous week in tears. She wouldn't tell me why. She'd only been working there ten days or so. This conversation gave me an inkling into what might have prompted her departure. I was angry. I told them if they wanted a poke, they should go poke each other." She firmed her lips.

"Ah-hah, and the word hit him like a cannon ball when you said it." Phillip smiled. "It didn't mean anything to anyone apart from him so no one else reacted. It caught him off guard. He wasn't expecting you to do anything other than be passive this morning. For you to open with a salvo, well, it put him off his stride. He might have regarded it as a threat, or a warning you knew things he didn't want made public. Well done. It worked today, but it won't work in court. Ah, here's the coffee. Thank you, James. How are things going in Scotland, Lachie?"

"There's the problem. I have a business that won't run itself for much longer."

"Surely you have people who can manage in your absence?"

"Aye. I do, to a degree. Iona is the marketing manager and she does a good job. The guys in production are a bit soft, though, when it comes to getting things finished, orders checked, goods dispatched. Iona will be on her way here soon to give us some help with any arguments we choose to build around the way the pâté business is hurting us, meaning two of us will be unavailable."

"Who is Iona?"

"She's my little sister, lass. Didn't I mention her?"

"You said you have twin sisters. You didn't give me their names. Phillip," she swung her gaze from Lachie toward the lawyer, "what are we looking for amongst Gran's things? If I have a focus, I might be able to set aside the emotional stuff. If I find a photo of my mum, say, with nothing to do with pâté, I can leave it and not be a blubbering mess twenty times in an hour."

"You're on the right track there. If you have photos of you making pâté with your mother or whomever, or letters referring to it, anything will help. If the recipe has never been put to paper, we would need to find some way to verify what you make is the same pâté McK-ells produced, for example. We also need someone who knows this stuff. Not some random person who likes the taste of yours. Someone who can be sure it is the same recipe."

"My great-aunts," Lachie said. "They're both national judges. They recognized the flavor of Catriona's pâté when they were here."

"Can you get them to Australia?" Phillip asked.

"I'll phone Iona now. She'll organize it if she hasn't left already."

"Make sure they can prove their credentials if possible. Are there any independent judges? Australians perhaps?"

"The aunts would know."

"I've done what I can for now." Phillip stood. "When you have sup-porting evidence, contact me. We can file from there. Make sure it's watertight. Have a good weekend, everyone."

"'Bye, Phillip."

Lachie's gut clenched at the smile Catriona sent the lawyer as he left the suite. Instead of letting go of the snarl hovering at the back of his throat, he swiveled to James.

"Since Iona will be here by Monday, can ye make sure there are meetings arranged for her with potential outlets and on-sellers? In fact, I'll leave it to ye to contact her. Tell her what happened today and ask her to bring the aunts if they're willing. Check what accommoda-tion they prefer and get it organized too, please."

"That's not what my job usually involves, sir, but I'll handle it."

"Good man." Feeling calmer now he'd dispatched tasks to be com-pleted, Lachie turned to Catriona. "Let's go. We'll get back to yer place to get the search started. Ye're chewing your lip again, lass. What's bothering ye?"

"Um, I think I want to do this on my own. Give me a couple hours to see how I do. You can come by at three o'clock, say. If I haven't made progress, you can help."

"It would go faster with us both."

"Mmm, there's the trouble. I don't want it to go faster. I prefer to have the time to sit with them, to feel the ghosts if you like. They'll guide me to the information. We can go to visit Gran later."

"Okay. I'll give ye a lift home, then."

"Um, I'll take the tram. It'll be quicker. By the time you call for your car to be brought from the parking garage, I'll be home. Thanks anyway."

She gathered her jacket and handbag. "I'll see you later. 'Bye, James."

"Goodbye, Miss Cameron."

She was putting distance between them. Lachie didn't like it but there wasn't much he could do. He satisfied himself with the reminder he'd be with her again in a few hours.

"She's an independent sort, isn't she?" James said.

"She surely is." Like the women before her, she was feisty but fair, not one to stand for injustice, and when she fell in love, she'd fall heavily. He'd have to make sure he was the man standing in front of her when it happened.

9

Chapter Nine

Cat breathed deeply of the Melbourne air. Though not necessarily fresh in the midst of the central business district, it was not as testosterone heavy as the room she'd left.

She recognized they were fighting with her and for her, but sheesh, she needed to breathe.

It was just her luck her tram pulled away from the stop in the middle of Collins Street just as she emerged from the hotel's driveway. She sat on the metal seat inside the clear Perspex shelter, resting her head against the back wall.

It had been a stressful day, albeit an anti-climactic one. The worst was yet to come, if the blokes upstairs knew their stuff. She glanced at the hotel building across the street. If there was any movement on the fiftieth floor, she was too far away to make it out.

A dinging bell drew her attention to an approaching tram. Although this one wouldn't go past her door, she'd be close enough. She boarded, burrowing her way through the crush of people already standing inside, and found a swinging overhead handle to grasp.

The ride was quick, and then it was a short walk home. She contemplated the task ahead, slowing her footsteps. There was a reason she'd been avoiding the box. It hurt. The memories lashed, like a whip on bare skin, slicing into her.

Her great-grandmother was already old when Cat was born. To

Cat, she was an angel. Little Gran lived at Gran's house, a fair step away from where Cat lived with her mother. Whenever visits happened between the two homes, Little Gran made sure Cat was cherished.

She would sit for hours telling stories of Scotland, how beautiful the land, how special the people. She held her lilting burr till she died. Whenever Cat heard it, it seemed as if Little Gran was in the next room. The appearance of Lachie's great-aunts in the café had the same effect, reminding her of her sweet great-grandmother.

There'd be memories of Little Gran in the box. Maybe she held the answers.

Cat accelerated her pace.

The boxes were waiting on Gran's bed, just as she'd left them. The photo of her mother and herself confronted her again as if defying her to venture further. She sat on her grandmother's bed staring at it.

There was so much love locked into the image on the glossy paper. It took her back to the hot, sunny day on St Kilda Beach. The salt tang in the air bit her lips and her mother's laugh rang out as she struggled in vain to control her hair whipped by the breeze. Cat smiled in salute to the happy memories of the day even as a tear leaked from the corner of her eye.

It was right for her to do this alone. No one else would understand, except Gran maybe. Not someone who'd never met her mother, studied her wry wit, or been held in her ever-loving arms. She set the photo aside.

Cat dragged the box nearer, hauling out a handful of papers, skimming them. She ordered them into family photos, pictures of people she didn't recognize, bank statements, letters, and "unknown."

Once she set her categories, she disbursed the contents of the box into their respective piles without thinking twice. There was nothing there that spoke of pâté or the McKells, unless the pile of "unknown" held some hidden gems.

She moved on to the shoe box. This was packed with letters, some in her mother's handwriting. She pulled one out. Addressed to her great-grandmother, it held a photo of Catriona as a two-year old. The inscription on the back read, *Catriona Alyce, Simone of the 21st century, aged two.* Her mother knew about the *Simones.* Why hadn't she told Cat?

Returning to the box, she focused primarily on the mail addressed to Little Gran. Most held photos of Cat in various childish poses or pursuits, including one where she'd tried to learn ballet when she started school. Cat and ballet did not make a successful partnership. She'd long ago relegated those memories to the mists of things best forgotten.

She opened an envelope with yet another photo of herself. This one was pay dirt. Startled from her study of it, she raced the length of the house and flung the door wide open to find Lachie frowning at her.

"Ye've been crying, lass."

"Have I? I didn't notice." She dragged one hand across her face to smooth away the moisture. "I think I've found the proof we need. What do you think?" She handed him the photo of herself standing on a wooden box at the stove stirring something in a pan.

"It might be anything."

"Until you turn it over. *Our little Simone—her first attempt to sauté livers for the pâté. Aged seven years.* Will this do?"

His face softened into a broad smile. "I think it's a good start, lass. Do ye have any more?"

"Come with me. Take a look. The shoe box was full of letters. Some from my mother to my great-grandmother, others between Gran and Mum. I haven't finished going through them yet. Only a few relate to the pâté. A lot have images of me growing up. If you take the photo you're holding, although it says *Simone*, really, it's me...*Simone* is a code for something else. Maybe it's a place to start with Gran this afternoon. If she can confirm that *Simone* is who or what we think it is, we're on the right track," she said.

"We know what *Simone* means, lass. I've told ye who the *Simones* are."

"I'd never heard about it until you came. I need to be reassured it's real, not something my family made up. For example, what if Rhona wasn't a *Simone* but she desperately wanted to be? When she came to Australia, what was to stop her from creating herself as a *Simone*?" Cat shrugged her shoulders close to her ears.

"Not many people are aware of the *Simones'* story. Our customers, even our workers, would only think it's a brand name we conjured. They wouldn't think it applied to a person. The *Simones* have kept a tight rein on the knowledge." His tone was matter-of-fact, as though he was trying to keep her grounded rather than succumbing to imaginary obstacles.

"You know," she insisted.

"Because I run the business."

"Your sister knows, too, and your great-aunts."

"Iona knows because she has to handle the marketing. She's trying to find an acceptable reason to give our customers for why the pâté's flavor has changed. The customers want the original recipe back. It's Iona's job to appease them until we can find it." He massaged his cheek with the palm of his hand. "My great-aunts understand Simone was an ancestor, not someone who is here now. They think it's a recipe we've lost. Prior to marrying McKell brothers, they were outsiders. Alethea and Elspeth recognized the pâté ye made as one made from the Simone recipe rather than a *Simone* who made it."

"So, will any of this help? If we can't tell people a *Simone* is a person, how do we handle it?"

"We keep it as a recipe. We follow along the line of ye making the pâté to Simone's recipe, and so yer forebears called ye Simone for a bit of a joke, like."

"I'll go to visit Gran with these photos. She might be able to tell me who the people are and if they're relevant to what we're trying to establish."

"The car is right outside."

"Thank you. If you stop at the supermarket on the way, I'll buy more sweets. Did I thank you for getting some the other day? How did you find them?"

"I didn't. I went for a hunt in the shops nearby without any luck. I asked the receptionist at the hotel. She knew what I meant right away. By coincidence, she had some she was taking home to her children and kindly let me have them. Ye don't get such service at home."

Her heart swelled. That he should go to such bother for her Gran was special. She placed one hand on his chest without thinking. "Thank you."

His hand moved to cover hers. "Nothing to thank me for, lass. It's my pleasure."

She smoothed her fingers over his shoulder as her heart did the two-step thing again. "Thank you, anyway."

"Don't tempt me, minx. If we don't leave this room now, I may not be responsible for what comes next."

"Ah, right," she conceded with a slow smile, acknowledging the power she held over him, and turned back to the bed. Gathering half a dozen photos from the "unknown" pile, she stashed them in her handbag on the way to the car.

The second he unlocked the car, she opened her door.

"My job, lass."

"Hmm? Oh, the door. It's not necessary." She seated herself, changing the subject. "Tell me about Phillip. He seems like an impressive guy. A bit serious, then out of the blue, he gives me a wink to settle me. There must be a wicked humor lurking there somewhere."

"I don't know a lot. James recommended him, says he's one of the best senior counsels in Melbourne. I did some research using the usual channels and found he has an excellent track record for litigation, no red flags. Since I'm a visitor in this country, I have to let others take the running."

"Now I understand why you were quiet, but nowhere near calm in the meeting this morning." She grinned.

"What makes ye think I wasn't calm?"

"You have a tell."

He squashed his bottom lip against his teeth. "What did ye identify as my tell, lass?"

"Nope, not saying." She shook her head. "It's information I might need another time. If you know what it is, you can control it. There goes my advantage."

"Ye're a wicked one, aren't ye? What are others ye've noticed?"

"Charles pinches the inside of his wrist. James pulls his ear. Gabrielle flexes her jaw. It makes the muscles in her neck jump."

"Our mediator was stressed?"

"I don't know. The flexing began when Charles became obnoxious. Maybe she's not used to people challenging her in her mediations. Here's the shop. I'll be two minutes."

Lachie was holding the door for her by the time she returned. She made no comment and climbed in, enjoying the quiver passing through her as she brushed against his chest on the way. Even better was that his breath hitched with the contact.

When they arrived at the care home and were walking to Isla's room, she heard her name being called. She pirouetted in the direction of the voice, and a carer strode toward her.

"Catriona, Isla's not good today. She's been fidgety, even a bit aggressive. She keeps yelling, 'Where are they? Who stole them?' We don't know what she's missing."

"Thanks, Narelle. I'll try to find what the problem is."

Lachie and Cat turned into Isla's room to find her sitting in her usual spot, her fingers manically plucking at her trouser leg.

"Gran?"

The angry look on her sweet Gran's face startled Cat. "They took them away, and they won't give them back."

"What have they taken, Gran?" Cat asked.

Isla made jerky movements, imitating putting something in her mouth.

"Your chocolates?" She nodded.

"We've brought you some new ones. Will they do?" Cat opened a bag of sweets and handed it to her grandmother.

Taking one, Isla popped it in her mouth, heaved a great sigh, and settled back in her chair.

"Would you like me to ask someone about the sweets you're missing?"

"What's missing?" she asked.

"It doesn't matter." Cat handed Isla the photos. "Gran, do you recognize these people?"

She tucked the bag of chocolates between her thigh and the side of the chair and accepted the pile. "Yes."

"Can you tell me?"

Isla started singing, "I dream of…" She closed her eyes, and her head lolled to one side. Cat sat on the side of the bed while Lachie took the visitors' chair. As they waited, he retrieved his phone, appearing to check emails. She sat, allowing her body to relax into a state bordering on a trance.

After fifteen minutes, his deep voice attempted a whisper. "Should we let her be, maybe come back tomorrow?"

Isla's eyes flew open. "Catty, dear, hello."

"Hello Gran. How are you?"

"I'm well, thank you sweetheart. You've brought your young man with you again. How nice." Her hand fell on the bag of sweets she'd tucked away. "There they are. I couldn't find them earlier. Would you like one, dear?"

"No, thank you. Gran, can you tell me who these people are?"

"Oh dear, yes. There's my dear Jimmy with his brother, Max. Jimmy was your grandfather. Such a lovely man. He used to sing all the time. When your mum was born, he'd sing, 'Jeannie with the light brown hair.' I'd remind him her name was Jeanette. He'd laugh and keep on singing. Such a lovely, lovely man."

"This is Granddad, too?"

"Uh-huh. Who else do you have there? Oh my, I haven't seen this one in an age. These two are sisters, Elspeth and, um, let me think…"

"Let me see," Lachie demanded. "This is Elspeth and Alethea?"

"Alethea, yes."

"How did ye know them, Mrs. Jenkins?"

"Call me Gran, young man, since you're going to be part of the family." Isla appeared not to notice the bombshell she'd dropped in the room. Lachie's gaze met Cat's. *Smug.* She frowned at him, tuning into what her grandmother was saying.

"My mother's best friend was their mother, Ethna, was it? I think so. The girls wanted to travel to Australia before they married. Ethna asked mum to keep an eye on them. They came to stay with us for a few weeks. They were a bit older than me, but they included me in trips to the city and to Luna Park. Lovely girls. They married brothers, I think." Gran's posture slumped. In a wistful voice, she commented, "They'd be gone by now, I suppose. Everyone goes, Jimmy, little Jeannie. They all go. Gone to God."

"Alethea and Elspeth haven't gone yet, Gran. In fact, they might come to Melbourne again. Would ye like them to visit?" Lachie asked.

"Ooh, yes please, son. They were a lot of fun." She took another of her sweets.

His phone burred in his hand. Glancing at the screen, he rose to his feet. "I'll go outside to take this."

As he left the room, Cat leaned in to her grandmother and whispered, "Gran! What makes you think Lachie will be part of the family?"

"Your auras are connected, dear. Yours is whole when he is near. It won't be smooth sailing. There are troubles ahead for both of you. Be warned."

Gran's words sent a chill down Cat's spine as her predictions had a habit of being right. She'd apparently tried to warn Jeanette a life of loving Brad Cameron wouldn't be easy. Her vision was proven correct when Brad left once he learned Jeanette was pregnant. She'd predicted Cat's broken arm. She'd even expressed her doubts regarding Charles Sopworthy, though she'd never met him. Gran's predictions were not to be dismissed lightly.

"What sort of troubles?" Cat frowned.

"I don't know everything, sweetheart. It's not good for us to know everything. We have a journey to make. If we take shortcuts, we won't learn what we're meant to learn. It will be all right if you hold your nerve."

Lachie came back into the room. "They're coming. Elspeth and Alethea are on their way. They'll be here on Sunday."

"It's nice to have good news," Gran wiggled her shoulders and grinned broadly.

"It is, isn't it? Gran, why do the photos call me *Simone?*"

"I won't talk about *Simone.* It causes trouble. I think I'm tired now." Gran pursed her lips and flung her head into the back of her chair.

"Do you need anything, Gran?" There was nothing to be done once her grandmother closed a conversation. She knew from experience.

"I'm fine, petal. Will I see you tomorrow?"

"Tomorrow is Saturday. Would you like to go to the beach for lunch?" Cat placed one hand on her grandmother's.

"Can we get fish and chips at the café?" Gran pulled herself erect again.

"We sure can." "Great. I'm in. Bring the boy. He needs some sun." She chuckled at her own comment.

Cat hugged her and kissed her cheek. "Love you, Gran."

"Night, night, petal."

10

Chapter Ten

"Ye should give in to my charms now, ye know," Lachie said as they exited the facility.

"Listen buster, I'm not such a pushover. You want me, you fight for me. Understand? Though, you might not win. That's all I'm saying."

He pulled her into a one-armed hug. He wanted her like he'd wanted no one, ever. She was strong and feisty, and definitely not a pushover. She'd never be one to quail if he lost his cool, not like the timid girl he'd married. It would likely be him backtracking from her onslaught.

The idea of the McKell being forced on the back foot by anyone, let alone this sprite, made him grin. It hadn't happened yet. With her, there were new experiences around every corner. He hugged her harder and she wrapped an arm around his hips. Oh, the joys of a short woman. If she stretched her hand a little bit more—his body hardened at the image. Pulling his mind back to the reality of the moment, he stepped away from her and opened her car door.

They drove toward the city in companionable silence until he turned his face to her briefly. "What would ye like for dinner tonight?"

"I haven't given it a thought."

"Italian, French, Japanese?"

"There's an amazingly good Chinese restaurant upstairs in a laneway near your hotel," she said.

"Aye. Okay." He nodded.

"I'll need to change though."

"Ye look good to me." He grinned at her.

"The place I mean is upmarket. Seriously upmarket. Maybe it's a bad idea. We probably can't get in anyway, not on such short notice."

"Leave it to me. If it's as posh as ye're implying, I'd better get myself gussied up." Lachie's grin widened.

"Who says 'gussied up' in this world?" she said, with a giggle.

Her laughter hit him in the groin. He was going to have a rock-hard member if she kept it up.

"Business suit is fine. You don't need a tux or anything. I'll have to raid Gran's wardrobe for something decent. Or mum's, maybe."

"Ye still have yer mother's clothes? Hasn't she been gone seven years or so?"

"No one needs the room, so we haven't bothered to clear it out. I'm okay with it. Gran's okay with it. We don't have to answer to another living soul."

"Right, that's me told." He chuckled.

He pulled into her driveway and she scrambled from the car before he moved. "I'll come by at seven," he called.

"Thanks, I'll be ready." At least she smiled.

He pondered the depths of Catriona on his drive back to the hotel. She was straightforward in most things, but she was hesitant around anything to do with wealth, giving the impression she wasn't quite good enough, or she wouldn't fit in. He'd have to show her otherwise. If they were going to be together, she would live a privileged lifestyle. He didn't flaunt his wealth or take it for granted. He was who he was. It's the way things were.

He arrived to collect Catriona fifteen minutes before the hour. She was barefooted, dressed in a longish, flowing red dress snugly molding her breasts.

"Come in. I've found some mail addressed to Rhona, my great-grandmother, from someone called Ethna Salter. Is she the person

Gran referred to? Is she the mother of the two girls who visited? In the letters she says, 'No one needs to know, Dear Heart, you are keeping your family tradition alive. Your pâté is divine. I only wish you could teach me how to make it, but I'm not supposed to know, am I?' She goes on to talk about the girls coming to Australia. 'They'll take a train from Edinburgh to London and Southampton where they'll board the ship.' What do you think? Is this the magic bullet?"

"It may be, if we put it together so it makes sense to someone totally unfamiliar with the ins and outs of it." He stroked his chin.

"I'll work on it tomorrow before I take Gran to lunch. She said for you to come. Are you able to?"

"I'm free as a bird until my sister and aunts arrive on Sunday evening, or until another bombshell hits." He held his hands out to his sides expansively. He'd offer her any part of himself she wanted.

"So, you'll join us?"

"I will. I'll play chauffeur too."

"Great." She grinned. "Let me get my shoes."

When she was ready, he took her hand to walk to the car. She didn't pull away. It was a tiny victory on the path to winning her. He was a lovesick fool, there was no denying it. "I like the dress."

"Thank you. I found it in my mother's wardrobe. She was taller than I am, slimmer too, so the dress is longer than it should be, and a bit firmer in some places. It's the best I could do on short notice." She tugged at the fabric on the side of her midriff.

"It's grand. If ye wanted it less tight at the top, ye might undo a button or two."

"I'd look like a tramp!"

"One button then. No one would ever be thinking ye're a *hoore*, lass. Ye've too much class."

She frowned at him but loosened the top button and flipped the sun visor for the mirror.

"How is it?" he asked.

"It's more relaxed without exposing any more flesh," Catriona conceded.

"Try the second one." A sideways glance showed him the release of the second button, exposing the shadowy valley between her breasts. "There ye go, better?"

"You know your women's clothing, Scot. I'll have to keep an eye on you."

"And ye'll find my eyes are only on yer bonny self, lass."

She swung to him. The warning in her eyes was clear, but the tip of her tongue darting between her lips was a definite come on. His body reacted of its own accord.

The restaurant was quiet for the first wee while, though it didn't take long to fill. The level of service impressed Lachie. Looking around, he understood how Cat would have felt out of place in her normal, casual clothes, even if it didn't bother him what she wore—or didn't. Perhaps he should keep those notions to himself.

The waiter presented them with menus more like a novel in length.

Lachie scanned his briefly, then placed it on the table. "Ye've been here previously, lass. How about ye order for both of us?"

"Is there anything you don't care for?"

"Whatever ye choose will be fine with me." He sent her a wink and a grin. She rolled her eyes in return but quickly decided on a selection of dishes.

When the food arrived, he followed her movements as she checked the flavor of each mouthful. The tip of her little pink tongue kept making an appearance, and he watched for it.

Before he knew it, they were being offered coffee. She gave a minute head shake, so Lachie handed over his credit card and waited for its return, smiling at Cat's enraptured face.

She caught him staring and tilted one corner of her mouth. "This has been a lovely evening. I've only been here once. Gran brought me here for my twenty-first birthday. It's still wonderful. Did you enjoy the food?"

"Aye. It were well tidy scran."

"You'll have to translate for me."

"Ah," he chuckled, "the food was delicious, I said."

He stood, and as he held her chair, he wasn't able to resist sliding his gaze to the valley between her breasts. The shadows suggested an invitation to come and explore. He could barely wait.

They were quiet on the ride back to her place.

"Would you like to come in for coffee since you missed out at the restaurant?" she asked.

"I would like to come in, aye."

Inside, she dropped her keys on the hallstand and pivoted toward the kitchen. He pulled her back and twirled her to face him, holding her loosely in the circle of his arms. "It's not coffee I want, but a taste of the wee pink cat's tongue you've been teasing me with all night."

She slid her hands across his abdomen and chest. "Is this you asking for a kiss, then?"

"Aye, exactly what it is, ye canny lass."

"Alrighty." When she stretched onto her tiptoes, he grasped under her buttocks and hauled her up to sit around his hips. Her hands moved to his shoulders as a beatific smile lit her face.

With her legs wrapped around him, her mouth was within reach.

Her tongue peeped out, offering pure devilish temptation.

"Ah, lass." His throat was tight.

She placed a hand on the back of his head, leaned in to him, and skimmed her tongue across his bottom lip.

Tightening his hold, he pulled back to look at her as her hands framed his face.

The feel of her body curving into his brought him close to exploding and she teased his lips again. Retreating less than a centimeter, she returned, crashing her mouth against his. His hands were full of her, leaving her in total control. Never had he surrendered so completely to another person.

She nibbled his top lip, and her tongue darted into his mouth luring his to follow until she was sucking it like her life depended on it. Letting go, she kissed him again while her touch roamed his face until she wound her fingers into his hair.

Moving to the sofa, he sat with her legs still astride him, her knees bent against the chair as she knelt around his hips. The strength of his hard-on rested between her legs. She didn't seem to mind, settling onto him fully.

His body was on fire, his hands traveled up her back to capture her head, to coax her to kiss him again. Even as a teenager finding his way, he'd never experienced such urgency. This woman, this wee sprite, was kissing him like there was nothing to be afraid of, not his size, nor his physical strength. There was just this, this passion. The kiss went on and on, driving him forward with a desperation he wouldn't have imagined.

He could live on this, on her. The sensation of the soft fabric of her dress against his palms heightened his awareness of her curves as his hands explored her from her buttocks to her head. His thumbs barely skimmed her breasts, enough to realize they were as full and inviting as the enticing valley between them suggested.

Leaning closer, she deepened the kiss even more, her tongue roaming the inside of his mouth. The little jiggle when she changed her position on his cock made his manhood want to burst through the fabric containing it.

Never wanting the kiss to end, he groaned deep in his throat when she sat back on his thighs. Her eyes were huge in her face and she looked as shell-shocked as he was.

Sliding off his body, she extended her hand. "Coffee or bed?"

"Ah, lass. I've no protection."

Placing her hand on his chest, she peered into his eyes. It took a moment, but her mouth curved into a small smile. "Coffee it is then."

Leaning forward, she kissed him hard. She took his hand and led him to the kitchen.

Refusing to deflate, his member chafed against his underwear when he walked. This was the right outcome for now. He believed it in his head, though other parts of his body weren't so sure.

The kitchen table was surrounded by half a dozen chairs. Dragging one out, he sat and let his gaze follow her moving around the space. As though an invisible string linked them, he sensed he only needed to tug on the connection, and she'd be back in his arms.

Temptation was a foul tease.

"Here you go." She placed the coffee on the table, taking the seat kitty corner to his. Their knees banged together. Her eyes were close to normal size again, but the pulse hammering in her neck belied her attempt at making things appear like he was just any guest sitting at her kitchen table. She was as affected as he was by their passion.

"If you're going to seduce a maiden, you need to be prepared."

"Aye, lass. I'll remember next time," he said, trying to appear chastened. "Will a string around my finger help, do ye think? On the other hand, I got the powerful feeling I was the one being seduced. I don't believe I have ever been kissed so thoroughly. Does the maiden have the same preparation obligation?"

"Hmm, I see what you mean. We both have homework to do then."

He laughed at the serious frown she adopted, drained his mug, and stood. She joined him. Together, they moved to the front door.

"Lass, I...," he ran one hand through his hair. They should pull back, at least until they sorted the legal stuff. She'd have enough on her plate without a relationship with him, a man for whom relationships didn't work. It was selfish, but he wanted this, her, for as long as he could have her. His hesitation lengthened.

She touched one hand to his face. "Lachie? It's okay. We'll get there or we won't. Let's wait and see, shall we?" *Does she read minds too?*

"Aye, lass. We shall." He leaned across, brushing a kiss onto the top of her head. "Can I collect ye to fetch yer Gran tomorrow? Eleven o'clock?"

"Okay, perfect. Thank you for a lovely evening."

She stepped backward into the house, out of range, though he sensed the touch of her gaze on him when he was climbing into the car.

She was a *Simone*. What was he thinking? He'd trodden that path before. When she put two and two together like Meredith, what would she think of him then?

11

Chapter Eleven

Cat sat reading the news on her phone with a cup of coffee and a piece of toast on Monday morning, when the instrument rang in her hand. "Miss Cameron, this is Myra from Phillip Walker's office. Mr. Walker was wondering if it would be possible for you to come in this morning?"

"I can. What time will be convenient?"

"The sooner the better is the impression Mr. Walker gave me."

"Um, it's a quarter after eight now. I'll aim for nine o'clock. Will that suit?"

"Excellent. Thank you. I'll see you then," Myra said. There'd been no mention of Lachie being part of the meeting. Should she contact him? She decided against it, hurrying to her room to find something respectable to wear.

She'd handed a dossier of photos and letters to Lachie on Saturday which told as much of the story of the provenance of her right to hold on to the pâté recipe as such things were able. Lachie said he would pass the material to Phillip straight away.

His confidence gave her pause. What sort of man had access to a senior counsel on the weekend?

For Phillip's office to be phoning her at this hour on a Monday morning meant he'd received the package between Saturday afternoon and now.

Deciding black slacks paired with a silver-gray blouse was as good as it was going to get, she slipped her feet into a pair of black, kitten-heeled pumps and headed for the tram stop.

She arrived at the high-rise block in William Street with seven minutes to spare and presented herself to the security desk in the lobby. Myra was waiting for her when she emerged from the lift.

"Mr. Walker is in the meeting room, Miss Cameron. Please come this way."

"Ah, Catriona. Thank you for coming in so soon," Phillip said as she joined him. "We might get a jump on these buggars, pardon the French. Take a seat. The material you've provided, laid beside the stuff the McKell has given me, is pretty darn convincing. My intention is to file a complaint in the magistrate's court this morning. We will allege Sopworthy is making spurious, unfounded allegations against you, and improperly attempting to impose an unfair restraint of trade. It's a strategy to put the onus on them to prove otherwise. We will be the complainants. I believe it will put us in a stronger position."

"Will it be resolved quickly?" Catriona pressed a hand to her midriff to calm her nerves.

"How long is a piece of string? It will depend first on when we can find a spot in the court. It has a notoriously heavy workload. I can try to apply some pressure, but there are no guarantees."

"I don't have the finances to fight a case like this." She grimaced. Money and power went together, and she had neither.

"It's not your problem, Catriona. The McKell has everything covered."

"He does?" She didn't know what to think about that. The man was an enigma sometimes. Her focus snagged on Phillip's words. "Why do you keep referring to Lachie as 'The McKell'?"

Phillip wrinkled his brow for a moment. "It is who he is. Now, what I'll need you to do is to read through these affidavits. If you're happy with them, sign where I've indicated, and Myra will get it filed."

Cat read through each document with care, seeking clarification on unfamiliar terms.

"These are quite thorough. What's my liability in this? What happens if we don't win?"

"There may be a monetary settlement. They might require you to give them the recipe and prevent you from producing the pâté ever again, even for private consumption."

"Ridiculous. I've been making the pâté since I was seven. For nearly twenty years, I've sautéed the livers, blended the ingredients, and worked the food mill. I've only been making pâté for Charles to sell for three years."

"We'll need to convince the magistrate. It won't be a walk in the park. I'm confident, though. That's not just brash lawyer-speak." He smiled with one corner of his mouth. "You must prepare for them to tear your character to shreds. They may already have investigators tracking your every move. Be careful whom you talk to, whom you invite into your home, and with whom you're seen."

"Does Lachie count?"

"Most definitely. He has a pecuniary interest in the outcome. If the court finds your recipe is the one produced by Lachie's ancestor, two things can happen. He might be the one to sue you into revealing the recipe so production can recommence with the original recipe, or he might apply some other inducement to encourage you to comply."

"Seduce me into it, you mean?"

Phillip tilted his head to the side. "Is it likely?"

Her cheeks warmed. "It hasn't happened yet. Who knows? It might have been possible without the forewarning. Thank you."

"Look, I don't want to throw a spanner in the works or even to impede true love, but you have your own interests to consider here. Once this dispute is settled, you can worry about the next one, if indeed, there will be one."

"Hmm. The other day, Gran said she wouldn't speak of the pâté or *Simone* because it always caused trouble. I can see what she meant," she frowned.

"How is your grandmother? Would she be able to testify on your behalf if the need arose?" Phillip tilted his head.

"On a good day, she would. By the same token, she may be on the stand for five minutes, then forget where she was or why she was there."

"Another way to handle it would be to depose her in stages when she is comfortable to do it."

"Good luck. She is rather resistant to talking about it."

"I can be charming, Miss Cameron." He made a parody of batting his eyelashes.

"Ha, yes, you can. I was most grateful for said charm last Friday."

"Would it be possible for me to meet your grandmother?" He was serious again.

"Certainly. Let me know when it will work for you. I can meet you at the care facility."

"I'll check my availability and contact you. Do you have any questions on what happens from here?" he asked.

"It's probable I will when I can think straight. My head is spinning with how fast this is moving."

"Understood. Give Myra a call anytime. She'll take a message for me to answer your questions when I can."

Cat stood. "Thank you, Phillip. I just want this whole thing to go away."

"It will—though not today. I'll be in touch regarding a meeting with your grandmother."

She nodded, offered Myra a perfunctory smile as she passed her desk on the way to the lifts. She'd told Phillip her head was spinning, but that was an understatement. Her mind was dazed like she was punch-drunk and all she could do was to operate on autopilot.

Marching toward the tram stop in Collins Street, thoughts and names bombarded her. Lachie, "The McKell", whatever that meant, Charles, Gran, Phillip, Lachie suing her, using her? She boarded the tram and arrived at her home stop with no conscious memory of the trip.

12

Chapter Twelve

Almost stumbling through the front door of her home, Cat veered left, throwing herself onto her bed. She let the muted sound of the traffic passing on the major road half a kilometer away lull her for several minutes.

She stood, pulled her phone from her handbag and ambled across the hall to the lounge room. Dropping onto the sofa, she shot off a text to her best friend, Lori. *"Busy?"*

The phone rang in immediate response with Lori on the other end.

"What's up?" Lori asked.

"Um, I've met a guy."

"And…?"

"He's a Scot, and he likes my pâté," she said.

"That's lame, Treena. There's got to be more to it. How'd you meet him?"

"At the café because his aunts liked my pâté." Cat laughed.

"Geez. Let me pass the baby off to Brian and get a glass of wine. I'll call you back."

Cat relaxed into the chair. Good friends understood when a chat was likely to morph into a marathon.

The phone rang again. She put it on speaker mode and set it on the coffee table in front of her. She feared if she kept holding it her grip would crack its screen. Tension still coursed through her body thanks to Phillip's warnings.

"Now, I'm ready. Give," Lori commanded.

"First tell me how things are with you. Are you still loving living in Canada?"

"Ooh yes, except the winters are brutal. Brian keeps me warm though." Lori snickered. "Drene is a dream baby, so bubbly. I wouldn't have believed life could be this good. Now we have the pleasantries out of the way, tell me about your guy."

Cat recounted the story of Lachie as she knew it—how he worried for his workers, his mind-blowing kisses, and how he found the chocolates to take to Gran.

"He sounds like one of the good guys. What's the issue?" Lori asked.

Cat heard her friend take a sip of wine and wished for a moment it wasn't so early in the day in Melbourne so she could join Lori in a glass. "I think it's the lawyer's warning Lachie might be the next on the list to want to sue me to get hold of the recipe. Is he just another guy who wants what he wants? Someone who doesn't care who gets hurt along the way?"

"You're not still hung up on Steven, are you? He was a bastard, Treen. I warned you right at the beginning not to open a joint bank account with him. I guessed what would happen, and it did."

"He was convincing, though. If we both worked at getting our savings together, we'd get better interest to have more to spend when we went to Bali with the group. He made it sound like this was the start of our life together."

"Yeah, right. When your Gran went into care, we knew you wouldn't be going overseas any time soon. What did your caring partner do? The bastard took the opportunity, grabbed your money, and ran. He was a taker, Treena. A shit-faced user and a shit-faced taker. Thank God he didn't go on the trip with the rest of us or I might have been tempted to drown the mongrel."

Cat giggled at the ferocity of Lori's voice emanating from the phone. "You probably would have too."

"You'd better believe it, but not every man is like him. Your Scot doesn't sound like he's short of a quid. He's not going to rip you off like Stevie-boy did. Plus, he seems okay with you having responsibility for your Gran. Not like shit-face."

"I thought you liked Steve at the beginning," Cat said.

"Yeah, he was a charmer, but when he hurts my BFF, his very soul is condemned for eternity in my opinion. What about this Lachie character? Does he look like Steve?"

"No, Lachie is huge. He's built like a rugby forward, only taller. The muscles on him are amazing, rock hard, not a skerrick of fat."

"You've been closely assessing these attributes?"

"I can hear your eyebrows waggling." Cat laughed. "I might have undertaken a perusal—just for scientific purposes, you understand."

"Huh! And?"

"Neither of us brought a condom to the party, for goodness' sake. We had to stop."

"Oh dear." Lori giggled. "So, you shared a cold shower?"

Cat's teeth dug into her bottom lip. "Not quite."

"Treena, for you to allow a guy to get close, he must mean something to you. Go for it," Lori advised.

"But what if it's only because of the damned pâté?" She fisted tufts of her hair.

"Hmm. Was he kissing the pâté? Was he molding his hands around the pâté? Did he want to get into bed with the pâté?"

"Eww, gross, you make him sound like a pervert. I didn't say anything about molding and hands." Cat dragged her hands over her rapidly warming face, glad Lori couldn't see her.

"We're grown-ups here. What you're asking is, would he want you without the pâté? You'll probably never know. Do you like him?"

"I've fallen for him like a ton of bricks, but with this other stuff going on, I can't work out whether it's love, lust, need, or safe harbor. It's confusing."

"I wish I was able to be there for you, love, to check this dude out face to face. What does your Gran say?" Lori asked.

"Our auras are connected."

"Hey, that's what she said about Brian and me. She was so-o-o right," Lori said.

"She usually is, but—"

"I understand why you're hesitating—sort of. I'd say get the legal shit off the table, and go to Scotland. Observe the beast in his natural environment. Take it from there. In the meantime, enjoy his body, especially if he's huge all over." Lori snickered again.

"You are wicked, but you're the closest thing I have to a sister. I love you for it."

"Love you too, BFF. Call me when it washes through. If your Gran is right, invite us to the wedding," Lori said.

"Ha-ha. Give my god-daughter a kiss from me. Hugs to Brian too. He's obviously loving you right," Cat said.

"I will. You look after yourself, Treena. Love you. 'Bye!"

13

Chapter Thirteen

Cat needed a distraction, but what? She wandered aimlessly through the house. The silence pressed on her. That was strange. Even living alone, she often sensed her family around her. It was as if there was a change in the air. Something just out of reach. Logically, it would be the impending court case affecting her spirits. Or maybe the chat with Lori, who now lived half a world away, left her feeling bereft.

She drifted into her mother's bedroom and yanked on the wardrobe doors. It'd been over seven years since these items had been worn by anyone, except for the red dress. Perhaps now was the time? She slumped onto her mother's bed, staring into the clothes-filled space. She wasn't sure what she was looking for. Whatever it was, it didn't come.

There was the answer, perhaps. Her mother wasn't here anymore. The clothes, the shoes, the handbags—all these things her mother treasured no longer had life in them. They were dead, inanimate, useless.

Whatever she wouldn't use was going to go.

She sped to the kitchen before her resolve failed her and snatched a roll of black plastic garbage bin liners.

Her mother's shoes were at least a size too large for Cat's petite feet. With frenzied haste, they went into one bag. She slowed her pace for the clothes hanging on the rails, withdrawing each garment and assessing it closely.

Her mother always preached economy in clothes came with buying classics. A stylish dress, skirt, or jacket would pay for itself several times over compared with cheaper fashionable items discarded after one season. As usual, she was right.

There were many blouses, frocks, and jackets Cat could use here.

Hems might need to be adjusted, but the fit wasn't too far off, and the styles were timeless.

The clothes she was keeping, she set aside to launder. She hadn't time with the red dress on Friday night when she went out with Lachie. There was opportunity galore now.

Anything else she found in good condition, she folded neatly into another garbage bag to go to the bargain shop. Empty clothes hangers went back onto the rails. Before long, she'd cleared the lower wardrobe.

She flopped onto the bed again. Was she doing the right thing? An image sprang to mind of a hoarders' decluttering program on television from a couple months back. The presenter spouted the adage, "If it's not paying rent, it can't live here." This stuff stopped paying rent seven years ago.

Carting a large armload through to the laundry, she sorted a washable load of skirts and blouses and set the machine going. She retrieved the small step ladder she stored in the laundry cupboard, hauling it back to her mother's room.

The wardrobe's top shelf revealed half a dozen handbags, two valises, some gifts wrapped in Christmas paper, and a small safe she didn't remember having seen.

She tugged on the safe. Although heavy, it moved easily. Pulling it out, she tucked it awkwardly under one arm and eased herself off the stool. She set it on her mother's dresser to examine it. It closed with a keyed lock rather than a combination. If she wanted to know what was inside, she'd have to find the key.

The logical place to start was the dresser where the safe was perched. She removed the small side drawers that were part of the stand supporting the mirror and revealed some minor jewelry.

In the top right-hand drawer was her mother's makeup collection. She spread a garbage bag on the bed and tipped the drawer's contents onto it. There was a small key there, but it would not be large enough to fit the safe. The rest was makeup, probably out of date even before her mother's passing. She rolled up the bag, dumped the lot into another one, and left the key on the dresser.

Underwear and personal clothing from the next few drawers went into another bag for disposal.

The bottom drawers held some knitted goods. Easing them out, she shook each one individually, refolded it, and placed it back into the drawer. In Melbourne, a person could never have too many good quality pullovers and cardigans.

She'd cleared the dresser, and still there was no key to fit the safe.

After surveying the upper shelf of the wardrobe, she climbed the ladder, and retrieved first one valise and then the other. Both were empty.

Her search of the handbags proved as fruitless in terms of finding a key, though they yielded several hundred dollars amongst them. She kept the money, leaving at least a gold coin in each bag. Her mother, like Gran, held a handbag, or purse, should never be empty. She replaced the valises and handbags where she found them and reached across into the far corner, retrieving the Christmas gifts. They were neatly labeled in her mother's fine script. Four were addressed to her and one to Gran. She set them aside.

She was reaching to take hold of one of the bedside drawers when her toe struck something under the bed. Cat drew it out to find an old-fashioned suitcase with locked, time-rusted catches. Seizing the small key she'd found earlier, she tried it in the locks and was rewarded with the hinge catches flipping open.

She hesitated. There was a reason her mother locked this one and stored it out of sight under the bed. For the first time during her de-cluttering, she paused. She bit her lip. Should she violate her mother's privacy? Her stomach growled. She'd have some lunch and then decide what to do.

The tomato and cheese sandwich satisfied her physical need, but offered no advice on whether she should breach the sanctity of the suitcase. She trudged back to the room and stood in the doorway, staring at the red and yellow form on the other side of the bed.

Ridiculous. She stomped across the room and flipped open the top. There was a key taped inside the lid that looked the right size for the safe. She eased it away from its hiding place, leaving it to one side. In the lower part was a collection of covered books.

The first she extracted was her mother's wedding album. She appeared truly happy and very much in love. Her husband was older than Jeanette, handsome and smiling. Cat didn't think of him as her father because she'd never known him, and he'd chosen not to know her.

She flicked through the remaining albums, finding wedding cards in one, her mother's memories of the early days of her marriage in another, and some of herself during various stages of her life.

Right in the bottom of the case were two large yellow envelopes. In the first, she found the death certificate for Bradley Raymond Cameron. Her father died when she was ten years old. Sitting heavily on the bed, she grasped the certificate. She was an orphan. Her mother never encouraged her to hope he would someday come back to claim her, but knowing he was dead stopped her heart.

Sitting quietly for a few moments, she let the knowledge sink in. Curiosity about what else she might find roused her back into her exploration and she delved further into the envelope. She extracted a tightly bundled sheaf of papers that proved to be Brad Cameron's Last Will and Testament prepared by a solicitor in one of Melbourne's outer suburbs. Cat was the sole beneficiary. Any settlement was held in trust for her until her twenty-first birthday.

Gran mentioned a legacy for her when she turned twenty-one, is this what she meant? Was this truly a legacy? If he were a man who wasn't responsible enough to be a father, what did he leave for her to inherit? Debts?

Still, she'd call the legal firm to discover what she could.

The second envelope held more surprises. There was an old-fashioned bank book in her name. Someone made the last deposit a year before her mother's death. If her eyes weren't deceiving her, the amount read over half a million dollars. *Holy Moly.* Was it real? Would it still be valid if the account were inactive for so many years?

If all this was here, what was possibly left in the safe?

She took the albums and the envelopes to the kitchen to study later. If the morning's meeting with Phillip was a shock, the revelations from her mother's bedroom were more stunning.

She picked up the key and slid it into the lock of the safe. The door swung open on silent hinges.

Inside were stacked four black jewelry cases. Each held a complete parure. She didn't know where she learned the word, but she understood what it meant. A set of jewelry—necklace, earrings, brooches, and head piece—intended to be worn together. One, which appeared to be made of diamonds, included a tiara and a Scotch thistle brooch set with a large, purple-colored stone. There was a parure with what might be sapphires, one with emeralds, another with rubies or garnets and diamonds. If they were real, they were worth a fortune and not a small one either.

With shaking hands, she reached for a smaller cube. This one held what must have been her mother's wedding rings. She recognized the engagement ring from her mother's wedding photos. The wedding ring was engraved and promised love forever. Huh! She'd never seen her mother wear it.

Cat was trembling. *Gran.* Gran could tell her what the hell was going on.

Everything went back into the safe, and she locked it, wondering what to do with the key. It lay undisturbed for years inside the suitcase. Putting it back there, she locked the case, slid it back under the bed and, taking her mother's lead, hid the other key amongst her own makeup.

She struggled back up the stepladder to return the safe to where she found it and stacked the handbags in front.

It made no sense. If there was the possibility of converting the jewelry to cash, why hadn't her mother done so? Why not use the money in the bank account to buy the extra treatment that might have kept her alive instead of leaving her daughter to grow into adulthood without her? Anger spurted through Cat. Maybe Gran would make sense of it.

The Christmas gifts beckoned. She wasn't sure how much more she was able to handle today.

Falling sideways on the bed, she was ready to burst into tears. This was her mother being her mother. Whatever was in here, her mother had chosen it especially for her. With that thought, she dragged the heaviest package toward her.

She tore off the paper and opened the cardboard box inside to reveal a pair of purple Doc Martens. Shooting bolt upright on the side of the bed, holding a boot in each hand, she let her tears flow. Cat wanted these so badly when she was younger, as her mother knew. Her mum gave no inkling she'd bought the boots, waiting for the big reveal at Christmas. It'd been a quiet and lonely Christmas that year for Gran and Cat. Neither was in a celebratory mood and neither bothered with gifts.

The next parcel was a long black skirt accompanied by a black bolero. They made her chuckle. You had to have a skirt like this to wear with Docs. Then she found the backpack with the university study diary inside. It all made sense now. These were the things she was to use when she started university, but her mother died, and university didn't happen.

There was one more gift. She unwrapped this one to reveal a diamond tennis bracelet and a pair of earrings. The note inside read, *For those times when you have to be a lady.* There was a big, hairy, smiley face drawn next to it.

Her mother despaired of Cat fitting the lady mold. She was too outspoken and too independent. Cat must have learned how to conform to society's rules by osmosis from her mother, because she could, when necessary, conduct herself in the way her mother would approve of.

She placed the jewelry on her own dresser and headed to the shower.

14

Chapter Fourteen

Lachie was waiting at the care facility when Cat emerged from a taxi in the home's forecourt. For a pint-sized being she sure packed a whale-sized whump to his gut each time he saw her. He knew better than to get involved. Hadn't Meredith told him he was a threat to small women? She wouldn't even be in the same bed with him in case he squashed her to death. Here was another petite lass he should leave alone, but something about her called to his soul. Keep it light, that might be the key. "It's a bit early for Christmas, isn't it?" He pointed to the package she carried.

"Mmm. Have you been in to visit Gran?"

He didn't care for the suspicion in her eyes. "Briefly. I took my aunts in to see her. Ye'll recall she wanted them to visit. I introduced them and left."

"How is she?"

"She was well when I was there, excited to have her visitors. When I introduced them, she recognized them straight away and called them by their maiden names. They are reminiscing on the things they did together when she was a teenager. Everyone was fine, so I came outside to wait for ye. How are ye? Ye look like ye've been through the mill." He rubbed one hand down her arm.

"I met with Phillip, then went home to do some spring cleaning. I'm exhausted." She stepped backward.

He noted her retreat. "Ah *m'eudail*, don't work yerself into the ground."

"If I'm not working and I'm not making pâté, there isn't a heck of a lot for me to do otherwise. I can't sit twiddling my thumbs in the middle of the day. It wouldn't feel right."

"What did Phillip decide?" Lachie shoved his hands into his trouser pockets.

"He hasn't discussed it with you?"

"I've been engaged with my aunts and my sister today. I switched the phone off until we arrived here. If ye needed me, ye knew where to find me. Anyone else was irrelevant." He shrugged, drawing the phone from his pocket to turn it on.

Her eyes narrowed at him, measuring him in a way she hadn't previously. It made him glad he used the Gaelic to call her his sweetheart rather than English.

"We'll talk later. I want to see Gran," she said.

"Shall we go rescue her from my aunts?"

She didn't answer except to walk into the building, leaving him to follow. Laughter flowed into the hallway from Isla's room.

They walked in to find his two elderly aunts screeching with laughter, and tears streaming down Isla's cheeks.

Catriona hurried to her matriarch. "Gran! Are you all right? Why are you crying?"

"Oh Catty. It's nice to talk to people who don't think I'm senile. It's been a wonderful afternoon. Have you met Elspeth and Alethea?"

"Hello, I remember you from the café," Cat said.

Again, Lachie sensed a wariness in her, even though she smiled warmly enough.

"We've been remembering the naughty little things we did when we were girls. There were many things our sweet mamas didn't know." Elspeth wiped a tear from her eye.

"I'd love to go back to Scotland," Isla said, echoing her desire from when they'd discussed Lachie's homeland previously.

His reactivated phone burred in his pocket. Retrieving it, he glanced at the screen, nodded an apology to Catriona, and left the room. "Phillip? Give me a moment to get outside." He didn't wait for a response, holding the phone to his side while he exited the building.

"Right. Sorry. I'm visiting Catriona's grandmother with my aunts. I don't know what the rules are for phones inside. What's up?"

"You won't believe this, but I've taken a call from the magistrate's office. With the material we presented, they think this case is pretty well cut and dried in our favor. They're prepared to schedule a preliminary meeting tomorrow to get it off the books, hoping to tick off a completion. The court's workload is horrendous with cases dragging out. They'd be pleased with a quick result. Can we do it from your end?"

Lachie frowned. "That will depend on Catriona."

"I tried contacting her first, since she is technically the complainant. I wanted to tell her I won't need to depose her grandmother, but I couldn't reach her. Do you know where she is?"

"She arrived here ten minutes ago. I'll have a chat with her and get back to ye when I can. What's their timeline for a yay or nay on the time slot?"

"Today. They can't have empty slots and will need to fill it." "Give me five minutes." He ended the call, striding toward Isla's room. "Is it Christmas?" he heard Isla ask.

"Not yet, Gran. I found this in the top of mum's wardrobe. There were presents for me too. Mum meant them for Christmas when she died. Open it. Let's see what she left for you." He slipped behind his aunts in silence.

Isla slid off the ribbon encircling the package and tore the brittle-sounding paper to expose what lay inside.

Catriona knelt beside her grandmother, gathering her into a one-armed hug as they stared at a photo in a silver frame.

"It's perfect. So perfect. Ah, Jeannie."

"Can we see?" Alethea shuffled closer to Isla.

Isla hesitated as if the moment was too precious to interrupt. Then, she swallowed. "When sweet Jeannie was diagnosed, she was aware the treatments would affect her appearance whether or not they were successful. She arranged for the photographer to take portraits of the three of us. I remember the photo shoot. I thought no more of it because afterward, her health declined rapidly. The effort it must have cost her to organize this, well…"

Isla handed Alethea the frame. The picture was a relaxed one of the three women in a garden setting with their arms around each other.

There was an ageless knowledge, even acceptance in the eyes of the woman who must have been Catriona's mother. She recognized she didn't have long to live. The image of Isla was of a confident woman in her prime. Beside her, Cat projected the innocence of youth with a surety everything would be fine in her world.

Isla was right. The picture was perfect. He lost track of time waiting while the aunts oohed and aahed over the photograph.

He caught Catriona's eye, tilting his head to the door. She stood, gave her grandmother's shoulders a squeeze, and eased behind her to move to him.

"What is it?" Her tone was low. She didn't want to disturb the scene inside the room any more than he did.

"Phillip is offering us a preliminary hearing tomorrow. Are ye okay with it?"

"So soon?" Her face bloomed bright pink, then became deathly pale as her body swayed.

"Hey. Don't faint on me." He wrapped a hand around her upper arm. "Are ye all right?" Her nod didn't reassure him fully. "Phillip says the court believes this is a case they can conclude quickly and tick it off. Can ye manage it tomorrow?"

"Um. Yes…I think. Um." She chewed her bottom lip, drawing his attention to her luscious mouth. Her gaze flitted around anywhere but at him. She drew in a deep breath, then looked him in the eye, her expression hard to read. Determined? Independent? "Yes. Let's get this dealt with so I can get my life back." She shrugged out of his hold.

"And ye can come to Scotland to learn why we need ye."

"We'll see. Your problems are not mine. I'll consider Scotland when I've cleared my own path. Don't assume I will fall in line with your plans whatever the outcome." She spun on her heel, retracing her steps into the building.

He followed more slowly, puzzled by her brusqueness.

The aunts were gathering their handbags when he returned. "Ah, Isla, it's been grand to visit with ye. Absolutely grand. May we come again? Or would ye like to come to lunch with us tomorrow or the next day? We can discuss getting ye back to Kellburgh. That would be smashing, wouldn't it?" Elspeth clutched her bag, her eyes shining with delight.

Isla's face reflected her visitor's excitement. Catriona's was closed.

"We'll see how Gran feels tomorrow. Today has been a lot for her to take in," Cat said.

"Ah." Elspeth's face fell.

"It would be grand." Isla's eyes shone. "Don't worry about Catty. She frets too much."

Catriona's body stiffened, and she swung her gaze to Lachie's, telegraphing a warning.

Now he was sure of it. Something set them at a distance from each other. He would have to find out what the problem was. She reacted every time anyone mentioned Scotland. Did it mean she wouldn't help them or was it him she was rejecting? After the kiss they'd shared, he thought they had something of an understanding.

He wanted to take her in his arms, smooth away her fears. Instead, he bid Isla goodbye and escorted his aunts to the car.

Rejection was not something new to him. With Catriona, though, the thought of it scored a deep furrow in his soul.

15

Chapter Fifteen

Catriona was probably overreacting, but Phillip's words from the morning played on her mind all day. Lachie being here with his aunts did nothing to allay her fears.

She wouldn't be coerced into doing anything. Her body might want him, and her heart might already have fallen at his feet but neither inconvenience would detract her from protecting her grandmother or herself. If he tried to use her grandmother's affection for his aunts as a noose around her neck, he'd soon find out how wrong he was.

The room was quiet with the visitors gone. Her grandmother sat staring at the picture.

"Gran." Cat hesitated. "Gran, would you like to come home?"

Isla raised her gaze to her granddaughter. "I am home, dear."

"Would you like to come back to our house to live with me?"

"Away from here, you mean?"

"Uh-huh, home with your own things."

"What about your work?" Gran frowned.

"I don't need to work for a while. I found the bank book. We have enough money to keep us going for a long time."

"We kept the money for you. To set you up, for you to go to university, do the things you want to do."

"What I want is to have my Gran back."

"And this?" Isla rotated one finger against the side of her head. "Will you send me away again if it gets too much?"

The statement stabbed Catriona with guilt. She never intended for her grandmother to be "sent away." Gran needed to be cared for when Cat was not around to do it. The care facility was the most practical solution.

"How about if you and I can't manage on our own, we hire someone to help? Do you think we can make it work?" Her grandmother remained silent.

"Gran?"

Isla's fingers plucked at her trouser leg. "I'm scared. How would we pay for the someone?"

"We can afford it. We own the house and we don't have any other debts. You and mum saved a fortune. Mum should have used it for her treatment, but she didn't. I think she's made me angry for not spending it to find a cure for herself."

"Don't be. Jeannie knew it was end game at the outset. She put on a brave face for you. More treatment would not have given her any more time, just false hope for you. Your mum knew what she was doing, little one."

Cat's chin wobbled. "Gran, come home. I want us to be together."

"I don't want to be a burden, dear. You're young. You have your own life."

"And you're a very big part of my life. Did you think I was a burden when you were caring for me all those years?"

"Of course not. It's what grandmothers are for."

"You've made my argument. Watching out for grandmothers is what granddaughters are for. Besides, you're able to care for yourself most of the time. You just need backup every so often."

"If you're sure—"

"Do you want to come now or tomorrow?" The puzzled, hopeful look on her grandmother's face nearly broke Cat's heart. "It's okay, darling. If you don't want to come home today, it can wait till you've decided."

"Let's blow this joint." Isla's smile beamed.

Cat laughed with relief. "You put the stuff you want with you in a bag. I'll tell the staff I'm taking you with me."

"Deal," Isla said.

The director of the center raised warnings about living with a dementia patient. Cat thanked the woman for her concern and for the care the team provided for her grandmother, but was firm in her resolve to have Isla at home.

At the front desk, she asked the receptionist to call a taxi since she didn't have her own phone with her.

Isla was dithering over what she needed to pack in the suitcase when Cat returned. "We'll do it together. You get your knickers and bras. I'll get your pictures."

Isla followed the directive with alacrity.

"Now, get your frocks and slacks. I'll clear the bathroom." Cat kept the momentum going.

"You get my shoes. I'll empty the bedside table."

Catriona grinned at the command and was following orders when the bedside phone rang.

Isla answered, then addressed Cat. "They say the taxi's waiting."

"Tell him to start the meter, we'll only be a few minutes," Cat said.

Isla replaced the phone, then brought her two fists to shoulder height, wiggled her upper body, and danced from one foot to the other. Her smile was luminescent.

"Do you know, Gran, if we put the shoes in a shopping bag, I think we'll have everything."

"Way to go, Supergirl!"

"You carry the handbags. I'll bring the rest."

"On the run, honey bun."

Isla picked up the bags and scampered from the room. Cat took a moment to check for anything they may have left behind before following suit. It seemed unreal for a woman's whole world to be contained in one room and her belongings fit into a suitcase and a couple of shopping bags.

The room already appeared dull and lifeless, and Cat was glad to leave it behind.

At home, Isla went straight to her room. She threw herself on the bed, bouncing on it and grinning like the Cheshire Cat.

"Shall we get you unpacked, Gran?"

"There's nothing I need from those bags, Catty."

"Cool, I'll put the kettle on," Cat said.

"Yes!" Isla bounded off the bed. She stopped dead when she peeked into Jeanette's room. "You've done a clean out? It's about time."

"You're okay with that?"

"I would have been okay with it a fortnight after your mother died. You needed time. I didn't think it would take seven years, though."

"I left it because I thought you needed it," Cat said.

"Silly duffers. Both of us."

She sounded like Gran in her heyday. Cat hugged her, hard. "I love you, Gran. So much."

"That is mutual, honey bun. What have you got to eat?"

"Not a lot. We might have to order in, unless you'd like to go out?"

"I'm not leaving again for a while." Isla shook her head. "Does the Indian do delivery?"

"They sure do."

"Good." Her eyes lit up. "I want spice, lots of spice. And Naan bread, and raita, and some saffron rice." She heaved a great sigh and grinned.

"Didn't they feed you in the home, Gran?" Cat chuckled.

"Oh yes. They catered to the lowest common denominator, though—healthy but tasteless." Gran screwed her mouth into a tight moue.

"You should have said. I'd have brought you anything you wanted."

"It was bad enough you traipsing out to the home every other day. I didn't want to be more of a—"

"Gran. You are not a burden. Never have been, never will be. Tea's made. Get it while it's hot. I'll find my phone to ring through the order."

Cat finally located her phone on her mother's bedside table. The battery was flat, so she took it to the kitchen and plugged it into the wall socket to make the call. With the order placed, she called a car hire company to rent a small vehicle for the next two weeks, to be delivered immediately.

If something were to go wrong with Isla in the middle of the night, she didn't want to wait for a cab or an ambulance to get her to hospital.

The bonus was she'd have transport to dispose of the stuff from her mother's room.

She made Isla's bed with fresh sheets, put fresh towels in her ensuite, and headed back along the hall. She joined Isla at the kitchen table and took a sip of the tea.

"Shouldn't you be making pâté for Charles?" Gran asked.

"No, I don't work in the café anymore."

"Why?" Isla grabbed Cat's arm and stared into her face.

"I told Charles we were going to Scotland to visit our relatives. He got angry. He said I was going to Scotland to help the McKells make pâté. Now we're going to court."

"To court?" Isla squawked. "Why on earth?"

"Because Charles says the pâté recipe is his so he's fighting with me. He says I'm not allowed to leave the country and I'm not allowed to produce the pâté for anyone else." Cat stirred her tea.

"That's preposterous."

"When it's done, I think Lachie wants me to go to Scotland to help them make the pâté. The last *Simone* has died, apparently. They don't have the recipe anymore." Dropping the spoon into the saucer, she picked up her cup and wrapped her hands around it.

"The last *Simone* has not died. We are both still here."

"But do we want to go to Scotland to make pâté, or do we let the recipe die? Is it something we should live our life around?" She set her cup down. "It's a bit like a prison to me, now. I like Lachie, Gran. I like him a lot. I wonder if he's interested in me, or just the pâté. Grr, I hate this. I hate not knowing, being uncertain."

The doorbell rang. Catriona snatched her wallet from her handbag and strode to the front door. The delivery driver was waiting uncertainly, shuffling from one foot to the other. She wondered for a moment if he needed to use her bathroom until she registered Lachie's hulking form standing off to the side.

Her heart flipped at the unexpected sight of him. "Good evening, Lachie. Go on in. Gran is in the kitchen." With the giant gone, or at least not a looming presence any longer, the driver relaxed, received the cash Cat proffered, and thanked her effusively for the higher than usual tip. She figured he'd earned it.

She carried the bags of food through to the others. "We're having Indian tonight. Would you like to join us? I'll warn you, Gran wanted spicy, so two of the curries will be quite hot."

"If ye have enough to go around, that would be great, aye. I'm a bit of a curry man myself."

"You unpack the food. I'll gather the plates and cutlery. Gran, would you like a glass of wine?"

"I'd like a red from the back cupboard, please dear. A good high alcohol wine will make the food even spicier." She chuckled wickedly.

The back cupboard? Cat bought some time by collecting utensils.

"Where do you mean, Gran?"

"The back cupboard. You haven't drunk it, have you? I'll go check." Cat trailed behind her grandmother in puzzlement as she tottered along the hallway. She went into the spare bedroom at the back of the house and flung open the door on the far side of the wardrobe to reveal four boxes of red wine stored on their sides.

"Goody! There they are." She opened the flap on the box at her eye level and withdrew a bottle. "We'll try this one. If it's not corked, it should be magnificent." She teetered back to the kitchen.

How did Cat not know the wine was in the cupboard? What other surprises were in this house? She mostly stuck to the areas she used every day. Even living here on her own, she'd found no need to come to this part of the house, except for a whip round with the duster or the vacuum. It didn't involve ferreting through the cupboards. Crikey. If there'd been a drug lab in the back wardrobe, she wouldn't have known.

She scooted after her grandmother and saw her hand the bottle to Lachie. "Would you open this for me please, son? We don't have time to let it breathe properly. We'll compromise. You'll find an aerator in the second drawer. Perhaps you should decant it instead, Catty?"

Cat nodded, took the aerator from Lachie, and returned it to its hiding place, then retrieved a decanter from the old-fashioned lead light sideboard in the main lounge room. She chose the carafe with a funnel and filter sitting in the neck. Gran had a distaste for the sediment of old yeast and bits of grape accumulated in the bottom of an older bottle of wine.

She decanted the wine with care, leaving a small amount with the dregs in the bottle, and pulled some wine glasses from the cabinet and set them on the table.

Lachie set out the plastic food boxes and searched for an extra plate for the Naan bread.

"What a treat!" Gran said.

"Be careful, Gran. It's been a while since you've eaten food this spicy. Go easy."

"I'll go easy when I'm dead, my girl. This, I want now." She took a mouthful of vindaloo. "Whoa! It's amazing. I'd almost forgotten how good this stuff makes you feel. The after-burn is like an orgasm in your mouth." Her eyelids fluttered, and she flapped a hand in front of her face.

"Gran?"

"Oops, sorry. But it is, really," she whispered in a conspiratorial tone.

Cat glanced at Lachie and saw his eyes bulge slightly. He was trying not to laugh, if his clamped lips were anything to go by.

The wine Gran chose was superb. "Not many pinot noir made by Italians anymore," she said, sniffing the contents of her glass and taking a sip. "Ah, that's so good."

Cat grinned. Her grandmother was right about the extra depth to the spices. Cat reached for her water glass more often than she did for the wine.

Not all the food was eaten when Gran declared herself replete and was taking herself off to bed.

"Do you need a hand with the shower?" Cat checked.

"No thank you. I manage on my own. Goodnight, dear. Goodnight, young man."

"Good night, Gran."

"Why is yer grandmother here?" Lachie asked when they were alone.

"This is where she lives."

"Ye brought her back from the care home?"

"She was only in the home because I was working. Now I'm not, she can be here with me." She gritted her teeth but held her temper.

"She has dementia, Catriona. She will need a lot of care." He frowned.

"Don't treat me like an idiot, Lachie. If it gets too much for us, we'll hire in some help." Her jaw ached with tension.

He narrowed his gaze. "Is it because I took the aunts to visit her?"

"You're being absurd. She was happy to see them. It's highlighted security issues at the home, however, if total strangers can walk in any time," she snapped.

"The staff recognized me from being with ye and were okay with me going through."

"I won't discuss it. She's home now. This is where she will stay if I have my way." She stood to gather the plates.

"I'd still like ye to come to Scotland with me."

Cat clamped her jaw. When the doorbell sounded a clang into the room, she stomped through the house to answer the summons. The car rental clerk confirmed her driver's license and credit card, then happily handed her the keys to a small white compact sitting on the street behind Lachie's rental. "Do you need a lift back to the office?" she asked.

"No thanks, ma'am. The support car should be right behind me. Ah, here it is. Goodnight, ma'am."

Dropping the keys into the hallstand drawer, she returned to the kitchen where Lachie was replacing lids on containers and stacking them on the table. The dishwasher drawer was open, with plates and cutlery arranged within it.

"You didn't need to clear the dishes," she said.

"I didn't need to sit doing nothing, either. It's a few plates, lass."

He grasped the back of his neck with one hand. "What's going on, here, Catriona? Ye told Sopworthy ye were going to Scotland to visit relatives and now what? Ye've brought yer Gran home from care. Why? An excuse not to come home with me? What of the court hearing? What will ye do with her when ye're busy? Ye remember we'll be at the magistrate's court tomorrow?"

"I'll take Gran with me. It's me who has to be at the court, Lachie. There is no we." *What kind of domineering jackass did this guy think he was?* Her chest was fizzing, and it was not with lust.

Lachie's body jerked as though she'd struck him. "Lass, I'm sorry if I've offended ye. Ye need to tell me what I've done." His accent was quite broad when he was upset, she noted in passing, and his tell, the little pulsing pull on the edges of his mouth, was in evidence.

"You're second-guessing my choices. I don't answer to you in any way. My decisions are mine. I'll acknowledge you're trying to help, but I live my life my way." She took a calming breath. "Look, I like you.

A lot. You might have noticed I gave you a hint on Friday night, but I don't know where this…us…we, where we're heading. If this is an antipodean fling for you, find someone else. If it's seducing me into handing over the pâté recipe, you won't get your way there either. If it's a genuine thing between us, will it morph into me going to Scotland and being guilted into making pâté, living like a prisoner for the rest of my life, bound to something I have no control over? What the heck is it?" Cat flung her arms out to the side and dropped them with a clap against her thighs.

"These are questions ye'll need to sort for yerself, lass. I don't understand where they're coming from. I hoped ye reciprocated my feelings. If ye're asking these questions, maybe ye don't. I'll back away. I will be in the courtroom tomorrow whether or not ye believe ye need me. For the record, I think ye've made a mistake upsetting yer grandmother's world to make a point. I'll see myself out."

He stalked away and closed the front door behind him.

A cry erupted from her grandmother's room. Cat raced along the hall, swept open the door, and flicked on the light. Gran was sitting bolt upright in bed, staring in front of her. "Gran, what is it? Can I get something for you?"

"Who are you? I want Jeannie. Get Jeannie. I want Jeannie. Now."

"Gran?"

"No! Don't you come near me. Get Jeannie. Get Jeannie. Jeannie!"

Cat backed from the room. How to make her mother appear? She dashed to her mother's room and searched about. Grabbing a pullover from her mother's drawer, she threw it on and scurried back to her grandmother. "Mum! What is it?"

"Jeannie, Jeannie. Where am I? Nobody will tell me anything. I haven't had my supper. Do you think they're trying to starve me to death? They do that with old people you know."

Cat half-lay on the bed, drawing an arm around her grandmother's shoulders. "Would you like a cuppa? Do you want to come to the kitchen with me?"

Gran's eyes went wide. "Oh, they don't let you into the kitchen, dear. No, no, not at all. I went to find an apple one night, and they yelled at me because patients weren't allowed in the kitchen. I'm not a patient. I'm a resident. Patients are sick people."

"We've brought you home, darling. Catty and me. You're here at home. You can come to the kitchen any time you like when you're at home. Do you want to be brave and come have a hot drink? Tea, hot chocolate? What would you like?"

"No, no, I'm tired. I'm going to sleep now."

"Would you like me to leave the light on?"

Gran was already asleep.

Cat slipped out, leaving the door ajar for the light from the hall to penetrate the room. She would make herself a cup of tea.

Lachie might have been correct in thinking her move to bring Gran home was precipitous. However, she and Gran had made their decision.

She would make it work.

16

Chapter Sixteen

Lachie unbuttoned the jacket of his woolen suit, wishing he could take it off altogether. He ran one finger around the inside of his collar but kept walking toward the magistrate's court in William Street with his aunts in tow. Their lightweight frocks were far more suited to the stifling hot Melbourne weather than his business attire. His sister, Iona, was somewhere with James working on a plan to introduce McKells Whisky to the Australian market.

She'd come to Australia to support Catriona in his place. He should return to Scotland to run the business. Even with Iona here, though, he was disinclined to leave while his young relationship with Catriona was at risk. He needed to understand why she was withdrawing from him. Was it like Meredith all over again? Was it she didn't want to be with a man like him?

He held the door for his aunts to precede him into the blessed cool of the air-conditioned building and located Phillip, Cat, and Isla seated outside a courtroom door. Phillip was holding an earnest conversation with Isla as Lachie and his aunts approached.

His gaze tracked to Catriona, noting the dark smudges under her eyes and her pale complexion. She hugged both of his aunts without needing to bend down. He got that the lass was tiny compared to himself, most people were, but he thought of his aunts as miniatures and she was the same height!

118

He looked her over. She was wearing a long black skirt, a silvery mauve singlet with a black half-jacket thing, and purple boots. This was nowhere near the image she projected at the mediation. At mediation, she'd been the demure, serious businesswoman. Today's look was a "mess with me at your own peril" persona.

He bent to kiss her cheek. It wasn't enough. Not nearly enough.

She didn't pull away. If the flutter of her fingertips on his forearm was any sign, she was equally affected by the contact. There was hope yet.

Phillip drew his attention. "The other team haven't arrived and we're due to be called."

"What happens if they don't show?" Lachie asked.

"The magistrate can rule, anyway."

The court door flew open and a youthful woman stood searching the assembled group. "*Cameron v Sopworthy,*" she called.

"That's us," Phillip said, raising one hand. "Lachie, you can go through to the gallery with your guests and Isla. I'll take Catriona with me."

They trooped into their designated places to be seated. Lachie was unable to hear what Phillip and Cat were saying with their heads bent close together. A rush of pure jealousy infected him, even if the discussion was business related.

The clerk announced the magistrate, calling everyone in the room to stand. She was a woman of about forty, much younger than Lachie thought a magistrate might be.

They took their seats again. There was a flurry at the door as Sopworthy's team filed in to take their places.

"Mr. Baxter?"

"I do beg your pardon, Your Honor. We were delayed this afternoon. I assure you we are now ready to proceed."

Lachie picked up the counsel's tones as toffee-nosed smarminess. The man was patronizing the magistrate. Lachie was sure such a tactic would not work in the man's favor.

"Mr. Walker, you may advance your position."

Phillip presented the argument they agreed on. Troy Baxter responded with Sopworthy's contention Catriona worked as his employee, thus the original pâté recipe was his. Further, Baxter asserted, Sopworthy labored to improve the product through research and development. The intellectual property rights accrued to him. Miss Cameron's behavior was unconscionable in seeking to claim the pâté. The magistrate's lip twisted to one side, looking skeptical.

Phillip called Catriona to the stand, asking her questions designed to elicit the story of the history of the pâté. She was calm and composed, serene. She projected an elfin beauty as she spoke with certainty of her legacy. Phillip asked where she made the pâté and how she provided it to the café. Cat explained she made the product at home as always, never at the café.

Troy Baxter took over from Phillip, immediately going on attack.

"The story you have given us today is nothing but a story, isn't it, Miss Cameron?" He waited. "Isn't it, Miss Cameron?"

"I beg your pardon. Was there a question?" Cat raised her brows, keeping her focus trained on her interrogator.

"You have provided a fictitious parody of the truth of this matter, haven't you, Miss Cameron?" He waited again. "Haven't you, Miss Cameron?" The man's badgering irritated Lachie, though Cat appeared to be handling it well.

"I'm sorry. I'm not sure what you're asking."

"Your Honor, please direct Miss Cameron to answer the questions."

"I'm afraid, Mr. Baxter, I am of a similar mind to Miss Cameron. You are making statements, anticipating agreement. They do not constitute questions."

Baxter's face was a thundercloud. "Miss Cameron," he snapped. "Did my client teach you to make pâté?"

"No."

"Did my client teach you to cook anything?"

"Yes."

"Miss Cameron, please tell us what my client taught you to cook." Catriona listed a variety of pastries and cakes.

"Miss Cameron, do you have any proof the recipe you use is indeed more than two hundred years old?"

"No."

"What do you mean, 'no'? Isn't that the whole point of the dispute?"

"I beg your pardon, sir. If you will recall from my earlier testimony, I explained my forebears have handed down the recipe through the matriarchal line of my family. They never committed it to paper to make sure no one could steal it. Thus, I can't prove its provenance." She clamped her lips tight and shrugged one shoulder.

"If this court requires you to commit it to paper, what then?" the magistrate interjected.

Catriona's expression fell into a worried frown as she swiveled her head to face the woman. "I would struggle to do that, Your Honor. Keeping the legacy secret is a responsibility I have held throughout my life." Her gaze pleaded for understanding.

"How convenient your claim is, Miss Cameron, that you're the only one who holds the key to the secret portal. Woo woo," Baxter said, waggling his hands around his ears.

"Mr. Baxter, your theatrics are wasted in this courtroom," the magistrate said.

The glare he directed to the magistrate was one of disdain bordering on disgust. He focused again on Catriona. "Is there any other living soul who can corroborate your story, Miss Cameron, or do we need to commune with the ghosts of your dead ancestors?"

Cat's chest expanded, taking in a deep breath. "There are others who can confirm the history I have recounted is what we know with certainty."

"Where are they? Bring them on, Miss Cameron. Let me see them."

Catriona looked to Phillip, who in turn, nodded to Lachie. Lachie helped Isla to her feet.

"There are two present, Mr. Baxter. Let me introduce my grandmother, Mrs. Isla Jenkins, and Mr. Lachie McKell of Kellburgh, in Scotland. Like me, both are direct descendants of Simone de Salignac."

Baxter's eyes widened. He seemed stunned for a moment, but recovered.

Lachie eased Isla back into her seat.

"All this bother about pâté. My bet is a person can't taste the difference between one pâté and another. If I set your pâté against one I bought at the supermarket, how would I tell the difference?" Baxter demanded.

"It's not for me to say, sir. I don't know how astute you are with taste." Cat's mouth widened into a smile. "Are you able to tell the difference between red or white wine if I blindfolded you?"

Baxter aimed his gaze to the ceiling before continuing. "You believe the flavor is so well differentiated from others?" He sneered.

"Yes." Cat raised her brows but maintained her calm demeanor.

"Let's put it to the test, shall we? Your Honor, I propose Miss Cameron provide us with an example of this celestial food. We can then compare it with generic brands from the local deli."

"Miss Cameron, are you able to provide a sample of your pâté by nine o'clock tomorrow morning?" the magistrate asked.

"Yes, Your Honor."

Phillip sprang from his seat. "Your Honor, my esteemed colleague has implied he can differentiate a red wine from a white wine blindfolded. We can't be sure whether he can discern a shiraz from a cabernet. If we are to proceed with a comparison, I contend we need expert tasters. People who would recognize the true recipe and not say, 'Oh this one's very nice and so is this one, they must be the same.'"

"Do such experts exist, Mr. Walker?"

"Yes, Your Honor. With us today are Mrs. Elspeth McKell and Mrs. Alethea McKell. Each is an accredited expert in her home country. Indeed, these ladies recognized the pâté, served to them at the defendant's café some weeks ago, must have derived from the McKell's long-lost recipe. Thus, this whole saga began. These ladies can taste the difference, blindfolded if need be."

"Would those ladies stand, please?" Lachie's aunts bounded to their feet. "Ladies, are you prepared to be our judges in the morning?"

"Oh yes, my lady. We'd be happy to do that for ye," Alethea said.

"Thank you. Please be seated."

The women sat, giving each other a nudge with their elbows, and smiling broadly.

"Your Honor, these women are part of the conspiracy. Surely there is an independent judge?" Baxter interjected.

"Mr. Baxter, we need accredited people who can recognize the original recipe from a time preceding when Miss Cameron started working for Mr. Sopworthy. If you can produce such a person at least half an hour ahead of the time we reconvene tomorrow, I'll consider them. Mr. Walker, please present your judges' credentials to my clerk by eight-thirty a.m. tomorrow.

"At nine in the morning, Miss Cameron will provide a sample of her pâté, and Mr. Sopworthy will provide a sample of his pâté. My team will provide two outside varieties for comparison."

"What? No."

"Is there a problem, Mr. Sopworthy?" the magistrate asked.

Baxter stared at his client who subsided with a meek, "No, Your Honor."

"We are adjourned."

Lachie guided his aunts and Isla to the outside corridor. He heard Sopworthy complaining to Baxter for proposing such a stupid idea. The volume of the argument spilled into the hallway when Phillip opened the door to usher Catriona through.

Again, Phillip was bending low to talk to Cat in muted tones. As before, Lachie's jealousy rose like bile to choke him. It worsened when Cat beamed a mega-watt smile on the man.

"Can I give ye a lift?" Lachie asked, trying to draw her attention back to himself.

She turned to him, her face lacking the smile she'd offered her counsel. "No thanks, we're good. We have a few things to take care of while we're in town. Then we'll go shopping for chicken livers. We'll see you tomorrow."

He was dismissed. He read the message as, "Don't come near me tonight." She moved away, and his heart dropped.

17

Chapter Seventeen

Catriona's hands were shaking. Her stomach reacted as though she'd eaten concrete for breakfast. *Lordy, lordy.* She gulped a breath of air. She'd prepared the pâté in the same way she always did, but no one had judged it before, at least not officially. The customers liked it, but was it as strongly differentiated as she intimated in court yesterday?

No one specified how much she should bring so she opted to bring a small, disposable, plastic butter box. The clerk could turn the pâté onto a plate for serving, then place it back into the box for storage, if necessary.

Catriona and Isla emerged from the multi-story carpark to walk to the courts. Just ahead, Phillip approached from the opposite direction, hailing them with a bright smile.

"Is that the pâté? If it's as good as everyone claims, I'll want the leftovers," he said, with a wolfish grin.

"Deal," she agreed. His vote of confidence brought a lightening of her nerves, and she smiled. She noticed her grandmother was somewhat perplexed this morning, less steady on her feet than yesterday. Managing Gran, her handbag, and the pâté was difficult for her. Phillip's assistance was welcome when he took Isla's arm.

Phillip guided them away from the public areas of the courts into the area where the magistrate's office was located. The attending clerk accepted the pâté and Cat watched as the clerk labeled her contribution "pâté 3" and placed it into a refrigerator alongside two other offerings. One of the pâté products already there was in a store-bought package, while the other appeared fresh.

Cat and Phillip took their waiting positions as they did the previous afternoon. Lachie, his aunts, and another woman about Cat's age with similar features to her own soon joined them.

Did Lachie have a thing for petite women with long dark hair? Alethea and Elspeth bounded over to Isla like twenty-year-olds and started chattering. Isla reared back, her brows drawn together in a puzzled frown.

Cat turned her attention from her grandmother as Lachie touched her arm. Gazing into his eyes, an intense hunger for him swept through her. Blood warmed her features. The harsh angles of his face softened into a slight smile.

"I'd like ye to meet my sister, Iona, *m'eudail.*"

Cat extended her hand to the other woman and noticed a speculative look in her eyes. Lachie's sister seemed to size her up, assessing her by some secret criteria.

"How do ye do, Catriona?" The woman's pronunciation of Cat's name gave an emphasis to the "o" Cat herself didn't use, always pronouncing it as Catreena. She liked Iona's variation.

"I'm well, Iona. It's a pleasure to meet you. Will you stay for the hearing?"

"Yes, I want to observe how they do the judging."

Their conversation was interrupted by a plump woman of late middle age hurrying along the corridor with a beaming smile. "Elspeth. Alethea. What are you doing here? Why did they call on me, if they have the experts?"

"Sharyn. How lovely to see ye. Ye must be the independent judge for the pâté, right?"

"Yes, dear Elspeth. I got a phone call, ooh, around ten last night. Someone had a list of pâté experts. They specifically wanted someone who tasted or judged Simone's Pâté from more than five years ago. Of course, I had. I sampled the real thing in Kellburgh when you were training me to judge. Is it true there might be someone making it here in Australia?"

Phillip jumped into the conversation. "That's what this morning's exercise will determine, madam. We ought not discuss the pâté in any form at this time. I advise you to engage in your social chat once you've completed the judging."

"Oops, sorry. I didn't realize we were on different teams." Sharyn looked crestfallen.

"It's all right dear. We should be through by elevenses, we can catch up then unless ye have to drive straight back to Warragul?"

"No, I caught the train. You can never trust there won't be an accident on the Monash Freeway at this time of day to make me late. There are trains throughout the day. I'm in no hurry."

At Phillip's scowl, Sharyn nodded jerkily and widened her eyes. "I'll back away now." She laughed, taking three dramatic paces backward, turned, and found a seat further along the hallway. She gave a little wave back to the group when she settled.

He turned to the aunts. "Is this woman a reputable judge?"

"Oh yes. We trained her ourselves, didn't we, Elspeth? She has an excellent nose and can judge the graininess of the pâté with perfection. She can tell ye if the livers have been overcooked by one minute or five. She was one of our best pupils. Wouldn't ye agree, dear?"

"Yes, Alethea." Elspeth's response was distracted. Her gaze was on Isla. "Catriona, Isla is struggling."

Alarm streaked through Cat. "Gran, are you okay?"

"Oh yes, dear. Who are these people?" Isla's head shrank into her shoulders as her glances darted around the group.

Cat's heart sank as she took in her grandmother's confusion.

"Let's go next door to get a cup of tea. Come on, dearest."

"Do they have fruit scones?"

"We can soon find out, Gran. I am sure there will be something delectable for you. Phillip, you won't need me until after the tasting, will you?"

"Um, we do need you, Catriona. You will verify the offering they labeled as yours is correct."

"Oh."

Iona touched Cat on the arm. "I cared for my own mamma, can I help?"

"Um…"

"Look Jeannie, there's Catty. She's all grown up!" Isla flung her arms around Iona.

"Hiya Gran." Iona's raised eyebrows signaled a query to Cat, who nodded. "Shall we go find those scones, eh?"

"Ooh, I love the way you're talking, Catty. It sounds like Scotland. I'd love to go back to Scotland. Do you think we can?"

"Surely we will. We just have to work out things like passports and plane tickets, a whole bunch of stuff."

Cat was apprehensive until Iona expertly maneuvered Isla to the outer doors. The warm security as Lachie slid his arm across her shoulders nearly made her cry. She wanted to bury her face in his massive chest and let the world go by around her. She arched her neck and he placed a kiss on her forehead.

The same young clerk from the previous day stuck her head out the door of the courtroom. "Good morning. All the pâté has arrived, and the defendant is already inside. Please join us. I need to find the Australian judge, then we can start."

Phillip indicated where Sharyn was seated.

"Oh good. Her Honor wouldn't be happy if we were delayed again."

They walked into the space to find several people clustered by the clerk's table at the front of the room. On it, someone had draped a black cloth to cover the objects beneath.

The magistrate observed them as they moved forward. "These are the Scottish judges we met yesterday, correct?"

"Yes, ma'am," Phillip replied.

"Where's your judge, Mr. Baxter? We will not wait." Baxter seemed momentarily flummoxed, as though he'd overlooked a minor detail capable of spelling disaster for his client.

Phillip intervened. "A lady called Sharyn Brierly is being collected by your clerk, ma'am." He finished speaking as Sharyn and the clerk joined them.

"Good. We have three blindfolds, so you won't have to share. Two of you will wait in the other room, while one tests the pâté. We'll present the submissions in random order. You will not receive them in the same rotation as the person ahead of you. We may offer you the same product more than once. After you have tasted, you will remain in this room toward the back. Do you understand?" She waited as each of the judges nodded in turn. "Good. Mrs. McKell and Mrs. Brierly, you can go with the clerk."

"Mrs. Alethea McKell, ma'am, or Mrs. Elspeth McKell?" Phillip asked.

"Oh, there are two. Okay, Mrs. Alethea McKell can go. Mrs. Elspeth McKell will be the first tester."

When the others were gone, the magistrate trained her attention on Elspeth. "Are you comfortable wearing a blindfold, madam?"

"Oh yes. Ye can tell too much from the appearance of a product, whether it's fresh, too raw, or grainy. We usually wear a blindfold."

"Thank you. We will present you with a good chunk of each pâté on a gluten-free potato wafer. The wafer is bland to the point of being tasteless so as not to affect the flavor. There are tissues here for you to dispose of any unwanted product. Perhaps you should hold the tissues since we won't know how urgently you might need them. There's a glass of water which we can pass to you as required. Ready?"

The clerk, who had returned, placed the blindfold on Elspeth's eyes and checked she'd fit it correctly. She removed the cloth covering the pâté to reveal four different submissions. A woman wearing blue plastic gloves and a disposable hair net prepared a wafer with the pâté labeled "2".

Elspeth sniffed the product and popped it into her mouth. She declared it a pleasant pâté with good texture, but not Simone's. It was made with brandy, she determined. The second one, "pâté 1", Elspeth said was bland, a bit rubbery, probably commercial. Pâté number four was next. Again, Elspeth sniffed, giving a slight grimace. She sniffed again. "I won't put that in my mouth. It is two weeks old and has not been stored well. It has elements of Simone's Pâté, but it's a health hazard."

"Noted, Mrs. McKell, here is the next sample," the attendant said.

"Ah, this one is Simone's. Yes, indeed." Her lips broadened into a smile as her tongue roamed the inside of her cheeks, savoring the flavor.

"Here's another."

"It's the same as the second one." She pursed her mouth, and her tongue peeked out as though rejecting a product not up to Simone's standard.

"Correct."

"It's stale though not offensive like the other. It's bland. It's definitely not Simone's."

The attendant refitted the black cloth to hide the trays of product.

"Thank you, Mrs. McKell. You can take the blindfold off now."

Catriona smiled at Alethea when she made her way to the back of the room. She'd identified Cat's pâté as being Simone's.

The process was repeated with the other two judges who gave consistent results. The dodgy pâté brought forth a similar tirade of abuse from each.

Sharyn tasted pâté number four. It didn't last long in her mouth. Her face contorted and she stuck out her tongue to rake away the offending mixture. "Water!"

Phillip passed the glass into her hand.

"Your verdict, Mrs. Brierly?" the magistrate asked.

"I'd say it was Simone's once, but a fortnight old. It's off. Someone is trying to kill me. Yuck! You said you might offer the same product twice; well you can bin that one. I don't want it anywhere near me." She shuddered.

If the product was Simone's Pâté, only aged, where had it come from? Cat was confused. The only person who would have access to any of it other than herself was Charles. Surely, he hadn't tried to pass off her pâté as his?

"The verdict is unequivocal. Pâté number three is the recipe identified as the original. Whose entry was it?"

"Mr. Walker's client provided product number three, ma'am," the clerk confirmed.

"Who provided pâté number four?"

"Mr. Baxter's client, ma'am."

"Right, then. Mr. Baxter, Mr. Sopworthy was deliberate in his attempt to deceive us into an acceptance he produced this pâté overnight.

All three judges have declared it an abomination." She narrowed her gaze on the hapless lawyer. "Mr. Baxter, Mr. Sopworthy has attempted to commit fraud against this court. I do not take deception lightly. I'll come back to that later. In your opening statements, you asserted your client's ownership of the recipe. Again, the evidence is that is not the case. Instead, he has attempted to lay claim to a product from a supplier, not one he produced himself; another example of fraudulent intent." She heaved a breath through her nostrils, keeping her lips firmly closed.

"I am not happy. I'll decide today on whether to charge your client for these transgressions and what form of restitution I will require him to make to Miss Cameron. This case is dismissed."

Baxter's face reflected a furious thundercloud. Sopworthy's mouth hung open. Baxter spun on his heel to storm from the area with a twittering Sopworthy in his wake.

The magistrate leaned against the bench. "Mrs. McKell, yes, both of you, and Mrs. Brierly, you can come back here now. Ladies, the second pâté was mine. I thank you for your complimentary judgement. Pâté is one of my private passions. I find it difficult to get a good fresh one, hence I make my own."

"Yers was indeed a pleasant product, but we were here to find Simone's. Thanks to ye, we have. Thank ye, Your Honor. Keep making yers," Alethea said.

"Thank you for your service, ladies. Good day."

Cat was in a state of shock. Three judges found her pâté was the original Simone's. Where did that leave her now? Did she travel to Scotland to make pâté for the rest of her life, or did she stay in Melbourne and ignore the plight of Lachie's people? What should she do about her feelings for the man?

He caught her eye. *Could he read her mind?* She felt drawn to him by a silken thread. She almost took a step in his direction. *Silken threads are also traps. Ask any fly caught in a spider's web!*

She spun on her heel. "I'll find Gran."

"Lass!"

She ignored his summons and sped from the court.

18

Chapter Eighteen

Lachie's gaze followed Cat's exit. This was wrong. He cared for her and, given her response this morning, he believed she cared for him. What was the problem? Was it him or the blasted pâté? The door slammed closed behind her, and he pivoted to search for Phillip.

The lawyer was in close conversation with the magistrate. He smiled and gestured to where the remains of the pâté rested. He smiled more broadly, and strode to the bench.

"Come, give me a hand, Lachie. I'm taking this back to the courthouse staff room to put some cling wrap on the good stuff. I'm determined to try it. Her Honor said I can have hers too. Drinks and pâté on the twenty-third floor tonight," Phillip said.

"I want to try some now. Are there any crackers left?" Lachie asked.

"Plenty. You grab those trays. Put the cracker box on top of pâté number four. It's bin-bound, any damage to it won't matter."

They collected the food, transporting it to the staff room in one go. Lachie dropped the box of crackers onto the table and scraped the maligned pâtés one and four into the nearest garbage container. He wrapped pâté number two with some plastic wrap.

Phillip located some plates and a knife, and seated himself at the table. "Pâté number three is the real deal, yes?"

"I'll soon tell ye." Lachie scooped some pâté, spreading it onto a wafer. He sniffed it first, studied its visual appearance, and popped it into his mouth. "Ahhh. This is the one. It's the best batch I've ever tasted, and I've tried a lot."

"Give me a go then. Hand over the knife." Phillip didn't bother to sniff or study. He ate the cracker straight away. "Holy Toledo, that's good!"

"Let me try the other one," Lachie demanded.

Phillip retrieved the magistrate's version, passing it across to Lachie.

Lachie spread a generous serving onto a cracker. "Smell is good, texture is fine, color is right." He took one nibble and followed with the rest of the cracker. "Mmm, nice. I would eat that."

"I'll take your word for it. You've had your share now." Phillip grinned. He re-wrapped the remaining pâté in cling film and snaffled the box of crackers.

"Will you come to my office with me or do you need to be somewhere else?"

"Iona has the aunts. I'm free to come with ye. Ye can give me a plan of what happens next."

They stepped into a cool blustery wind with a hint of rain in it. "What happened to the hot weather from this morning?" Lachie asked.

"This is Melbourne. We have the ultimate four-seasons-in-a-day weather. You get used to it. We should hurry if we don't want to get caught in a downpour." They strode the block and a half back to Phillip's offices, past security, and up the lifts.

He handed the pâté to Myra with a request she refrigerate it and guard it with her life.

His secretary took the bundles with a quizzical expression. "Pâté?"

"Sshh." Phillip looked over his shoulder as if to check for lurking intruders. "Don't let anyone know we have Simone's Pâté in our fridge. The magistrate's version too."

Myra laughed aloud. "I take it you won the case?"

"Did you ever doubt it?" His tone was smug.

She shook her head. "Shall I bring through some coffee for you and Mr. McKell?"

"Yes, please. Right this way, Lachie."

Phillip's humor was catching. Lachie grinned like a loon.

"Do ye always react like this to a win?" he asked.

"When I get one over the high and mighty Troy Baxter, I do. Man, that was great. Even being in the magistrate's court is beneath his dignity. And to lose? Yes!" He laughed and punched the air. "Catriona was magnificent."

Lachie suffered the tightening of his groin at the mention of Cat's name and held back the urge to punch something—maybe Phillip's nose?

"She was calm on the stand yesterday. Her polite non-answer to piss-head Baxter's questions was superb. Then, to produce a world-class pâté by her own hands overnight? What a woman."

"Aye, she is that." Lachie stood with his legs firmly planted, his arms across his chest.

Phillip raised his brows. "Warning me off? Is this you doing the lord of the manor thing? Do you demand *droit du seigneur* too?"

"Don't be crass, Phillip. Ye're already aware of how I feel about Catriona." Lachie let his arms drop to his sides.

"What if she doesn't reciprocate?"

"Aye, I'd have a problem. I would like her to visit my home, my people, to see how much they depend on a credible pâté maker." Lachie fingers edged into his hairline.

"The pâté is what's important for you, is it? What of the girl?"

"It's not one or the other. They are indivisible. If it had to be one, it would be Catriona herself. The recipe holder is a bonus. Enough of my personal life. What comes next in this whole sorry saga?"

"The magistrate was clear she found in our favor. She was not impressed by Sopworthy's attempts to pass off some stale pâté as something he'd made himself. He probably had some of Catriona's on hand, figured no one would notice it wasn't fresh. In my humble opinion, the magistrate is keen to teach him a lesson. I am to send her a copy of my invoice. She will include my costs in the restitution she will order Sopworthy to pay. I suggested she might consider the damage to Catriona's reputation since Sopworthy accused her of industrial espionage and lying. There was also the matter of inconvenience caused to Catriona by preventing her from leaving the country and loss of income since she hasn't been able to work. It should come to a tidy sum in Catriona's favor."

"From which ye'll take your share."

"We all have rent to pay, Lachie." Phillip raised his brows.

"Aye. And ye did a good job."

The lawyer rested a hip against the desk. "I can't take the credit on this one. Baxter shot himself in the foot, insisting Catriona produce the pâté. His client was beside himself. Now Sopworthy is likely to have a fraud slash perjury case to defend."

"Mmm. Baxter was dismissive of the magistrate. She was ready to show him who was boss and Baxter's client handed him to her on a plate."

"Rumor has it," Phillip folded his arms across his chest, "Baxter wanted the magistrate's job but missed out to her. Why would he bother, I wonder? He earns more as a senior counsel than the magistrate, and her workload is humungous."

"Probably power-hungry. Woe betide anyone who stands in his way." Lachie grunted.

"What's your plan now? Will you take Catriona to Scotland?"

"She'll have to decide." Massaging his chin with the thumb and forefinger of one hand, Lachie wished there was no question about it.

"I can advise you not to use any form of emotional blackmail. She might agree to please you in the beginning. Then bitterness and resentment will set in. Neither of you will be happy," Phillip warned.

"I'll bear it in mind. Well, thank ye, Phillip. Ye've set Catriona's mind at rest over this matter, and for that alone, ye've earned yer keep. I'll be in touch with ye again when we establish our markets here."

As he reached the lifts, he pulled his phone from his pocket and dialed his sister's number. "Where are ye?"

"We're at Catriona's celebrating with pâté and a champagne. Are ye coming over?"

"Aye. I'll be there."

"See ye then."

Lachie stashed the instrument back inside his coat as the lift doors opened. The city was once again bathed in sunshine from a clear blue sky with no sign of the rain that threatened such a short time ago.

He strode to the undercover car park to retrieve his vehicle, set the navigation system to direct him to Cat's home, and drove onto a quiet side street. He was not relaxed. Waltzing into an environment holding the most important people to him in the world would take some fancy footwork. Iona and his aunts would forgive him a misstep. They always had, even when he married Meredith and accepted her daughter. He was less certain of Catriona, and didn't want to get her offside with a thoughtless comment. He wanted her in his life, but at what cost to him, to her, to the business?

"Ah shite!" he muttered. "Can nothing be straight forward and go the way it should?"

19

Chapter Nineteen

Cat left the courthouse and went to the café next door to find her grandmother sitting alone at a small table. The reason for her isolation became clear as Iona returned to the table with a chocolate lamington.

"Here y'are, Gran. This was the only chocolate thing ye've not tried. Is it okay? I haven't seen these before."

"Of course you have, dear. We used to make them a lot when you were little. Jeannie would bake the sponge cake to cut it into big cubes like this one. You'd get chocolate icing all over yourself when you rolled the cake in it. My job was to finish them with the coconut. I do love lamingtons."

"Hello," Cat chimed in, joining them.

Isla appeared confused for a moment. "Hello, Catty. All done? I was telling—"

"Iona," Cat prompted. "Iona is Lachie's sister."

"Yes, I remember, now. I was telling Iona how we used to make lamingtons."

"We haven't made them for some time, have we?"

"No, not since Jeannie died. She made the best sponges."

"I make excellent sponge cakes. Would ye teach me to make lamingtons?" Iona asked.

"Oh yes, we'd have so much fun. Can we do it Catty?"

"Whatever you say, Gran. Shall we head home? Where are Elspeth and Alethea?"

"We're right here." A voice came from behind her. "We were showing Sharyn where we bought our sneakers. She wanted a pair too."

"They're gorgeous, so bright. You'll see me coming when I'm on my evening walks in these," Sharyn said.

"I'm taking Gran home, now," Cat informed the group. "If you would like to join us, you're most welcome."

"I'd like to come. I want Gran to teach me to make lamingtons," Iona said.

"I'm a wiz at lamingtons," Sharyn said. "I can help. I don't have to be home 'til later. If someone can get me back here to the station by three-thirty, I'll be set."

"In that case, we'll all go," Alethea decided for her sister.

"Sharyn, ye can ride with us," Elspeth stated.

Cat typed her address into Iona's maps application on her phone. Gran wrapped her lamington in a fresh paper napkin and slid it into her handbag. "Waste not, want not," she advised.

With a flurry of activity, they vacated the café.

Traffic was light and the six women arrived at the house in minutes.

Gran took point on the top step at the front door, waving the visitors inside. "Welcome, welcome. Come along, Iona. Let's get started on making those cakes. Alethea, you can put the kettle on. Elspeth, can you and your friend get the nice cups from the sideboard, please?"

"What about me, Gran?" Cat asked.

"You can pop to the post office for the mail. Check if the bakery has anything edible we can serve until the lamingtons are ready. And, dear, fetch some salad or something for lunch."

"Will you be fine on your own?"

"I'm not on my own, dear. We have these lovely guests."

"I'll be as quick as I can."

"All right. Get some fresh coffee too. There was none this morning," Gran said, already moving to the kitchen.

"I rarely drink coffee at home. I finished it the other night."

"Well, you'd better get some."

Cat collected her keys, handbag, and the sack of reusable shopping bags, then left.

When she returned twenty minutes later, the kitchen looked like a bomb had hit it. She didn't mind. Everyone was in high spirits.

The sponges were in the oven and the nice cups were neatly stacked at the far end of the kitchen table. Isla had found one of the two bottles of champagne in the bottom of the fridge, and the second, larger loaf of pâté.

The ladies sat around the dining table with cloth napkins, champagne flutes, and the side plates from Gran's collection of Royal Albert. Gran was in hostess mode. Cat could have wept with joy, seeing her this way again.

"Come, have a drink with us, dear." Gran passed her a flute half filled with bubbly wine.

Cat juggled her shopping sacks into one hand to take the glass and set it on the table. "I'll be back in a sec, Gran. Let me put this stuff in the kitchen." Dropping the bags in the only place available—on the floor in front of the kitchen sink—she shook her head at the mess, then returned to her grandmother, raising her glass with a broad smile. "Welcome everyone, and thank you so much for your help this morning, including you, Mrs. Brierly, er Sharyn. You convinced the magistrate my pâté is Simone's original recipe, not something Charles Sopworthy created. Thank you all. Cheers!"

"Cheers!" The ladies' voices rang out around the room and glasses clinked.

Cat leaned on the doorjamb, smiling at the assembled guests. The chatter was of Kellburgh and the people. Isla commented yet again she wanted to visit, and the aunts encouraged her. Even Sharyn insisted the opportunity shouldn't be missed.

Their stories drew Cat's imagination.

A trip to Scotland loomed in her near future, it seemed. Isla wanted it. The aunts wanted it. And the lovely Iona, who had cared for Gran, wanted it. Visiting the place did not constitute a commitment to stay there forever. And, if she was being honest, she wanted to see Lachie's home.

She jumped as Iona's phone rang beside her. Iona spoke into it briefly and announced Lachie was on his way.

A buzzer sounded from the kitchen. Sharyn bounced to her feet. "The sponges. I'll go." She sped into the kitchen and Cat followed.

Sharyn drew one cake-filled lamington tray from the oven and touched it in the center. "Excellent. Do you have a cake rack?"

Cat found a couple in a high cupboard and set them in a cleared space on the table. Sharyn transferred her prizes from the oven to the wire racks. "They'll be perfect for the lamingtons. We have to wait until they're completely cold. We should wait until tomorrow but, if you're careful, you can handle them in a couple of hours or so."

Um, I know. Cat refrained from saying anything aloud and smiled instead. This woman was not aware of Cat's history, and she had been helpful this morning.

With the cakes left to cool, Sharyn returned to the party while Cat started cleaning the mess. It didn't take as long as she feared. She was doing a final wipe of the bench tops when the doorbell sounded. "I'll get it," Iona called.

Cat recognized Lachie's deep rumble as he greeted the ladies, then asked for her.

Gran piped up, "She's in the kitchen, dear."

Lachie spoke behind her as she rinsed the dishcloth under a running tap.

"Congratulations on yer win."

"Thank you." She pivoted to face him, clutching the edge of the sink behind her. "It's a vindication, not a win, exactly. I've worked with Charles for years. I don't wish him ill."

Lachie folded his arms across his titan's chest. "I understand yer feelings. I also understand from James that Sopworthy was aware of the problems we were having with Simone's Pâté. He was planning on using yer pâté to fill the hole in the market. It's why he wanted yer recipe."

"Bloody hell. That would be right. He was always one for the main chance in anything business related." She slumped backward, heaving a sigh. Her gaze flicked to his. "It appears they've made a decision in there." She jerked her chin toward the dining room. "Gran and I will travel to Kellburgh to visit. Are you okay with the idea?"

"When can ye come?"

The timbre of his voice had her heart beating a tattoo.

"It will take me a week, maybe a fortnight, to get things organized. I'll have to check on Gran's passport and sort a few personal matters. The neighbors will keep an eye on the house. How long should we plan to be away?"

"Ah, *m'eudail,* ye know my answer. I want ye to stay with me for-ever."

Cat melted at his words.

"I'll buy yer seats tonight; one-way to Edinburgh."

"I'll buy our tickets." Her voice firmed. "This is a sightseeing trip for Gran and me. I won't have any strings attached. I will not be beholden to you or to anyone else. I'll go. I'll explore. I'll come back."

"What if ye find ye don't want to come back?" He strolled across and placed his hands on her shoulders.

She moved her hands to his chest without conscious thought. Her neck strained backward to scan his face. "Whatever happens, Lachie, I have to come back. There are loose ends here. The house included."

"Ye'll keep yer options open? About Scotland? About me?"

Her nails curled into his jacket. She went on her tiptoes to feather a kiss across his lips, then stood back. "I will, I promise."

His arms wrapped around her fully, pulling her into the most exquisite bear hug with her cheek flattened against his jacket lapel. "Thank ye, *m'eudail*."

She backed away with a slight smile. "For now, I have a family to feed. Go join the ladies."

"Yer wish is my command." He grinned.

"I'll remind you later. Now, scram."

Laughter filtered from the dining room as she put together a couple of large vegetable frittatas. Once they were in the oven, she prepared a sizable Greek salad.

Lachie returned with an empty bottle in hand. "They've finished the champagne. What would ye like me to offer them now?"

"Check the fridge. There may be another bottle of sparkling wine unless Gran has already found it. There will definitely be some Sauvignon Blanc. It will pair well with the frittatas in the oven. Quit that!" She smacked his hand as he stretched to steal an olive.

He rewarded her with a kiss on top of her head. Her mind went blank as an intense need for him to hold her swamped her body, but he'd already turned to the refrigerator.

"Aye. There's another bottle of what they've been drinking. There's the white wine too. Ye've a flagon of chilled water here. Shall I take it?"

"In the cupboard above your head, you'll find a table-service jug. Fill it from the flagon. I'll put more water in the fridge."

She set the salad aside and spun on her heel to find the wineglasses in the dining room. She kept a couple in the kitchen for her own use but they wouldn't be stylish enough to use for guests, Gran would say. She brought the glasses to the kitchen, gave them a quick rinse, and dried them with a clean tea towel. With four glasses suspended from one hand and three in the other, she took them to the dining room and set them on the coffee table.

As she cleared the pâté and gathered the plates, Iona jumped to her feet, offering to help. Cat thanked her with a smile. From the bottom drawer of the sideboard, she extracted a floral tablecloth. Squeezing between the aunts, she flipped the cloth onto the extended table, then arranged the wine glasses at each place setting. Lachie followed with the open wine bottle and water jug.

They lay the table without a break in either the conversation or the laughter.

Iona waited in the kitchen to help carry the food. "Yer Gran has been wonderful with everyone here. She was distressed with the strangers this morning."

"I haven't thanked you. You said you wanted to witness the judging. Instead, you took responsibility for Gran. I didn't expect you to do that," Cat said.

"It helped she thought I was ye."

"You can't blame her. We look similar and you have a familiar air about you. It's hard to explain. It feels like you've been part of the family forever."

"What a lovely thing to say. Ye know, I—"

"Anything I can do?" Lachie strode back into the room.

Iona tilted one corner of her mouth and turned to her brother.

"Um, bread rolls," Cat said. "If you put the bread rolls on an oven tray on the shelf below the frittatas for five minutes, then we'll be ready. I hope no one is allergic to eggs."

Lunch passed in a whirlwind of laughter and much wine, though Cat noticed, like her, Lachie and Iona stuck to water.

As the meal ended, Isla rose, guiding her guests to the lounge room to relax. Lachie took orders for tea or coffee while Iona and Cat cleared the table.

"Cat, Iona and I have some meetings this afternoon. Is it fine with ye if the aunts wait here?"

"Of course. They can snooze in the recliners or on the lounge, if they want to. Can you take Sharyn back to the station?"

He bobbed his head. "We'll go now. I'd like to confer with James ahead of the meeting. We'll be about an hour and a half to two hours."

"No rush, everything is fine here."

His eyes burned into hers. "Why is it, *m'eudail*, it breaks my heart every time I leave ye?"

She grinned. "The kitchen cleaver in your back, perhaps?"

"Minx." He leaned in to her and kissed her hard and fast on her open mouth.

The kiss lingered on her lips for a long time afterward.

20

Chapter Twenty

Cat wandered into the lounge to check on Gran and the aunts. The discussion had calmed to a desultory comment here and there.

"Catty, put some music on, dear. Are Mumma's Nelson Eddy and Jeanette McDonald records there? I'd love to hear their *Indian Love Call.*"

The records were stored in an entertainment unit housing an ageing television, an even older record player, and Cat's Bluetooth speaker. She flicked through the stack of records to find the soundtrack for *Rose-Marie,* which featured the song Gran requested.

Soft music filled the room. "Oh aye, aren't they magnificent?" Elspeth mused. "I didn't realize ye could still find records like this."

"My mother bought these when they were released." Isla rested her chin in the palm of one hand. "She took care of them. I grew up listening to these songs. So did Jeanette and Catty here. Didn't you, dear?"

"I sure did, Gran, and I loved it. Would anyone like more tea or coffee?"

"I don't think I can have another thing." Alethea folded her arms over her stomach and gave a contented sigh.

Cat set one hand on the doorjamb. "Call me if you do, I'll be in the kitchen making some phone calls, or across the hall in my room."

Her first call was to the customer support center of the bank relating to the old passbook she'd found.

"We have suspended the account, ma'am, and we require authority to reopen it," the operator said.

"Whose authority?" Cat asked.

"We would need a direction from the person who opened the account, or the account holder, if they are different."

"I'm Catriona Cameron, and I'm the account holder. The person who opened the account died more than seven years ago. Are you able to provide me with a current balance on the account?"

"We would need some identification, Catriona. May I call you Catriona?"

"Yes. I have another account with you, one I opened myself," Cat said.

"That would be a great help. Can you give me the number, please?"

She rattled off the number for her account and heard the operator keying it in.

"I have it. Can you give me your full name and date of birth please? Thank you," she said as Cat relayed the information. "And your mother's maiden name? And the name of your first pet?"

"Dog or cat? We got Zelda and Zeus at the same time."

The bank assistant chuckled. "Okay. For future reference, Zelda is the name we have recorded."

"Right. And my mother's maiden name was Jenkins."

"Thanks. The details on this account match those for the account you are enquiring about, so there shouldn't be a problem. I'll reactivate it for forty-eight hours. You won't be able to make transactions on it until you get to your local branch with the bank book. I'll give you a reference number to provide the teller. You can make any further inquiries on the account after we confirm your identity. Please make sure you have identification documents with you, birth certificate, passport, driver's license, medical card, any two of those."

"Thank you. Can you tell me why we didn't receive a letter or any query for the account during the last seven years?"

"Give me a moment." Catriona heard the rattle of the keyboard again. "The account holder marked it no mail. Sometimes people open a secret account they want to hide from a husband or wife or from themselves if they're saving for a particular goal."

Catriona chuckled. "Ah hah. Thank you for your time. I'll go to my local branch tomorrow."

"Is there anything else I can help you with today, Catriona?"

"No, thank you," she said, ending the call. She'd organized the bank account as much as possible for now, so she dialed the number she found on her father's papers.

"Smith and Jones Legal. Melanie speaking."

"I'm sorry. I thought I called McAllister Legal."

"Oh yes, we're McAllister too. We changed our name two years ago. How can I help you?"

"I found my father's will, and I wanted advice on what to do with it."

"Your name?"

"Catriona Cameron. My father was Bradley Raymond Cameron."

She swapped the phone to her other hand and flexed the fingers she'd held in a death grip on the instrument.

"Yes, I know the name. Let me put you through to Mr. Benjamin Jones. One moment, please."

"Miss Cameron? This is Ben Jones. It's good to hear from you. Did your mother change her mind about allowing you your inheritance?"

"My mother passed away, Mr. Jones. I located the information relating to my father's will when I was clearing her things this week."

"I'm sorry to hear you've lost your mother, Miss Cameron. The last contact we had with her was at the time of your father's death. She was angry, I think, and forbade us from contacting her, or you, ever again. She wanted nothing to do with Brad's legacy. That can happen in the early stages of grief, especially for sudden deaths like this one. Clients wait until they need funds and remember the inheritance. Generally, these things clear themselves up in a few years. This one has taken a bit longer, but we're happy you've found us now. There's a portfolio of information I need to go through with you once I have verified your identity. Are you able to come in?"

"Not easily. I'm caring for my grandmother. I'm not sure how she would cope with a trip to the Mornington Peninsula." She bit the corner of her bottom lip.

"I see. We can come to you. Would early evening be convenient?"

"Today?" A *whump* of agitation hit her chest—a feeling of unpreparedness like the times at school when a teacher lowered the hammer of a pop quiz.

"If that suits you. At six?" Jones asked.

"I wouldn't want to monopolize your evening."

"No problem at all. I live in the city. Unless your home is in Bacchus Marsh or Tullamarine, it won't be much of a detour."

"We're in Kew." She gave him the address.

"Are you married or in a relationship, Miss Cameron?"

"No, why do you ask?"

"The beneficence of this estate predates any current relationship. We would seek to protect your inheritance from becoming part of a contested settlement."

"I see," she said, confused about what the man was saying.

"We can explain more when we get there. I'll have a younger colleague, Joshua Fredericks, with me. We'll see you at six this evening." He terminated the call.

She sat holding the phone until Alethea appeared at the door.

"Are ye all right, dear?"

"Yes, thank you. Just a few surprises. I have someone coming this evening. Can I get you a cup of tea?"

"I'm after the bathroom first, but a cuppa would be lovely. Wine in the middle of the day is not something I'm used to anymore. Though it is such fun." She chortled.

"The bathroom is around the corner, to your right." Cat directed her to the guest bathroom, then went to put the kettle on and rummage in the cupboards for the ingredients to complete the lamingtons.

She sifted cocoa and icing sugar, ready for the boiling water. The click of the auto switch on the kettle flicking off must have sent some magical signal to the universe. Isla and Elspeth shuffled into the kitchen and took a seat at the table as the doorbell rang.

Cat scooted around the ladies and welcomed Iona and Lachie back. "Perfect timing. I'm making the icing for the lamingtons. You can help," she said to Iona.

The next half hour passed with the older ladies drinking tea and being entertained by the sight of Iona jiggling cubes of cake into liquid chocolate icing, Cat rolling them in coconut, and Lachie gingerly setting the covered cubes on wire racks. The constant knocking of his hip against her side each time he reached for the cakes was a delicious distraction. She was sure there were far more bumps and rubs than were required. She smiled to herself.

"Gran, could we get away with putting some in the fridge, since we would like to try them today?"

"Yes, I suppose so. Enough for what we'll eat now. Eight or ten maybe?"

"Cool. Lachie you can put five each on two plates and pop them in the fridge for fifteen minutes. They may not be quite set by then, but it will be better than trying to handle them fresh. Spread them so the cold air can circulate. Shall we move back to the dining table, ladies? You'll be more comfortable in there."

The older ladies left their seats and waddled their way back to the other room, with Lachie herding them along.

"Hehe! That was great. I hope they taste as good as they look," Iona commented, licking her icing-covered fingers.

"They will be. If you like chocolate and coconut, you'll love these."

By the time they'd cleared the kitchen, Cat decreed they might risk trying the lamingtons. She made a large pot of tea and invited Lachie to make his own coffee.

The Scots visitors received the cakes with delight.

"Ye'll have to make these when ye come to Scotland, lass." The appreciation in Lachie's eyes made the butterflies in her stomach take flight.

She smiled at him. "I will."

His return smile sent wild sensations bouncing around her body. "Would ye like to join us for dinner tonight? Ye and Gran?"

"Oh, we can't. We have people coming by at six, and I'm not sure how long we'll be."

His brows drew together. "It can wait. Right, ladies. It's time for us to leave our generous hosts in peace."

With some shuffling and a lot of shambling, the ladies gathered their bags and Iona guided them to the door.

Lachie dropped a kiss on Cat's head. "Can I see ye tomorrow, lass?"

"I should be free after lunch."

The bedroom look smoldering in his eyes left her with a zinging awareness in her gut. "'Til then," he said.

She strode to the kitchen, tamping her emotions as she went. Clearing away the afternoon tea dishes reminded her of her days in the café. When she wasn't serving, she was clearing and cleaning tables. The routine was satisfying, and the task was completed with an efficiency born of years of training.

She helped Gran back to the lounge room and put the record on to play again. It sounded scratchy, though it wasn't too bad given it was more than eighty years old.

"Gran, where's your passport?"

"At the back of the drawer with my knickers, dear. Do you need it?"

"I want to check if it's current. You must have one if we're going to visit the McKells in Scotland."

"I'd like to go to Scotland again," Isla said.

"That's the plan, Gran. I'll go find it, if it's okay with you."

"Yes dear, whatever you like. I'm tired. I'll nap here for a while." She adjusted the angle of the seat to suit, leaned her head back, and closed her eyes.

Cat found the document where Gran said. It was current for another five years. She must have renewed it before her dementia became apparent. Her own passport was a little older. She gathered it and put both in her handbag.

Ben Jones and his colleague arrived on the dot of six. Cat eyed the briefcases they were carrying and directed them to the dining room table.

"Can I get you a drink or a cup of tea?"

"Tea for me, please. I have to keep a clear head."

"Joshua?"

"Tea for me too, please."

"I'll let you get organized while I fetch my grandmother."

She approached the chair where Gran was still resting. "Gran, are you awake? My father's lawyers are here. Do you want to be part of the discussion?"

"Poor Brad, he was never happy. He was so lovely, so sad," Isla said.

"Do you want to come?"

"No dear, I'm tired. You can tell me later." She waved one hand on a limp wrist.

Cat skirted the dining room to get to the kitchen and prepared a tray with tea and lamingtons and the nice cups. She carried it back to where the men waited. "Gran won't be joining us. Shall I get the will I found?"

"Not necessary, Miss Cameron," Ben said. "I drew it up for your father so it's quite familiar to me."

"Please call me Cat or Catriona."

"Thank you, Catriona. We've continued to manage your father's affairs, or your affairs I should say, and we've been happy to do so. We're thrilled you found us. We'll hand over to you only what you want to manage for yourself in terms of the properties or the investments."

"You'll have to start at the beginning. I know nothing of the man, save he left my mother when she was pregnant with me," she said, her tone grim.

"He did it to protect you and your mother both. He left some personal knick-knacks, his Rolex, some other little things for you. He'd always intended to write you a letter, but my guess is he never expected his life to be cut short so suddenly. If you have personal questions about him, you can ask me. I knew Bradley for most of his adult life, and most of mine, until his passing. He was born in Scotland and came to Australia on a project for the United Kingdom government. He decided to stay here after he met your mother. He was a good man, a solid man. And he loved your mother very much."

Ben leaned forward. "Bradley was determined you and she should be well cared for in the event he wasn't around. He regularly deposited money into an account for your mother. She, on the other hand, refused to accept anything if he wasn't living with her. It was a constant tussle between them. Jeannie used it to put pressure on Brad to come home, whatever the risk. She told him she wanted nothing from him if he didn't love her enough to be her husband. He was adamant he would not put her, or you, in peril. Eventually, they agreed the money would go from your mother's account into one in your name."

Cat nodded while hugging herself tightly around her midriff.

"Yes, I found a bank book for an account my mother opened in my name. It has a lot of money in it." She swallowed against the renewed sense of uncertainty and of life being turned on its head. "Why would we be in peril?" she asked, going back to the man's earlier comment. She'd never felt she was in danger, and if her mother did, she hadn't shown it.

"Because of the nature of his work. I'm not comfortable discussing it."

She hesitated. "All right." She'd leave those details for now.

Ben rested against the back of the chair and drew the sides of his business jacket together over his portly stomach. "In the end, Bradley left everything to you, because he wasn't sure what your mother would do if she was hurt or angry. So, Catriona, you have a portfolio of twenty Melbourne properties, two in New York, two in London, and two in Edinburgh. Bradley bought them gradually when prices were depressed, usually in suburbs other investors didn't want. Now each one is valued at over a million dollars. The New York and London ones are higher. The properties are tenanted with good income, except for one in Edinburgh which was vacated two weeks ago. Our agent there is seeking another occupant." He tapped the table with his interlocked hands.

"Bradley was keen to buy shares in start-up companies too. It was his way of giving others a leg up in the world. Many start-ups failed, but a good number succeeded. You'll recognize some names on the list; they're high-profile international companies now. There is a sizeable amount of cash in term deposits. We use those as receptacles for income across the portfolio. I applied for probate when Bradley died. We are ready to pass the entire estate to you when we verify your identity."

Cat was trembling, visibly shaken. "Catriona, are you all right?" Ben frowned.

"Um, I wouldn't know how to handle any of it. I found the bank book with the deposits, and I thought that was an amazing fortune. Now you're telling me it's small change. I can't think. Let me make a fresh pot of tea."

Staggering to the kitchen, she took huge, gulping breaths of air. Two days ago, she feared a court case would bankrupt her. Tonight, she was a multimillionaire? Things like this didn't happen to people like her.

She filled the kettle and plugged it in. Skirting the lounge where the men were, she stumbled to her room for her birth certificate and the bank book. When she returned, she made the tea and carried it through.

The men helped themselves to the lamingtons in her absence and were singing their praises, though she was too numb to appreciate it. She fumbled in her handbag to get her driver's license from her wallet and extracted the passports too, placing the lot on the table in front of the senior lawyer.

"Oh, you don't need Gran's passport, do you?"

The lawyer smiled for the first time when he opened Gran's passport. "No, it's not necessary, except it confirms she was Jeannie Jenkins's mum. Jeannie was the brightest thing in Bradley's life. Bradley didn't meet her until he was in his forties, and loved her at first sight. He was smitten, totally and irrevocably smitten. The man couldn't bear it if anything bad happened to her because of him. Ah, yes, Jeannie Jenkins."

For a moment, Cat thought the lawyer would cry, but he didn't. He coughed, closed her grandmother's passport, and gathered the other documents. Her birth certificate recorded Bradley as her father. Setting it aside, he checked her passport and her driver's license. Then he opened the bank book.

"Yes, this appears correct until seven years ago. We continued making the payments in accordance with Bradley's earlier direction. The later payments aren't here. Your mother must have done the transfers manually."

"Are you telling me there's yet more money?" Her hands shook as she poured the fresh tea, buying some time to unscramble her mind.

"Miss Cameron?" Joshua's tone was hesitant. "I work with Smith and Jones as a financial planner in cases like yours. I manage the portfolio and keep the profits turning over until the rightful heir comes forward. Of course, we take a percentage, so it works for us too.

"What I want to say is, ah, what Ben said earlier. You only need to do what you can cope with, or nothing, if you choose. If you want to walk away and have us deposit money into your personal account every week or month, we can make the arrangements. If you want to sell any of the investments, you can do it yourself or direct us to act for you. Don't be overwhelmed." Joshua's face was calm, concerned, reassuring. Cat relaxed with a heavy sigh.

"More to the point, Catriona," Ben said, "do you have enough to meet your immediate needs?"

"Um, I'm going to the bank in the morning to reactivate this account. If there are no problems and it happens immediately, we'll be fine. I'm taking my grandmother to visit relatives in Scotland." She smiled, hoping she conveyed the impression she was at least a little in control.

Ben's smile broadened. "You might like to inspect the Edinburgh and London properties while you're in the UK. I mentioned an Edinburgh property was vacant?"

"You did. Would you leave it untenanted for the moment? Gran and I might need an independent base. We would need some rudimentary furniture, I suppose."

"I can ask our agent to send you some photographs. If you want it refurbished ahead of your stay, he can arrange it. He can have it furnished to your specifications and provide linens and other support to the standard you would expect in a high-end serviced apartment. His staff will stock it with basic food items too, if it would help." Ben's avuncular practicality grounded her emotions.

"Wonderful, thank you. It might take me some time to process this." She waved a hand over the paperwork in front of her.

"We'll leave you with the material to go through at your leisure. If you have any questions at all, call us. Don't hesitate."

Cat drew the pile of paper close and laid her hands flat on top of it. "Thank you for your help. I'd never have imagined this."

The men stood from the table. "I would caution you, Catriona, not to discuss your changed circumstances with anyone other than ourselves. Fortune hunters are everywhere. You should also make time to prepare your own will, preferably prior to undertaking your proposed international travel."

She didn't want to consider the ramifications of what the man was saying—that her death might occur at any moment. It was too much to deal with on top of what this day had already brought. She needed time alone to process everything, so she nodded to signal the conclusion of the meeting and closed the door behind them, slumping against it. Then she smiled, a smile so big it stretched the muscles in her face.

She was an heiress! A real-life heiress. Not of Paris Hilton proportions, but more than she would need in her lifetime.

And they were going to Scotland. She'd book a flight with those fancy double suites in first class she'd seen the airlines advertise. Gran would feel safer sheltered from other people.

She danced on the spot. Who'd have thought it? Charles Sopworthy's café skivvy was an instant millionaire.

21

Chapter Twenty-one

Returning to his home country was always a pleasure for Lachie. Whether he'd been gone a week or a month, it was good to be back on home soil. The people here didn't ask him to repeat himself a dozen times because they didn't understand his accent. The weather suited his mood, and the food was predictable.

This time the return was particularly sweet. He was bringing home the woman he wanted for his bride. She was a stubborn wee thing. No surprise there. He'd known it from the outset. The obstinate woman insisted on doing the bookings for herself and Isla. She'd assured him she'd found a forgotten inheritance and was well able to afford her chosen seats. That was a puzzle for him, but all would be revealed in time, he figured.

Lachie made certain he was in the same cabin as the Australians for each leg of the flight. When she booked a suite, he booked a suite, where she booked first class, he booked first class. He couldn't leave his family back in business, where they usually sat, so they moved forward too. The exercise was costly, but worth it. There was always someone on hand for Isla, even when Cat was sleeping.

Reaching above her head, he fetched Catriona's cabin bag from the overhead locker and waited for her to precede him from the plane. In the other aisle, Iona was doing the same for Isla. Once they'd collected their luggage, they exited through immigration to find his driver waiting with the company limousine.

"Welcome back, my lord, my lady. Let me take yer things."

"Thank ye, Emerson."

"My lord?" Cat asked.

He raised one brow at her query. "A gesture of respect. Are ye comfortable traveling sideways?"

"Yes."

"Good. Ye'll find Emerson has supplied hot tea and shortbreads in case anyone is peckish. Here ye go, Gran. It's the last leg of the journey. It will take a wee bit more than an hour and a half. Make yerself comfortable."

Ushering his great-aunts into the car, Lachie slid in across from Cat. Every nuance of her expression fascinated him. Like the one a moment ago when Emerson addressed him by his title. There were many emotions flitting across her face—quizzical, impressed, disbelieving, and a wee bit fearful.

He dismissed Emerson's greeting, not wanting her to back away now she was close to his home. Besides what use was being a Marquis if he couldn't hold his community together?

"Will we go through Edinburgh?" Her eyes were alight with excitement.

"We're heading north; the city is south."

Her face fell as though a treat had been offered and then snatched away. He squirmed on his seat. The city was as familiar as breathing to him, but he should have realized it would be different for her. "If it's important to ye, lass, ye can come with me on my next trip. I'll be busy during the day so ye'll be on yer own. Edinburgh is a grand city. Ye'll find a lot to do."

"Okay, good." She relaxed back into the padded swabs. "Will we go to the highlands? And Loch Ness?"

"Ye'll see more highlands than ye can look at in one direction. Loch Ness is further north. We'll plan for it during yer stay."

"Are we on a bridge?" she asked as the car slowed.

He smiled at her enthusiasm, even for something as humdrum as a traffic snarl. "It's the bridge over the Firth of Forth. There's a bit of congestion today."

The lass was chewing on her bottom lip. Nervous or excited? He hoped for the latter.

After half an hour, Iona withdrew two flasks of tea, cups, and a covered plate of shortbreads from the center console and passed them around. Isla and the aunts had been napping, but woke to the sound of the crockery.

"Where are we? What are we doing? Catty, what's happening?" Isla jerked upright in her seat. Her gaze darted about, and a severe frown puckered her brow.

Cat placed a hand over her grandmother's. "We're in Scotland, Gran. You wanted to visit Kellburgh again. Lachie is taking us there now. Would you like a cup of tea? Iona has these lovely shortbreads."

"I want to go to Scotland," Isla said.

"Now we're here. Soon you'll see the places you remember."

Isla accepted the cup from Iona and sat back, apparently satisfied with the plan, drank her tea, and nodded off to sleep again. She stirred when the car slowed, and Iona leaned toward her.

"We're coming into Kellburgh, Gran. Do ye want to look? In another five minutes, we'll be home."

Isla blinked and peered out the window. "Oh yes, I remember this place. I was young, fifteen or so. We went to a house here, near the church, right next door."

"Whom did ye visit?" Iona asked.

Gran's face contorted into a sneer. "My uncle. Dougal McGill. Horrible man. I suppose he's dead now."

"Yes. His house was severely damaged by fire. His son, Doughal, still lives in town with his own son, Darro, a worker in the production room."

"Are they nasty people like Dallin and old Dougal?"

Iona chuckled. "I really can't say."

The aunts both snickered ruefully. They exchanged a glance with each other and with Iona.

"Hmph. We'll soon find out when they know we're here," Isla snarled.

"They do have a reputation, dear, but we stay well away if we can, so we can't say from personal experience, like," Alethea confided.

The car started up a sharp incline, and Isla held on to stop from slipping down the banquette. "Are we going to the castle?"

"I suppose ye might call it a castle," Iona said.

"Angus said he was from the castle. We weren't supposed to meet anyone from the castle. My uncle didn't want anyone to know there was another *Simone*. He hated *Simones*."

"Why?" Iona asked.

"Ah, who can say? Jealous, I suppose."

The car came to a stop in the courtyard of an impressive stone structure.

Lachie climbed from the car first, helping Cat out.

Her glance traveled over the façade of the building. "Not a castle, eh? So, what would you call it?"

"Somewhere ye might want to call home?"

Her warning gaze whipped to him. He realized too late he'd made a strategic error. "We're here for a visit, Lachie, and that's it."

He loved the way she was strong enough to stand her ground. "A man can hope, *m'eudail*." He raised his eyebrows and smiled, aiming to charm her out of her irritation.

She screwed her mouth to one side. "Right."

Two liveried footmen carried their luggage into the house. Iona directed them to place Isla's and Catriona's luggage in the peony and sunflower rooms. Then she asked the housekeeper for some tea and cakes, and led the troupe of travelers to a pleasant conservatory where a medium-sized table was already set with crockery for tea.

"There's a small bathroom over to yer left, Catriona, if ye need the facilities," Iona said.

"Thanks, we'll just be a few minutes. Gran?"

Isla nodded and took her arm, shuffling along beside her.

When they returned, Lachie scanned the group. Everyone seemed fine after the long journey, including Isla. He focused on Cat. She appeared relaxed and comfortable in his home.

He cared for her a lot, but the pâté shemozzle kept getting in the way. After the fiasco of a marriage he endured with Meredith, he'd seen no chance to ever find love.

"I'm tired," Isla stated abruptly.

Both Cat and Iona sprang to their feet.

"Let me show ye to yer room, Gran," his sister offered.

"I'll come with you," Catriona said.

"There's no need, dear. Catty will look after me," Isla said, linking her arm through Iona's.

"But—" Catriona's barely uttered objection fell on deaf ears.

Iona waved Catriona back to her seat. "We'll manage. Ye relax."

His aunts, too, decided the time had come for them to retire to their quarters, leaving him alone with Catriona.

"Are ye tired?" he asked.

"Not a bit. First class travel might even be worth the exorbitant amount they charge," she said.

"It's good value for a long haul. I'm happy further back in the plane for short hops."

She folded her hands, resting them on the table. "So, you're not a lord and this isn't a castle, huh?"

Lachie shrugged. What was there to say? "I'm a businessman, and this is my home. It's been my family's home since even before Simone arrived on the scene. I don't take it for granted, but I don't see it the way other people do. Does it bother ye?"

"I should warn you I would have voted for a republic in Australia if I'd been old enough. The entire aristocracy thing doesn't do a lot for me."

"My bloodline is yer bloodline, and, because we are part of the so-called aristocracy, it's our duty to take responsibility for our clan, for our people, to ensure they're housed, fed, and employed."

"Maybe for you. You can't generalize to other aristocrats, otherwise there never would have been revolutions."

"I'll give ye that, but it is the way my parents raised me and the way I will raise my children. It's a point of honor to care for others. It's why this pâté thing has been such a worry," he frowned. "We won't discuss it now. Ye've barely arrived. Let me show ye my home." He got to his feet and held her chair.

They wandered through the downstairs areas until they came to the library. Catriona stopped to stare at the portrait hanging above the mantelpiece.

"She is beautiful. Who is she?"

Lachie chuckled. "Let me introduce ye to Simone de Salignac McKell, late of this parish."

"She is the Simone? My great de-de-de grandmother?" She stabbed the air with her finger several times to show the generations the "de" represented.

"Aye. This was a portrait to represent her on her wedding day. In her journals she talks of the onerous effort required to dress in her wedding gown every day for weeks and weeks while she posed for the painting."

"And the parure?"

"Her husband's gift to her for their wedding. It's set with diamonds and has an amethyst for the thistle to represent her new home." He saw her swallow hard. Then she glanced at him sharply. "Where is it now?"

"We've lost it. We believe this collection passed to her eldest daughter for her dowry. From there, it's anyone's guess. There was at least one other set. It's gone too, more's the pity."

"Because of the value of the stones?"

"There is that, I suppose. They'd be worth hundreds of thousands of pounds today, probably, if ye consider the size of those gems. To the family, it would be priceless, because it would be a direct link to her."

Cat took a step closer to the painting. "She is so, so beautiful, and she fell in love with a Scot, hey?"

"It happens." He shrugged.

Swinging back to him, she swatted his arm. He caught and held her hand, taking possession of the second one to draw her to him.

"It can happen, *m'eudail,* if ye let it." His heart was pleading.

Her eyes widened, but she didn't pull away.

He lowered his face to hers. It felt like forever since there'd been a chance to kiss her. Here, in his home, there was a sense of rightness about it, a blending, a mutual ownership. *The wee sprite'd be none too pleased if she could read my mind.* He was tempted to chuckle. Instead, gathering her closer, the kiss went on. Her lips responded to his, her hands clawed into his sides. Lost in the dream of holding her, he was oblivious to anything but this.

"Pardon me, my lord. I have more logs for the fire." The voice of a maid intruded, bringing him back to reality. It didn't persuade him to let Cat go.

She dropped her hands from his waist and flexed one brow at him. "I forgot to ask again, hmm?" he said.

She flattened her lips and stepped back. Then she surprised him with a grin. "Can you direct me to my room, please?"

"Janet, when ye've taken yer load through, would ye show Miss Cameron to her room?" If he was the one to take her upstairs, even a kiss might get out of hand.

"Yes, my lord." A smiling Janet was quick to agree.

22

Chapter Twenty-two

"Good morning, lass. Did you sleep well?" Lachie asked.

"I did, thank you. I must've been more tired than I realized. A good night's sleep does wonders." She sat at the breakfast table. A maid offered her coffee or tea, and Cat chose the coffee. "Then, if ye care to, ye might like to stroll with me to the village. I've some people to see. That won't take long, and it'll give you the opportunity to orient yerself."

She took a sip of her coffee and eyed him over the rim of her cup.

"I wouldn't be in the way? It might put people off when there's a stranger around and they want to speak with you."

"Nay, lass. They'll be pleased as punch. Ye'll need to dress warmly. We're well into autumn here in the highlands. Ye'll notice the cold, coming from yer warm Melbourne spring."

"Okay. When do you want to go?"

"There's no rush. If we leave here by a quarter to ten, we'll have time enough."

An hour later, they met in the foyer near the front door. Lachie dressed casually in a dun-colored tartan kilt, white shirt, and a sleeveless jacket, something like a jerkin, she thought. She chose jeans, a long-sleeved blouse, and her favorite puffy coat.

Isla was still sleeping, the trip having been an arduous one for her, so Iona promised to keep watch should she wake while Cat was out.

Cat and Lachie wandered down the hill from the castle, past the church, and on to a strip with shops on either side of the street including a post office, supermarket, doctor's surgery, and various others. There was a large green area dissecting the street with more shops beyond it.

"This was the market square back in the day," Lachie said, as they followed a footpath across the space.

"Really? Is this where my great-grandmother met her Sassenach, do you think?" she asked.

"It's the only market square hereabouts, lass. I'm thinking this is likely the place."

"Wow!" She spun in a circle noting every corner, imagining a young Rhona being chatty with the young man Cat only knew from photographs.

She grinned. Lachie urged her forward into a quaint café proclaiming itself to be Hamish's Tea Rooms. Inside, the deceptively small exterior opened into an extensive area stretching into the back garden. The walls were a mix of painted wood paneling and colorful wallpapered panels adorned with work by local artists. Discreet price tags were tucked between the wall and the frame of each. The café was well lit, giving a gleam to the polished tongue and groove floor.

There were people scattered throughout at round tables which were topped with a red cloth and a glass overlay.

"Are ye warm enough, lass?" he asked as he helped her out of her puffy coat.

"It's beautifully toasty in here." She made a mental note to remember gloves next time as she rubbed her hands together to warm them.

"Good morning, Laird. Welcome home. We've kept yer usual spot." A dapper man in his early fifties directed them to a sizeable round table in the middle of the room, far enough away from the raging furnace of the open fire that they didn't melt, but close enough to feel its effects.

"Thank ye, Hamish. This is Miss Catriona Cameron, visiting from Australia with her grandmother," Lachie said.

"Welcome, Miss Cameron. We've heard ye were here. We hope ye'll be verra happy in our little corner of the world. What would ye like to drink? And to eat?"

"I'll have tea, please." She acknowledged the man's welcome with a smile.

Hamish gave a brisk nod and headed toward the kitchen area.

It didn't take her long to realize the community expected Lachie in the café on a Wednesday morning. A stream of people stopped by the table to say hello, to be introduced to the newcomer, and to bring the laird up to date on what was happening in their lives.

The range of topics was broad. There were complaints relating to a neighbor's barking dog, and concerns around political issues in the United Kingdom in a post-European Union world. Others asked Lachie to agitate for a new referendum for Scotland to secede from "the lot of them." The largest number of questions, though, were from people asking if the laird was progressing the pâté production, or what other industry he might have considered to provide employment.

The latter queries drew Lachie's gaze to hers. Every time it happened, she imagined prison bars being erected around her. She maintained a smiling façade, but her nerves were stretched.

After an hour, Lachie rose, waved a farewell to Hamish, and shuffled her outside. "Ye're peaky, lass. Are ye feeling all right?"

"You might have warned me. They probably thought we were a couple and I needed to hear their intimate stories."

He grinned. "Well, it is the first time I've taken anyone with me. I suppose they drew their own conclusions."

She stopped walking and looked at him. "You never took your wife?"

Lachie took her hand and tugged her lightly to continue their promenade. "No. Ye wouldn't be surprised if ye knew her. Meredith was pregnant when we married. After the *bairn* arrived, she focused her attention on the little one. I'm not sure she would've been able to talk to people they way ye do."

Cat squeezed his fingers, acknowledging his confidence in her, but also in sympathy at the mention of his lost spouse. "They ambushed me on the pâté."

"No one knows yer connection to the pâté, lass. But can ye understand why I'm worried? These people need jobs."

She stopped and looked at him. "Lachie, the surest way to get rid of me is to paint me into a corner on this. I'll come out swinging, lay waste to everyone in my path, and go without a backward glance. If that's what you want, keep parading this stuff."

"Look, lass. I only wanted ye to meet the folk here, to hear what's important to them. I didn't expect there would be so many queries about the pâté. I'd hoped the concern was settling, but it's not. It's their livelihoods." He let go of her hand and dragged both his hands through his hair, a sure sign she'd upset him.

"I will not brawl with you on a public street. Which way back, straight up this hill?"

"Aye. I'll take ye back."

"Don't. There's a man across the street who's doing a two-step to get your attention. I'll catch you later." She offered a half-smile she hoped appeared more genuine to their audience than it really was.

Turning, she waved to Lachie and strode toward the castle.

~ * ~

The next morning, Iona showed Cat and Gran to the area where the limited pâté making was under way.

"We've cut staff numbers because there's not much demand for what we're producing. The connoisseurs say they can't differentiate the new Simone's Pâté from any other freshly-made product. Worse still, sometimes they say it's too bitter."

"May I try some?" Cat asked.

"There's a whole refrigerator full here. It's what we've made in the past few days," Iona pulled a tray from the fridge.

Cat spread some pâté on a cracker for herself, then one for Isla.

"There's a slightly bitter aftertaste, isn't there? What do you think, Gran? It's palatable in its own right, though not Simone's."

"Too much lavender," Isla said.

"It hasn't been pretreated either," Cat mused.

"Pretreated?" Her eyes widened.

"It's part of the secret. Where's the flavored whisky used for this batch?"

Iona brought across a large porcelain flask, uncorked it, and poured some into three glasses. They each took a sip. "Hmm. The problem starts here." Cat frowned. "It has been steeped overly long. The herb flavor is too strong."

"We've made a lot of assumptions trying to get the product right. We found the whisky with the herbs in it after Meredith died. We used it the way we found it."

"It's been steeping for nearly a year? Oh my. May we have some straight whisky, please, and another container."

She blended the steeped whisky with the other, sniffing the new concoction for aroma until it satisfied her. She poured the blend into fresh glasses.

"Gran?"

"It's close. I can't taste all the herbs, though. It'll do until you start the process from scratch."

"I agree." Cat pursed her lips in thought.

Iona sipped the liquid. "It's mild. It softens the whisky without giving it too much flavor."

"Oops. Have we given Iona too much information?"

"Not unless you've told her what herbs to use in the first place." Isla chuckled.

"Ye can see why we need someone who knows how to make the pâté Simone's way. We're lost. Our reputation for the pâté is close to irretrievable. Can ye help?"

"We're only here for a few weeks. If Gran and I make pâté and you get your suppliers excited, the crash will be much worse when we leave."

Isla topped up her glass from the container of moderated whisky. "Ye can't stay?"

Cat heard the note of desperation in Iona's tone but firmed her resolve. "There's no reason for me to be here except to make pâté. It's not enough."

"My brother?"

Cat replaced her glass on the bench. "I want someone who will love me. Love me; not tolerate me because I can produce what he wants. With your brother, I'll never know."

Iona raised her brows. "Ye think my brother is a fortune hunter, except the fortune is pâté?"

"I don't know, Iona." Cat sighed in defeat. "I don't know."

"So, ye can't help us? Ye won't make the product?" Iona's shoulders drooped.

"I'll tell you what we will do," Cat began, her bracing tone as much for her own benefit as for her hostess. "We'll make pâté with your team just for in-house consumption. It would use some of the ingredients you have on hand and remind the team of the Simone's taste. What do you say, Gran?"

Isla nodded and downed the rest of her drink.

"It's a start, I suppose," Iona said. "What do we do with this stuff? Can we fix it? Can we make it more like Simone's?" She waved a hand across the pâté they'd tasted.

"You can't retrospectively make it into Simone's version. It's an all-right product on its own. It's just not Simone's. One idea might be to market it differently. Call it the Apprentice Blend, or some such. You're the marketing whiz, Iona, you've probably thought of those options already. Or you can freeze it to use in dishes like *boeuf en croute*."

"It has played on the edges of my mind." Iona chewed her bottom lip. "It was like admitting defeat, somehow."

"Not defeat, a new product," Cat insisted.

She fanned her fingers across her mouth. "Maybe," Iona conceded. "How many people do ye want to work with ye today?"

"This group will be enough. Do you have goats' milk?"

"Some. We freeze most of it. We didn't know how Meredith used it. None of the recipes we've tried called for goats' milk. But we kept the goats, and we've kept milking them." She shrugged.

"Meredith died last year?" Cat raised a hand to one cheek.

"With her baby girl," Iona said.

Cat's shoulders slumped. "Oh, how sad. Lachie said they were in a car accident."

"Lachie talked about her?" Iona raised her eyebrows. "How unusual."

She flipped the conversation away from the potentially troubled waters. "You can only keep the milk frozen for a few months. What do you do with it then?"

"We sell it at a month. It's on rotation until we find a solution to the pâté issue."

"You might make goats' milk soap, you know. It's in high demand everywhere. Add different herbs, honey, oatmeal. Precious!" Catriona said.

"Do ye think so?"

"Try it. It's easier to transport than pâté too. In the meantime, if you get me some goats' milk and cleaned livers, we'll prepare a batch to observe how your team works." She turned to Isla when Iona moved away. "Are you going to stay this morning, Gran, or would you like me to take you back to your room?"

"I haven't made pâté in a while. This will be exciting." Isla grinned.

"Great, I think we'll both need to supervise the sauté."

Iona returned with fresh goats' milk and introduced Cat and Isla to the women by the cooking stations. They were friendly enough on the surface, though a couple sideways glances gave Cat the sense of an undercurrent of suspicion, or perhaps resentment.

"Isla and Catriona have come from Australia to visit. They're both pâté makers. I've said they can work with ye this morning. Daphne, if ye give Catriona the cleaned livers, she can get started," Iona said.

"Thank you. Gran and I will work at this bench. You should heat the pans in an hour to medium heat," Cat directed.

"We have made pâté before, miss," one woman said in a disgusted tone.

"Emily, ye will follow Catriona's instructions, please," Iona insisted.

"Yes, my lady." The disgruntled Emily wasn't pleased.

Cat mentally listed any number of rejoinders relating to her opinion of the pâté they'd been making. Saying them aloud wouldn't help to win friends. Gran always drummed into her the adages, "Least said, soonest mended," or "What you don't say, you don't have to apologize for."

"If ye're okay here, I'll go and make a start on yer ideas to market our supply differently. If ye need me, Daphne will know where to find me. I'll leave ye to it and pop back later."

"Thanks, we'll be fine," Cat assured her. She'd never directed a team of cooks. Young waitresses yes, that was her job at the café, but a group of women all senior to her in age? This would be a new experience. With Gran's help, she'd manage. She straightened her shoulders and turned to the job at hand.

Cat asked the women to prep the onions and garlic. She and Gran took the livers to the far side of the room to work their magic with the goats' milk and herbs.

After an hour, they rinsed the livers, patted them dry, and brought them back to sauté. They divided the livers amongst the four women to handle and kept an eye on the work with the pans. Emily was scraping and tossing the delicate offal like she was cooking mushrooms.

"Emily, please be careful. If you're too rough with the livers, they become tough. It will make the pâté grainy," Cat warned.

"This is the way I do it, miss."

"Hmm. There's always more to learn, isn't there?" Cat smiled, hoping to defuse the situation. "Here's another way. Let the livers settle. When the blood rises, gently fold them, like this. Leave them alone for a while, then carefully flip them again. By then, they should be done. They should be a bit pink on the inside, do you see there? Not too rare, though. Okay?"

"We'll take all day, doing it yer way," Emily complained.

"Sometimes it does. Would you prefer to help with the onions? I'll take over here," she said, stepping in and taking hold of the pan's handle.

Isla walked along and checked each load of cooked livers. She nodded to Cat, who fetched the moderated whisky and added the right amount to each pan.

"Carefully, carefully, deglaze with the whisky. Let it boil off for one minute only and take the pan from the heat. Good. Who can clarify the butter for me? Thank you, Daphne. We'll cook the onions and garlic."

With the cooking done, the women emptied the ingredients into a large processor to blend them together.

"Where's the food mill?" Catriona asked.

"Why do ye want a mill? We've already given it a good blending." Emily frowned.

"Thanks Emily. This the part where Gran and I add our magic. We need a mill or a medium sieve. Is there one here?"

"We stored a couple in the top cupboard, miss." Daphne climbed a step stool to open a door above Cat's head. She passed down two large, ageing Mouli-style food mills.

"Ah." Isla grinned, "I haven't seen one like this for years. They work a treat. This will be good."

"Thank you, ladies. We'll be half an hour or more here. You relax with a cuppa. When you come back, we'll be ready to pot it up," Cat said.

Gran and Cat rinsed the equipment and set to work. First, they checked the flavor to see if it required any salt or pepper, or whisky. When they assured themselves the taste was right, they set to sieving the pâté. They made certain there were no fine sinew pieces or herb residue to detract from the fine finish of the product. When it was done, the sieved mixture went back into the clean processor. Isla drizzled butter melted with some goats' milk into the mix.

Cat finished rinsing the food mills as the workers shambled into the room. The processor bowl full of fresh pâté, she set on the bench where they'd mixed the whisky earlier.

"Each of you can try some. Let me hear your opinion," Cat invited.

There was a shuffle of feet as each woman took a cracker and spread it with the fresh product.

"Oh, this is lovely, miss. It's the way the old lady used to make it. Lady Meredith's mum, I mean. Don't ye think so, Gladys?" Daphne asked.

"Aye. Well tidy scran," Gladys enthused.

"Lady Meredith's was fine." Daphne tilted her head. "It was missing something, though. This is the genuine thing. Oh, it is wonderful to taste the true flavor again." She jiggled her shoulders.

"Thank you, Daphne. Gran and I have worked together making it since I was seven."

"Ye're from around here, then?" Daphne asked.

"Oh no. Gran's grandfather was Dallin McGill. He lived here."

"McGill, eh?" Gladys said.

Cat noticed furtive glances passing amongst the women again. She felt like she'd introduced the plague. There was a mystery here. "We can pot the pâté now. Daphne, you can cover half the pots with the clarified butter. The other half we'll seal with cling wrap."

Iona came back into the room. She waited to the side, watching the women return the benches to pristine condition.

"I'm here to fetch ye for lunch. Ye did all this today?" She scanned the array of pots. "May we try it?"

"We'll take this lot through to the kitchen. You can do what you like with it," Cat offered.

Iona's broad smile lit her face as she turned to address the other women. "Thank ye, ladies. We'll see ye tomorrow."

23

Chapter Twenty-three

The days settled into a routine for Cat. In the mornings, she would rise early and amble to the village for the simple pleasure of fresh air and exercise. After breakfast, she worked with Isla making pâté.

The stroll down the hill allowed her a view across the valleys and distant vistas. The return climb was challenging. She took her time, enjoying the full magnificence of the vast mountain range. It was all-encompassing and protective, like a natural fortress.

Her first few forays were met with questioning stares from the locals. After a week, there were faces she recognized and put names to. There were some she'd met at morning tea with Lachie. A few people introduced themselves on the third or fourth meeting. It gave her satisfaction to say good morning by name as they got to know her and she learned their stories.

Lachie gave her the space she needed to become familiar with her surroundings and kept his distance, except for those intimate looks across the dinner table.

He'd waved to her from where he stood in a pen, ankle-deep in mud, when she'd wandered by on her walk this morning. There were times a work-a-day kilt was more practical than jeans.

The sight of him sent tingles down her spine. Her lips remembered the touch of his with total clarity.

Ten meters past the fire-damaged remains of a house near the beautiful old church, or *kirk* as they called it here, she noticed a weedy forty-something man slouching toward her. She'd seen him around the whisky area, but didn't know his name. Every time he caught her glance, she felt uncomfortable, like she was confronting a dangerous animal. It made her shiver, and not in a good way.

He gave her a narrow-eyed nod as he passed. Cat breathed a sigh of relief cut short by an arm around her throat. The man lugged her backward in the direction of the ruined house. She didn't have enough air to scream. There was no one to hear her, anyway, on the quiet street this early in the day.

She slumped her body into a dead weight, but the man was strong. Tearing at his arms with her fingernails had no effect, so she scrabbled her feet in the dirt, trying to get some purchase. The arm at her neck didn't budge as he kept on towing her.

Throwing open a door at the back of the house, the troll tossed her inside. Cat landed in a heap on the dirty floor. Before she was able to orient herself, he put a boot into her side. Doubling up in pain, she drew her legs close to her chest.

"So, ye're the new *Simone*, are ye princess?" He kicked her again. "I thought I'd seen the last of ye when I dealt with the Meredith bitch. And fuck, here we are again." Dragging her head back by her hair, he snarled into her face, his fetid breath making her recoil. "I had a bit of fun with her first, like I will with ye. Like her, if ye tell anyone about me, I'll take care of yer Granny." He flung her head back to the ground so hard she felt as though her brains rattled.

The man stomped away a few paces then swung to face her again. She whimpered.

"So, she goes to the laird and tells him she's knocked up with no man in sight. What the fuck? The eejit marries her. To protect the *Simones*! He weds her, puts her in the fucking castle, treats her like a queen, all to protect the *Simones*. Fuck the *Simones*."

"How do you know about the *Simones*?" she gasped, hoping conversation might deter another physical onslaught.

"My great-grandmother, Darla McGill was a *Simone*. My family knows too well about their secret cult and how special they think they are. A brainless *bawheid* like Meredith gets the princess treatment because she's a girl, and her mother was a *Simone*. The rest of us poor shites, the men, we get nothing, nothing! Well, I tell ye that bairn of hers carried my blood in its veins. The bitch has my baby—my baby, isn't it ironic—the bairn is another fucking *Simone*. They had to go," he shrugged.

"What did you do?"

"I ran her off the road." The comment was unemotional, like he was telling her he'd bought some biscuits.

"But why? Meredith didn't tell anyone what you'd done, did she? Why did you kill her and her baby?" She wrapped an arm around the worst area of the pain. Keeping him talking might stall another kicking.

"Because they were the last *Simones*. I made sure they would be the end. Then those crazy old biddies come back from their jaunt to Australia and say they've found the fucking pâté. Fuck the pâté! We have more fucking *Simones*! Are ye the last of them? Tell me ye're the last." He stomped back toward her.

"I wasn't even aware they existed until a month ago." The words were thready. She shrank away.

"Bullshit! I'll bet ye were making pâté before they weaned ye, weren't ye? Weren't ye? It's time to cut off the head of the snake. There will be no more fucking *Simones*. I won't kill ye, bitch. But I will make damn sure ye'll never have children." He raised his boot again when the door slammed open. The man was thrown against the wall like a rag doll.

A mud-spattered, red-haired giant, bristling with anger and contempt, raised Cat's assailant to a height that left him dangling, and shook him with threatening ferocity. Two more men crowded into the room.

Lachie glanced over his shoulder and threw the man back to the floor with a whump. "Get rid of him. Get him out of my sight now! Quick, or I'll murder the wee *blaigeard.*"

The men dragged away her attacker. Lachie crouched beside Cat without touching her. "Lass, can ye straighten yer body? Tell me where ye're hurt."

"I can't," she moaned, staying curled in a fetal position. "Then hold on. Stay still. I'll pick ye up now. Are ye ready?" She whimpered.

He eased her into his arms and gathered her to his chest. Tears tracked down her face. Cat raised her gaze to his. "Lachie..." She fainted.

24

Chapter Twenty-four

Catriona had little memory of the days she lay in her bed. Wild dreams flashed through her mind—images of making pâté with her mother, cars hurtling off cliff edges, babies crying for their mothers, a ruined house with a menacing figure.

As the images receded, her eyelids cracked open and she took in her surroundings. It hurt to move her head, so she didn't. Her eyes scanned the room until she found a familiar giant sleeping in a too-small armchair by the window.

"Lachie?" Her throat was dry, her voice hoarse and quiet. She tried to lift a hand, but she had no energy. The slight movement must have been enough to disturb him because he opened his eyes, and his gaze roved over her.

Her lips twitched in a facsimile of a smile.

"Catriona, *mo leannan.* Ye're awake. What can I do? What do ye need?" He sprang across the room with surprising speed.

"Um, water."

"Can I raise ye a little?" He put one arm around her back, carefully hefting her into a half-sitting position, then raised a glass of water to her mouth.

She gulped half the glass then settled back against the pillows. "What happened? Feels like…I've been…kicked by a mule."

"Not a mule. A wee *blaigeard*, a bastard named Darro McGill. The McGills are known for causing trouble in the village, but this is worse than anything they've done 'til now. Do ye remember anything?"

The rush of fear, the dank odor of a dark space, and the acrid smell of the man raced back at her. Her body convulsed, and her stomach heaved. Lachie was there with a deep bowl ready for the emergency. She retched until there was nothing left, and then retched some more. When she finished, he set the bowl aside and helped her lie down again.

He took a small towel from a pile someone left on the dresser, tipped some water from the jug onto it, and wrung it into the bowl. He wiped her face clean and mopped some drips which fell onto the bed.

Cat cried, great wracking sobs. She wrapped her arms around her body to minimize the pain to her injuries, but tears streamed from her eyes.

Lachie kneeled beside the bed and brushed her hair out of the way. "Aye, *m'ulaidh*, let it go. Let it go. Ye're safe now. Ye're safe here with me. Let it go." He lay a kiss on her forehead and passed her a handful of whisper-soft tissues. Lowering his face to rest on the pillow beside her, he placed his cheek against hers. *"Chan eil caoineadh mo ghràdh."*

Though she didn't understand what he said, her tears quietened as she listened to the soothing balm of his voice.

The touch of his cheek drew the sorrow and pain from her. No one would get past this man to hurt her again. He muttered more lulling words in the language of his ancestry, and she closed her eyes, letting sleep take her once more.

She woke sometime later, refreshed and grateful the nightmares hadn't returned. She'd sensed she was held in safe arms, warmed through in body and soul.

Lachie was still there, sitting with a book in his hand. The shadow of his beard was more pronounced. His face drooped into exhaustion. He raised a smile when he noticed her watching him. "Ye're back?"

"Yes."

"How are ye?"

"My body aches like I've gone fifteen rounds with a prizefighter. My brain seems to have recovered though." She rubbed a hand across her midriff.

"Do ye want to talk about it?"

"Nope. It's gone. You sucked away the fear and anger. He won't worry me anymore."

"He won't. We have sent Darro McGill to Glasgow. *M'ulaidh*, when I saw yer puir body crumpled like wastepaper, my heart nearly broke in two. That this should happen to ye here in my village…"

"It could have happened anywhere. It's not your fault. You're not the man who attacked me." She rubbed her fingers on the back of his hand.

"He's well away now. He won't be bothering ye again. Are ye hungry?"

"Starving." She managed to smile.

"Let me call for something to eat. Is there anything ye would like in particular?" he asked.

"Scrambled eggs with toast, please."

He lifted the phone on the bedside table. "Janet, Miss Cameron would like some scrambled eggs, toast, and tea please."

"Did you hear him say he killed your wife?" she asked when he came back to her side.

"No." Lachie dipped his chin to his chest.

"He implied he raped Meredith, then, when she gave birth to a daughter, another *Simone*, he wanted to get rid of them both. He ran them off the road."

Lachie took a rasping breath. "I'd suspected the bairn was McGill's. He was always following her around. I thought she loved him. Why didn't she say something if he raped her?"

"Because he threatened to hurt her grandmother. He did the same with me. He said you married Meredith to secure the *Simones*. Is it true?" she asked with a frown.

"In part. She was a *Simone*, and she needed help. The safest way to make sure I protected her was to wed her. We weren't in love. We were man and wife for less than a year when she died. I feared she'd committed suicide rather than be married to a hulk like me." His face tightened into hard angles.

"No, Lachie. You're tired or you wouldn't think such a thing." Her heart cracked at the anguish in his voice and she grasped his hand to shake some sense into him.

"It's not tiredness, *mo cridhe*. It's…" He hesitated as a knock sounded at the door, then answered it to admit Iona carrying a tray.

"Well, brother dear, now Catriona is awake and conscious, ye can go freshen yerself," Iona said.

He cast a glance in Cat's direction. She raised her brows at him without contradicting his sister.

"First, ye can help the patient sit up to eat."

"Put yer arms around my neck, *mo leannan*. Let me pull ye high on the pillows."

She nuzzled her face into his neck on the side away from his sister's vision, breathing in his earthy smell. She didn't want to drop her arms from him until he carefully withdrew, and she had no choice but to let him go.

The expression he wore when he looked into her eyes was a strange mix of shame, desire, and caring. Straightening, he muttered, "I'll be quick."

"Ye'll be long enough to have a shave, a shower, and a meal. Don't come back any sooner. Off ye go." Iona was firm. "I'll stay here." Her last statement must have mollified him somewhat because he stomped away.

Iona balanced the tray in one hand, flipping the stand from beneath it and setting it across Cat's legs. Then she dragged a chair close to the bed.

"He's been here for the last three days. Can ye feed yerself or would ye like some help?"

"I'll be fine." Cat picked up her fork and scooped up some eggs. "Ah, bliss."

"Well, thank ye. I made them myself. I was in the kitchen when Lachie called."

"They're lovely. Where's Gran? How's she been?" she asked.

"Isla's wonderful. It's like she lived here in a past life or something. She's at home here. She's been making pâté. The team has found she's a firm taskmaster with everything from handling the sauté to prepping the onions. Daphne told her she used to help Meredith with the food mill. Gran has let her help away from the others. They're fast friends. Sometimes she calls me Catty or Jeannie. It's okay. To be honest, she hasn't noticed ye're not around," Iona said.

"I need to talk to her." Cat rubbed two fingers across her brow trying to stimulate her brain into action. "How many female direct descendants of Simone are there, do you know? Apart from yourself?"

"Ye mean any? Not only the matriarchal line?" Iona asked.

"Mmm."

"Not so many as ye would imagine. They seem to have bred mostly boys. Look at the McGills. Dallin, yer great, great-grandfather was the last one to sire a daughter. Let me think. There's me, as ye say. My sister, Ness. Daphne, whom ye've met. Um, two, three cousins max. Why?"

"I was thinking… Darro McGill attacked me because he believed it would kill off the *Simones*. It seems there's been a generational feud against them, probably dating back to when Dallin threw out my great-grandmother, Rhona, for falling in love with an Englishman. His son, Dougal, was not welcoming when Rhona returned home with Gran for her father's funeral." She put her fork to her plate again and found the food was gone. "I've eaten the lot."

"Would ye like me to make more?" Iona offered.

"I shouldn't risk eating too much, but thank you. You like to cook, then?" she asked.

"Love it!" Iona's face beamed. She removed the tray and set it on the side table before perching on the edge of Cat's bed.

Cat smiled a moment before becoming serious again. "Iona, the line of *Simones* is precarious. I believe it's time to recognize the other women who descended from Simone if we are to keep her legacy alive."

"What are ye saying?"

"If we can gather the other female descendants, we can offer them the choice to become a *Simone* or not. You haven't been raised with the whole pâté deal like I was, but you can learn. I didn't know the Simone connection until your brother came to Melbourne to find me. Gran did. She and my mother decided not to tell me. For them, their Scottish family history didn't hold much pleasantness. What do you say? Would you like to learn how to make Simone's Pâté?"

"Can we?" Iona asked.

"Since the recipe can't be recorded in any way, it's a matter of physically teaching you how to do it. How to choose the herbs, blend the whisky, prepare the livers, refine the pâté, and check the flavor is just right. It'll take some commitment. We'd need to get on it pronto. We don't have much time until Gran and I go back to Australia."

"Do ye have to go?" Iona asked drawing her brows together.

"I have things back home I have to sort through," Cat said.

"My brother wants ye to stay."

"Maybe. Or maybe he wants the *Simone* to stay. If there are other *Simones*, he won't need me." Emotions churned in her gut. She wanted Lachie to love her for herself. If it was all about the pâté, she'd be better off back home and away from the temptation of the man.

She wouldn't play second fiddle to chicken livers. Her fingers scored across her forehead again.

Iona's eyes widened. "Do ye believe that?"

"It is what it is. It's why he married Meredith, after all." She heaved a calming sigh. "Would the others be interested? They must keep it secret. No one else should know who holds the recipe. Can you trust them?"

Iona tipped her head to one side. "I'll test the waters. Ness will be fine, though we couldn't get her to come home for any extended period. Her life is in Edinburgh. How would it work? If there are six, or seven including yer grandmother, who is the *Simone*?"

"My mother, grandmother, and great-grandmother always worked together. There need not be one person. It would be better when there's a couple at least to share the workload and to double-check the flavor." She screwed her eyes shut against the threatening drowsiness descending upon her. "In fact, it should be an enterprise, like the whisky business. A healthy one, no matter who's running it, with a roster of *Simones*."

"The whisky enterprise hasn't always been solid. It was on its knees when Lachie took over. It's through his efforts it's strong now. He's a tough businessman when he's working. At home, he's just Lachie."

"I wasn't aware there'd been troubles with the whisky." Cat frowned.

"Yes, we faced the same issues of looming unemployment we have now with the pâté. Ye can see why it has him twisted in knots."

"Hmm. He can't have been very old when he began managing the whisky business." Cat crunched her eyelids tight to force energy into them before focusing on Iona again.

"He was barely out of his teens with a business degree under his belt. He'd been champing at the bit for years trying to get our grandfather to listen to what the workers were telling him—their concerns for the quality of the barley, the outmoded equipment, all sorts of things. Gramps was past it, poor dear. He was more interested in consuming the product than selling it. When Gramps died, Lachie stepped straight in. He wanted to do the same thing with the pâté, but he couldn't because we don't have the secret." Iona pleated the fabric of her cream and roses skirt with one hand.

"You might have let it go to make something else, like the soap, for example."

Iona stood, taking a couple of steps away before facing Cat. "Lachie's big on tradition and legacy, even if he doesn't use his Laird title unless he must. Simone is a big part of our legacy. He wants her gift available for the generations to come."

"I got a taste of that when I challenged him on the aristocracy thing," she said, stifling a yawn. It was getting harder to stay awake. "He doesn't spend the day actually making the whisky, does he? He's not hands-on in the production?"

"Oh no, he manages the whole operation. He's hands-on in terms of making sure the whisky makers have everything they need to do the work, then he mostly leaves them to it. Why?" She canted her head.

"It can be that way with the pâté. We need a strong manager who can get the production running again. There can be any number who hold the recipe. We'd only need one or two on the ground making it. It's not enough to have the knowledge, you need to be passionate, otherwise the product is poor. Meredith didn't have the passion apparently, because Daphne said the batch I made tasted the way Meredith's mother made it, not Meredith." Cat blinked hard a few times.

"Yes, the passion always shines in the food, doesn't it?"

"Just like it did with those eggs." Catriona's eyelids wouldn't stay open beyond half-mast.

"Am I boring you? Ye keep nodding off. I'd leave you but my dear brother would skin me alive if I left ye without company."

"Not bored, just can't keep awake. Sorry." Cat flapped a hand in apology. "I must talk to Gran. She'll know what to do about the pâté and who we can teach. She learned from her mother who'd come directly from here. Rhona was Darla McGill's daughter. The man who attacked me said he descended from Darla. He was resentful of the *Simones*." She yawned again, trying to keep a focus on the conversation. There was something just out of reach in her mind she needed to know. *Ah yes!*

"Lachie mentioned Simone's journals. Maybe there's something there to guide us. Are we able to read them?" Cat asked.

"He has them in a climate-controlled cabinet in his office. There's nothing to stop us from accessing them," Iona assured her.

"Unless there's something specific in there to stop us, it's my plan to expand the number of *Simones*."

Iona burst into tears. "What is it?" Cat asked, jolted into wakefulness.

"Ye don't know what this means to me. I've always loved Simone, her story, the image. When I learned the pâté connection, I wished I was a *Simone*. Ye are so generous, so wonderful. I hope my brother has some sense and makes ye my sister." Iona gave her a gentle hug.

$$25$$

Chapter Twenty-five

"Iny? Are ye okay? What's happened?" Lachie's voice broke into his sister's conversation with Cat.

Iona glanced at him. "I'm fine thanks, Lachie, just some girl talk. I'll go, leave ye two alone. Thank ye, Catriona. Ye're amazing." She gathered the used dishes, then scurried from the room.

Lachie sat in the seat his sister vacated and took Catriona's hand. He'd been away from her side long enough. He needed the physical touch again. "She didn't overtire ye, did she?"

"Nope, I was already tired. Um, I want to know—how did you find me that morning?"

"Old Gladys spied ye from her window and was coming out of her wee cottage to say good morning. She saw it happen and rang here to raise the alarm. The first I knew was when Iny rushed from the house, screaming Darro McGill was dragging ye into Doughal's ruined house. I don't think I've ever moved so fast, lass." He dragged a shaky finger down her cheek.

Remembering the man standing over his angel was enough to send Lachie into a rage again. He wanted to pummel the mongrel into a bloody mass. His workers' arrival restored his sanity. He left them to cart McGill away.

"You arrived like the cavalry to save me." She slanted her lips into a small smile, then she grabbed his hand. The unexpected contact sent the blood rushing to his groin.

"*Mo cridhe?*"

"You will teach me those words, won't you? What is mo crid?"

Lachie hesitated. He didn't think she was ready to hear him call her "his heart."

"What was the 'connection' one you said?"

"Connection?"

"Connection o grudge."

Lachie chuckled. "Do you mean, '*Chan eil caoineadh mo ghràdh*'?"

"Uh huh."

"I said, 'Don't cry, sweetheart.'"

"Hmm. Nice." Her eyelids fluttered as if they wouldn't stay open. "Lachie?"

"*M'eudail?*"

"Kiss me? Like you mean it?"

"My pleasure—and I do mean it." He smiled, and his heartbeat quickened as his gaze settled on her mouth.

His lips met hers hard and fast. Slowly, he let it settle into a serene joining that warmed his soul. He might have gone on forever, if she hadn't fallen asleep.

Lachie sat back with a chuckle. She had no consideration for his male pride, his wee elf.

These were a harrowing few days for him while he kept vigil by her bedside. He wished he held the power to take away her pain. If he was able, he'd turn back time to before she went walking that morning. He could have, should have, gone with her. Watching her become comfortable enough to familiarize herself with his home made him happy. Then, the McGill *blaigeard* diminished it to a place rife with terrible memories. He unclenched his fists as she murmured in her sleep.

She'd reached into his chest and stolen his heart the first time they'd met—before he'd tasted her pâté, before he'd accepted her connection to the *Simones* was real.

Cat stretched her arms toward the headboard. Her movement halted on a cry. Her eyes flew open.

"Ye canna do that yet, lass. It's yer ribs."

"Lachie, you're still here?" Her voice sounded relieved, if he needed to put a name to it.

"Aye lass, unless ye want me to go."

She shook her head lightly. "I don't want you to go." Her head relaxed into her pillows again. He thought she'd gone to sleep, but her lids flashed open. "Simone's journals. I need to read them. I understand they're old, but I'll be careful."

"No need to be careful, *mo cridhe,* they're in digital format. Ye can read them on yer tablet if ye like. Ye can even scribble on them. The originals are safe right where they are."

"Oh, you are clever. Wonderful. There's something I want to know but only Simone can tell me."

"I've read them all, lass. Maybe I can help ye?"

Cat's eyes drifted shut. "No, it's okay. I need to ask Simone myself. Why can't I wake up properly?"

"The drugs keep ye drowsy. The doctor said he wouldn't bandage yer ribs. It's not good, apparently. Ye've to take deep breaths so yer lungs don't collapse. He gave ye the painkillers to help ye rest while yer ribs heal. Ye'll be sore for weeks, lass, but ye'll be able to climb from yer bed whenever ye're ready now. There's no rush. Take yer time. Tomorrow or the next day, maybe." He smoothed her hair from her forehead. "Do ye need more painkillers now?"

"No, I want to wake up and use my brain like I did with Iona. Did she slip something into my eggs?"

"Ah lass, Iny wouldn't ruin her dishes with drugs. No, it'll come and go for ye 'til the drugs leave yer system. Drink plenty of water to flush the poisons from yer body. Ye'll be fine in a day or two."

Cat's chuckle was almost a whisper. "I'll hold you to your promise, *mo cridhe.*" Her breathing changed as she drifted off to sleep again.

His heart warmed at the words she attempted, even if she didn't understand the translation. She'd recognized an endearment and used it for him. "My heart," she'd said. He hoped she meant it.

He'd organize Simone's journals for her. He'd never translated them. Their mystique was they were in Simone's own words. He wondered if Catriona could read old French.

26

Chapter Twenty-six

Despite the soreness in her ribs, Cat resolved to get moving the next morning. She found it difficult to shift in some directions. Sudden movements reminded her with razor sharp precision her body was not in a good way.

It didn't slow her plans to create a new swathe of *Simones. More like a clutch if there would only be four.*

Isla was unsure of the plan when Cat explained it to her, but she came around when she comprehended Simone's legacy might die out completely, especially if Cat herself either bore no children, or sons but not daughters.

Lachie emailed the digitized journals to her. It surprised her to find they were in old French. It made sense though. Simone would have written her private thoughts in her native tongue.

Cat learned French from her antecedent mothers, who mostly used it when they were making pâté. She hadn't realized the French she'd learned from them incorporated a Scottish accent until she studied the language at school. She was set to take her French studies further in her Arts degree at university until her mother's death put paid to those ideas.

The journals were a treasure trove of life in this place during the early- to mid-1800s. Simone described the clearances and the British officers who came to dinner from time to time, few of whom impressed her. Cat understood why a woman from this area would've been scorned for falling in love with an Englishman as her great-grandmother, Rhona, did.

The journals mapped the pâté recipe's progression, including when Simone tested various herbs, and when she switched to whisky because the cognac she'd brought with her from France was finished. Cat wondered if the research team used the journals to recover the recipe when Meredith died. The elements were here, but not the quantities. Simone couldn't record the taste test in written form; it must be taught practically.

In one of the last entries before her death, Simone mentioned her various daughters who made the pâté well in the same paragraph where she noted demand for the product. She followed with the comment that the pâté was a reliable income source. Where men were able to find work anywhere, their sex constrained women from many endeavors. Kitchen work was an approved female activity. If women made their living from cooking, they would have some security. The knowledge of her pâté would pass only to her female descendants, never to a male. Her daughters and granddaughters would have available to them a manner of provision for their families, if required.

Cat turned to Isla. "She tells us her female descendants should hold the knowledge. Logically, her decree would mean passing it from mother to daughter, but it doesn't prevent other female descendants from being taught by their aunts or grandmothers. What do you say, Gran?"

"You're right, dear. Simone does say the cook must whip passion into the pâté or it won't taste right. Some of her daughters didn't have the passion and refused to make it. Their daughters would have been taught by aunts for the secret to continue."

"We can teach the others, do you reckon? We only have a few weeks until we go home. Can we do enough before we go?"

"Or we might stay, Catty. It feels right being here." Cat frowned.

"Our lives are in Melbourne."

"There's nothing for us there anymore. Everywhere here, I hear my mother's voice. They talk the way she did. It's like she meant for us to come." Isla's lips wobbled, and tears welled in her eyes.

"Oh Gran." Cat gathered her grandmother's frail body into her arms.

Iona knocked on the door, then edged inside the room. "Are ye okay?"

"Yes, we're good, aren't we, Gran? We've read the journals. It's been quite revealing, visiting early nineteenth century life through Simone's eyes. She didn't suffer fools, did she?"

"No," Iona grinned, "none of the McKell women do. Was there anything there forbidding ye from teaching others?"

"The recipe can only be passed to her female descendants. She doesn't insist they be daughters of daughters, though. I think we're cool. Right, Gran?" Cat encouraged Isla's opinion.

Isla sniffled. "My mother said the pâté only caused trouble. It's why we didn't tell you the history, Catty."

"She was right, particularly when there is only one or two who can make it. If we build the numbers, there's less risk of us being targeted. Did you find anyone interested?" Cat asked Iona.

"I did what ye asked. I checked the family tree and spoke with the cousins who are Simone de Salignac's direct female descendants. Only out of interest, I told them. There was no guarantee the training would, or could, happen. Two agreed to train to be alternate pâté makers, one was Daphne. Then there's me and Nessie, and our cousin Sheila who lives near Edinburgh. Another cousin declined. She hates the smell and taste of pâté!"

"She would never be a good *Simone*." Isla shook her head.

"Daphne will be excellent. She already handles the pâté well."

"They're all you found?" Cat asked.

"I warned ye. There are few girls born into the family." Iona shrugged.

"The sticking point for the project to go ahead is finding somewhere to do it," Cat said. "Trying to train the new team here in the castle would create too much interest and speculation. The entire project must be secret. You warned the others?"

"Aye. I told them if there was even a whisper, I would scratch the whole deal." Iona drew her forefinger and thumb across her mouth in a zipping motion that made Isla giggle.

"Great. We must find somewhere to work." Cat groaned. "I'm drifting off into la-la land again."

"You rest. Gran and I will go have a cup of tea. Coming, Gran?"

"Yes dear. It's not like Catty to sleep in the middle of the day." She rested her hand on Iona's arm. "You don't think she's pregnant, do you? I slept a lot when I was pregnant."

Cat's mouth curved into a wry smile as she lay on the bed and their voices faded away. She might create miracles with pâté, according to some people, but immaculate conception was beyond her purview.

She definitely was not pregnant.

~ * ~

Cat was unsure how long she slept. Images of red-headed boys with blue eyes and happy little girls who were a match for herself and Iona punctuated her dreams. Overhearing Gran's pregnancy comment must have been the prompt. Her mind decided the children were hers and Lachie's. There was no chance of that happening until she sorted this pâté mess.

She stumbled into the ensuite, grateful for its proximity, then returned to the bedroom, spotting the shiny shell of her suitcase the maid stored under the bed.

There was an idea tingling in the recesses of her mind. She reached to grasp the case, cautiously to avoid unnecessary pain, tugged it from its hiding place, then flipped it open. In the mesh pocket in the case's upper section was a sheaf of papers.

She withdrew them and skimmed across the text. She owned a property in Edinburgh; two, actually, though one was let. She had no idea of the place's size, what the kitchen was like, or even its location relative to shops or transport. Was it even possible to use it for the project she was considering?

Ben Jones had written Roderick St Clair's name on the paperwork as her agent. There was a phone number alongside it. She rummaged in her handbag to find her phone.

When she was transferred to Mr. St Clair, he welcomed her call. "Your father's Australian lawyer, Mr. Jones, informed us you are traveling in Scotland, Miss Cameron. We were hoping to hear from you. I was well-acquainted with your father. We've held your property vacant as you requested. The tenants in the second, adjacent property, have also given us notice they wish to break their lease. They will pay the ongoing rent until the contract expires. There'll be no income lost for you. You can decide what to do with the property."

"It's adjacent did you say?"

"Yes, they are townhouses with a common wall in a Georgian Mansion. Three levels plus basement, seven bedrooms, two bathrooms each. Can you come to Edinburgh to inspect them?"

"I'll see what I can arrange and get back to you."

"The sooner the better, please, Miss Cameron."

"I will let you know, Mr. St Clair." She was firm. She was the employer here; she didn't care to dance to anyone else's tune even if he was someone who knew Brad Cameron.

"Very well. Please make sure you have identification documents with you when we meet."

Cat ended the call, then shuffled out the door to find Iona. A few moments later, she located Iona sitting at a desk in a cozy sitting room. "Can you take me to Edinburgh for some shopping and stuff soon?"

"Lachie and I have meetings there on Monday. Are ye sure ye'll be up to it? Where do ye want to go?" Iona asked, gathering some brochures.

"Um, Princes Street?"

She gave a thumbs-up. "Perfect, that's where we're heading too. Is there anywhere in particular ye want to go?"

"Actually," Cat bit into her bottom lip, "I'm meeting with someone who knew my father. I'm keeping it under my hat because I don't want to mention it to Gran."

"And Lachie?" Iona raised her brows.

"I'd rather keep it between us for now." Cat firmed her mouth.

"Fine with me. When Lachie and I go to town, we're full on with meetings. We'll arrive by ten and we won't finish till four. Will ye manage?" A crease appeared between Iona's brows.

"Definitely. I expect there will be cafes or restaurants where I can linger?"

"Yes, there are many lovely places along there. I'll inform Lachie ye're coming. If he doesn't need the place for meetings, he will probably invite ye to use his permanent apartment in the Balmoral Hotel. Ye'll have Emerson at yer disposal too, if ye choose to do some sightseeing around the city."

"I don't want to bother anyone," Cat demurred.

"Catriona, ye're part of the family. There is no bother to anyone. Ye must manage yer injuries. What if ye become unwell? Or need to sleep like you did earlier? Especially if…" She rolled her hand as though she wanted to say something but shouldn't. "Anyway, the apartment is there. Ye should use it." Iona was definite.

"Thank you. That would be wonderful. Oh, Iona? You can ignore what Gran said. I can't be pregnant. No sex for a long, long time." Cat grinned.

Iona's smile was sad. She gave Cat a small hug before she left.

Cat shambled along to the sunny sitting room on the same level as her bedroom to make another call to Roderick St Clair. She informed him she'd be available to meet with him at eleven on Monday. The weekend offered the time for her to heal more.

~ * ~

The trip to Edinburgh was torture for Cat despite the benefit of the beautifully appointed Rover. She sat next to Emerson in the front while Lachie and Iona continued their business-related discussions in the rear seat.

Lachie wasn't happy Cat wanted to make the trip in her condition. He insisted on showing her to the apartment at the hotel when they arrived in the city. He ordered tea and sandwiches to be delivered before he and Iona proceeded to their meetings.

She was grateful for the opportunity to relax and recover from the travel. Her body was repairing itself slowly. It felt more bruised than broken today. She covered the colored patches on her face with makeup. The marks around her ribs were psychedelic.

The bruises reminded her of her resolve to put her plan into action. She didn't want the situation ever again where a woman was subject to the abuse she and Meredith endured because someone, anyone, wanted to finish Simone's legacy.

With the new *Simones*, the chances the line would fail were not destroyed, but they were drastically reduced.

The hotel was a short stroll from the lawyer's office. She left the sanctuary of the suite at quarter to the hour. When she arrived, she was shown to an office. A tall, spare man rounded the table to take her hand.

"Miss Cameron, I am Roderick St Clair." He showed her to an overly large, padded leather chair. She winced as she sat. "Are you hurt?"

"Recovering. I had an accident last week. What can you tell me of my father, Mr. St Clair? I don't know much."

Dark brown eyes speared her as if assessing her statement's veracity and measuring her worth. "What do you know, Miss Cameron?"

"Nothing. It seems the understanding I assumed of a parent who abandoned my mother when she told him she was pregnant was not true after all. Mr. Jones insists Bradley Cameron's absence from our lives was to protect us, not willful desertion."

"How was he protecting you, Miss Cameron?"

"I have no idea. What work would a man do that required his family's protection? Was he a drug runner? A hit man? What?"

"Do you have your identity documents with you?" His gaze narrowed on her.

She withdrew her passport, driver's license, her mother's passport, and a photo of her mother with a man Isla identified as Brad Cameron. The lawyer scrutinized the documents, turning them this way and that.

He studied the photo. "You have the look of your father—the dimple in your chin, straight dark hair, and the divot in your nose." He returned the material to her. "Right, then."

He sat on the sofa at right angles to her chair, crossing one long leg over the other, and rested an arm on the padded wing of the lounge.

The fingers of his other hand stroked down his cheeks to join at his chin. "Brad Cameron was my friend since boyhood. He was born outside Edinburgh. We went to the same school. In time, he wandered off on his adventures. I stayed here, but we never lost touch.

"Your father was, shall we say, an operative? Sometimes he'd work for government agencies. Sometimes he'd take on private assignments. He was always undercover, but not the grungy, dirty undercover the Americans like to portray on their television shows. Brad was debonair, if you like the old-fashioned term. He fit in with the highest and lowest echelons of society, and traveled like a wraith between the two." St Clair uncrossed his legs and bent toward her.

"He would follow a money trail, from a chop shop dismantling high-end cars to the mafia boss who was running the place, with no one realizing he was doing it. International money laundering, drug cartels, gun runners—he took on the lot, quite successfully."

The lawyer sat back and folded his arms, defensively, Cat thought. "He cultivated the fiction he was gay. He would affect the most dreadful stereotypical mannerisms. I am a gay man, and Brad's carrying-on made me cringe, but he was effective. No one took him seriously. He was a joke. He had the facility to get men and women to talk to him about the most confidential stuff. Brad was an artist."

Cat grimaced. "If he was so good at it, how was he killed?"

The lawyer's gaze narrowed on her again as he brought his hands to his hips. "Wrong place, wrong time, mistaken identity. An up-and-coming drug lord in Melbourne began to emulate Brad's style. When a rival gang member saw Brad leaving this man's house, he thought he'd hit pay dirt. Two shots with a silencer, head and chest, and your father was dead." Cat's hand flew to her mouth. Sandwiches and tea roiled in her stomach.

St Clair leaned forward. "You're not going to be ill. You are your father's daughter. You're made of stronger stuff."

Somehow, the world stilled at his words. Her stomach stopped heaving. Her imagination was caught on what he said. She was her father's daughter—her mother's too. Her mother never gave in to weakness, even when she was dying. "I was not acquainted with my father," she said.

"He knew you. He loved Jeanette, heart and soul. If anyone knew you or she existed, it would have destroyed his cover. Your family would have become pawns or targets. He protected you, even when your mother begged him to come home." St Clair was stern.

Cat nodded. "That's what Ben said, too."

"He did what he could to make sure you were secure, especially financially. Even before he met your mother, when he got a big bonus he'd buy property. He'd buy stuff no one else wanted when it was cheap. He had an eye for value. The properties he bought here in Edinburgh he acquired for a song thirty years ago when people despised Georgian Mansions as outmoded. They're now worth six times what he paid for them."

"What have you been doing with them since he passed away?" she asked.

"We've kept them tenanted, repainted, et cetera, as needed. We've made no structural changes, though both would benefit from an interior facelift according to our in-house designer. There are no amenities on the top level or in the basement, for example. Agnes suggests sacrificing bedroom space to make ensuites, maybe put in a lift, refurbish the kitchens in each property to make them more functional. I'll let her fill you in. Is there anything further you would like me to tell you, before we meet Agnes?" St Clair asked, shuffling his legs as though ready to stand.

Cat shook her head. "You've given me a lot of information to sift. Between you and Ben, my view of my absent, irresponsible, philandering father has been spun on its head. When I found his will and contacted Ben, truthfully I was expecting to find a stack of debts waiting for me, not that I would become a multi-millionaire overnight."

"Bradley was none of the things you described. He was a valuable law enforcement member who dismantled any number of illicit activities. A man to make you proud, Miss Cameron. He'll never receive public recognition like a war hero, but he was heroic, clever, savvy, and courageous. Come, I'll take you to meet Agnes. She can show you the properties."

He stood, and Cat gingerly followed his lead. They went along a corridor into a light airy office, in direct contrast to the dark formal tones in the room they'd left.

A young woman was there, dressed in an asymmetrical skirt, a long-sleeved blouse, and with a long Isadora scarf wound around her neck. She was bent over a bench covered in swatches of fabric and paint color charts, but swiveled to face them when they entered. Cat's breath caught in her throat.

"Agnes, this is Miss Cameron. I'll leave her in your capable hands."

"Thank you, Rod," the woman said.

As St Clair exited the room, Cat stood transfixed. "You're so much like—"

"Iona?"

"Yes!"

"She's my twin. You're Australian? Are you, Catriona? Oh Lord, how are you? Are you okay? Come and sit, please. Iny told me what that mongrel, Darro, did to you." Agnes took her arm and guided her to the chair. "The McGills have always been troublemakers but this…"

"You're Ness?"

"I am." Her smile was broad like Iona's and equally welcoming. "Rod just said there would be someone here to discuss the Cameron estate?"

"He was my father," Cat supplied.

"Oh." Ness rested her backside against the table. "Iny didn't mention your family name, or that you'd be visiting the office here. What a coincidence you are Bradley Cameron's daughter." Her gaze skimmed over Cat's face as though to take a moment to let the knowledge sink in, or maybe to realign her expectations of the Cameron heir with the woman Iona described as Lachie's love interest.

"Let's go review the properties. They're fifteen minutes away on foot. I have some brilliant suggestions for you." Ness flung her hand in the air.

"I'm not able to walk that far today," Cat demurred.

"Of course not, sorry. Did you come to town with Iny and Lachie?" At her nod, Ness picked up her phone. "Then Emerson will be around somewhere twiddling his thumbs. I'll call him."

Within minutes, Ness was letting them into what appeared to be the original main door to a well-maintained Georgian mansion.

"We've used this townhouse for offices. It won't take much to re-configure it into accommodation if you choose, or to re-let it for business space. I would recommend at least a bathroom and separate WC on the top level. And a lift from the basement to the top story. Those items, though moderately expensive, will enhance the income potential for the property."

Cat was listening with half an ear. Her focus was on the building's innate grandeur. The foyer was tiled in black and white diamonds. It rose to a domed, colorful lead light skylight two stories above them.

An imposing female nude sculpture holding aloft a shining chandelier dominated the entry. The nude appeared to guard access to an ornate marble staircase edged with an elaborate, black wrought-iron balustrade, highlighted with gold leaves.

"This is beautiful. Why did the tenants leave?" she asked.

"For the reasons I've outlined. There is no disabled access to the upper levels. Even getting in from the street is difficult. It doesn't suit a business environment these days. I put a case to Roderick to do some improvements, but he chose not to expend what would have been a sizeable amount of money without the legal owner's authority. You won't be able to make it up the stairs in your battered condition, so come next door. You'll be able to judge what this place can become. And it has a lift."

Half an hour later, Cat eased herself onto a straight-backed chair, one of a dozen sitting around a scrubbed pine kitchen table that might have been there since the mansion was built, two hundred years ago.

"So, what do you think?" a smiling Ness asked.

"Oh my, I had no idea what to expect, but this is amazing. With some furniture, I could move in straight away."

"You can. Your Australian agent put me on notice in case you wanted such an option," Ness said.

"Iona told you what I want to do? To teach Simone's other female descendants to make pâté?"

"She did. Iny would be perfect for it. She's always been a marvelous cook. I'm okay, but not a patch on her. I'd like to learn though, both to keep the legacy alive and to teach my own daughters when they appear on the scene."

"There are two other cousins?" Cat checked.

"You've met Daphne. She's been working in the pâté room for years. The other is Sheila. She doesn't live far from here. She's young, twenty-three. She lost her husband in a North Sea accident last year. Something like this might give her a focus for the future."

Cat leaned forward. "Would they be prepared to spend a week in Edinburgh, here in this house?"

"They'd love it, though Sheila might want to commute. She's still emotionally delicate and might want her own space at day's end. I can have the place furnished for you by the weekend, if you give me some idea of the style you'd like. The soft furnishings are reasonably new. We can leave them for now," Ness suggested.

"I don't have a style, since I've never furnished a place myself. I'm happy for you to decide what works well in this environment. Make it good quality and comfortable. The same goes for any appliances we need too," she said. "We'll get kitchen stuff first, including four sauté pans and food mills so each apprentice can have her own. And we must stock the fridges."

"Great!" Ness beamed. "I'll take you to the Balmoral and get started. I have furniture brochures in my office. I'll collect those to bring to the apartment. We can lunch while you tell me the things you'd absolutely hate. I'll give you a budget by day's end. With your approval, I'll draw on your escrow account to cover the costs."

"My escrow account?" Cat furrowed her brow.

"It's where we lodge your earnings from the properties." Ness smiled. "It'll save you from having to juggle money from one account to another."

"I see. Will there be enough available?"

"Heaps." She grinned. "We've only needed to use it for property taxes and other basics so there must be at least fifteen years' worth of income sitting there." She inclined her head toward Cat. "Are you okay? You look worried." Ness moved around the table to squat beside Cat's chair.

Cat dragged her teeth across her bottom lip and firmed her resolve.

"Actually, I'm fine. Everything lately seems to be one exploding bombshell after another, but this is my life now and I'll deal with it. How can we get this done?"

Ness patted her shoulder and bounced back to her feet. "You don't have to do anything, if you're happy to leave it to me after our discussion at lunch. I'll do the orders and then the providers will invoice the firm without needing to bother you directly. I'll use the suppliers I know can deliver quickly, especially the furniture. When I've got the furniture under control, I'll go shopping for the other stuff. Deal? Everything should be ready for you to start here on Monday, if that's what you want."

"Right," Cat said easing to her feet. "Let's get the project moving right away."

27

Chapter Twenty-seven

Lachie raised his head in response to a knock at his door. "Caelan, come in."

"My lord, I've got to talk to ye. It's the plant. With no pâté in production, like, I will have to let the rest of the women go. Without the women, we should sell off the goats too. Campbell says he must cull his hens if we're not needing livers." The man raised a worry-ridden face to Lachie.

"Let's not be hasty, Caelan. I will get the pâté back on track. It might take some time, maybe even some persuasion. We've been through some tough times before, when Meredith's mother passed. It was several weeks until Meredith was ready to do the work."

"Aye, sir, but it's close to a year now. We're spending money on power for keeping frozen stocks of the goats' milk we might never use. It's turning our bottom line, like, if not red, then a brightening shade of pink."

"Take a seat, Caelan." Lachie moved to a side table. He poured a dram of whisky into two glasses. "Here ye go. Ye're a canny business manager, man. I'm sorry things have been a worry for ye for the past wee while."

"Ach, it's not my worry concerning me. It's what it means for everybody else, like. Lady Iona says good things are coming. She said yer visitor suggested using the goats' milk to make premium soaps for high-end markets. It'll take time to establish. I can't say how many

207

people she'll need, what skills to teach, or even what the business proposition might be for it. I haven't been able to contact her this week to find what she means to do and if, or how, it can help the business." Caelan took a swig from his glass, his forehead puckered into a scowling frown.

"Iona has taken our Australian visitors to Edinburgh for a week. They're spending some time with Agnes. They'll be back on Friday evening, I believe. Tell me more about the soap notion." Lachie settled back in his chair.

"Ach, I canna tell ye much, only what I've read myself on the internet, like. Goats' milk we have a lot of, herbs we have a lot of. We'd need lye, olive oil, coconut oil, and even some stuff called babassu oil, whatever that is, because some folk are allergic to olive oil, like." He ticked the list off on his fingers.

"We'd need safety gear because of the lye. When all's said and done, it takes a month from go to woe until we can package the stuff, let alone send it out. It has a good price tag once it's done."

"It seems to me ye've all the ingredients to put together a business proposal for soap production. Ye might want to incorporate the whisky somehow, even a small amount for a McKell connection. Find what ye can ahead of the weekend. I'll discuss it with the family. In the meantime, let me know how much the pâté business needs to hold on to the workers we have for another two months. I'll put the money in myself."

Caelan drained his glass, set it on the table with a small snap, then stood. "Aye, my lord. I will. I'll get straight onto the proposal. Even if it comes to nothing, like, it'll make me feel I'm earning my keep for the first time in months."

Lachie got to his feet, too, extending his hand. "Thank ye. There are opportunities out there for our community. We must find them to make them work. And Caelan, tell Campbell to keep sending us his livers. We'll freeze them too, for when the time is right—even if we have to develop a fresh new line."

Caelan set his hand in Lachie's outstretched one, nodded, and left the room.

Lachie slumped into his seat. He'd been reading the business accounts when Caelan arrived. The man's revelations were nothing new. The soap idea was novel. It would be something they would be able to develop from scratch and put their own mark on with none of the succession-line caveats.

Caelan said the notion had come from Catriona. She was a canny lass even though she didn't realize it for herself.

Her face and voice invaded his mind constantly. His home was a lonelier place without her here. Even when she was lying in her bed, injured, her presence was everywhere in the house. Without her, the rooms seemed colder, the world gloomier, his heart sadder. He wished he knew what would persuade her to stay on past her deadline—to give them a chance at a life together, and not only for the sake of his workers.

He wanted her for himself and the family they might build together.

Instead, she'd taken herself and Isla off to Edinburgh with Iona. Maybe she was keeping her distance from him to prevent their relationship from developing. Perhaps she wanted to let him down easy. Who would blame her? He was a great burly brute and, according to his former wife, with no finesse, with or without his title. He was aware his money could buy someone to overlook his size and other shortcomings, but since Catriona appeared in his life, he craved more. If truth be told, he wanted the love his parents shared, the sort Malcolm and Simone had, a love which blossomed in the face of any challenges sent their way.

There was no chance to share his dreams with her while she was off shopping or whatever with Ness and Iona. It was an odd time for Iona to be out of contact for a week. Especially when things were so dire for the pâté enterprise. She must have needed the break. Although she was returning calls, she wasn't answering them straight away like she usually did.

The phone in his pocket rang. As though the thoughts of his sister communicated themselves to her, her name appeared on his screen. "Iny, what's up?"

"Everything's fine here, Lachie, but we've asked Alethea and Elspeth to join us for lunch on Friday for a ladies' day. Can Emerson drive them? Either tomorrow, to stay overnight with us, or on Friday morning?" Iona asked.

"Emerson is available on Friday. Tomorrow he's taking a small team to Dundee to check a new malt supplier," Lachie said.

"Friday it is."

"I'll drive the aunts to Edinburgh tomorrow, if ye like," Lachie offered.

"That's sweet of ye, brother dear. Ye've enough on yer plate. Friday will be fine. Emerson can drive us home after we finish. Tell him to bring the limo. Love ye." Iona ended the call.

Lachie frowned. Ladies' day? Curious. She'd likely tell him all about what they'd been doing when she got home on Friday night. Cat would return then, too. He'd wait.

28

Chapter Twenty-eight

"Which one is it? Which one is the real Simone's?" Iona demanded of her great-aunts, excitement flooding her voice.

"Ach, ye're kidding us, aren't ye? All these are Simone's recipe and ye know it. Ye shouldn't try to play tricks on old ladies." Alethea playfully wagged a finger in Iona's face. She turned back to the array of pâté on the table. "Catriona has been busy to produce this lot. None is the same as any other, would ye say, Elspeth? They're all Simone's, unmistakably. It just goes to show there's always some variation in different batches."

"I have been busy. I had Gran's help too." Cat hugged her grandmother with one arm around her shoulders. She scanned the team behind her, whose faces were glowing with pride. They shared glances with each other, stifling giggles. Only they were aware the work of more than one pâté maker was on display.

"Right," Ness took control. "I've booked lunch for us at the Balmoral. I've got to go into the office before we head to Kellburgh."

"Oh. Elspeth and I have a community meeting this afternoon. We were hoping to get home in time for it," Alethea said.

"I'd like to be home earlier too, if possible," Daphne ventured.

"Hmm. Would you be comfortable driving my car, Daphne?" Ness asked. "It's a medium-sized automatic. You can leave straight from lunch with the aunts. Emerson can wait for us and the luggage."

"Aye, of course, I'll drive yer car if ye trust me."

"We're Simone-sisters now. I have to trust you," Ness said, when the aunts moved beyond hearing range.

Lunch was an alcohol-free yet celebratory affair. The aunts regaled the group with their take on the trial in Melbourne when Charles Sopworthy nearly poisoned them with old pâté. They recounted the fun at the house with lamingtons and champagne. Daphne, Sheila, and Agnes were curious about the lamingtons, so Iona promised to make some the following week. Laughter flowed, and time passed quickly.

Daphne accepted the keys from Ness just after two and herded the aunts into the car to drive them to Kellburgh. They might be a little late for their meeting, but not by much.

"I'm off too," Sheila said as she headed to her own vehicle. She'd driven herself home each afternoon, preferring to commute from her cottage outside Edinburgh.

After waving off both cars, Ness declared she was going to her office to clear the work she'd left to accumulate during the day. She'd gone in most afternoons to keep on top of things.

With just the three of them left, Cat, Iona, and Isla slowly strolled back to the mansion. Cat's ribs were less sore than they were earlier in the week. The exercise felt good.

She and Isla had succeeded in bringing forth a new batch of *Simones*, if Elspeth and Alethea's reactions were anything to go by. The aunts believed there was one pâté maker, when in fact there were four. Neither Cat nor her grandmother made any of the pâté they'd tasted. Mission accomplished. Now she was free to explore a relationship with Lachie without the pâté issue between them.

Lachie—picturing him made her melt inside. The big man delighted her with his wry humor, surprised her with his insights. Every part of her body tingled at the mere thought of being near him. She wanted to crawl into his lap and lay her head on his chest, hear his heart beating. Her friend Lori's suggestion that he might be big all over had her fizzing in anticipation to find out for herself just how big he really was.

She'd done this for him. She'd manipulated the promises she'd made to her mother to keep the recipe secret except for her own daughter. Simone herself didn't specify any condition to teach only her daughter. Simone said her female descendants should be the beneficiaries of the pâté legacy; she'd placed no restriction for them to be daughters' daughters.

Still, Cat wouldn't have gone searching for alternatives if not for Lachie. She'd done this to ease his load. His workers would have employment. The business could continue to make its signature product. She sighed.

"Are you all right, Catty? There's a lot of sighing going on. Is the walk too much for you?" Isla asked.

She'd become aware, during the week, that Cat was hurt. Cat let her believe she was in a silly accident. She feared if Isla knew she'd been attacked because she was a *Simone*, she'd resume her belief it was the pâté causing yet more trouble. She might have withdrawn her support or her help to teach their apprentices.

"I'm fine. It's been a big week, hasn't it?" Cat aimed to deflect the query.

Isla's face lit up. "It's been good fun. I like Scotland."

"Our visit is nearly at an end. We return to Melbourne next week."

"Mmm, you said we would come back."

"As often as ye like," Iona invited. "We'll always be pleased to have ye here. Ye can check on our progress to make sure the product is exactly the way it should be."

"You are sweet, Iny." Isla said, adopting Agnes's familiar name for Iona. She wrapped an arm around Iona's waist for a moment and squeezed. "I like having extra granddaughters like you and Ness. Daphne's nice too, and Sheila. You'll be good *Simones*."

"Sheila says she'll relocate to Kellburgh," Iona informed them. "Since her husband died, she has nothing to hold her where she is.

She's still young. I hope she can find happiness again. Maybe working with Daphne as the *Simone* will help her."

"She's such a lovely person," Cat agreed, stepping forward to unlock the door to the townhouse. She helped her grandmother up the few steps into the entryway. "Gran, if you go pack your things, I'll square away the kitchen. Ness says she can have cleaners in early next week, but I'd like to leave things tidy."

"What can I do?" Iona asked.

"If you've packed already, would you like to go next door to look around? Ness has made some suggestions on how she wants to fit out the place. I'd like your opinion too, if you don't mind?"

"Ye want it like this place?"

"An updated version, I guess. It has a lovely entry foyer. I wouldn't want to lose it. We should modernize the kitchen. The house needs a lift, ensuites and so on."

"A blank slate? Great. Ness always has excellent ideas, but I can never picture what she's talking about."

Ness returned to the mansion half an hour ahead of the appointed time. She joined Iona in the next-door townhouse. When next Cat saw them, both were excited by the possibilities for the home.

On the dot of four, Emerson drove the limo onto the forecourt of the mansion. They stowed their luggage and secured the pâté in the onboard cool box. The four passengers climbed in. Emerson took his place in the driver's seat, and another celebration began.

Agnes cracked a bottle of French champagne and poured four glasses. "Here's to you, Gran. You've taught us to make wonderful pâté. We love you for it."

Iona followed. "To Catriona, for finding the solution to our problems."

Isla and Cat acknowledged the toasts, and Cat responded. "To the new *Simones*. May you each study Simone's history, remember to hold her secrets close, and pass them only to her direct female descendants.

You should practice your French by reading her journals for yourselves."

"Hear! Hear!" Isla applauded.

"What a week," Iona said. "I didn't realize how much history the work involved. Ye both have it in yer heads."

"Not me so much," Cat said. "My mum and Gran decided such knowledge was redundant. Your aunts arrived in the nick of time to resurrect it, accidentally. I'd grown up with the stories because my great-grandmother was still alive when I was little. She loved to share her memories of Scotland and Kellburgh." She smiled as she pictured Little Gran's face and remembered her voice.

"The significance of most of what she told me passed me by until Gran was teaching us this week. The pâté, on the other hand, I've been making all my life. There were three *Simones* teaching me, though I never knew it."

The small group enjoyed the champagne and snacks Ness provided, while the twins peppered Isla and Cat for information on every aspect of the pâté process, rehearsing what they learned during the week.

Isla wilted and confusion edged into her eyes. Cat quietened the conversation, advising her grandmother to rest. Isla was lucid, living in the moment through the week, and Cat was grateful for it. Isla loved sharing her skills. She'd participated fully with the new *Simones*. The ugly dementia word had wandered off into the never-never for a brief time. But Isla was tired now, and the beast raised its head.

The rest of the trip was mostly quiet. Isla dozed, and the peace persisted except for some desultory conversation around Kellburgh and the people who lived there. When Iona referred to the people who she would now rehire for the pâté production, a glimmer of satisfaction warmed Cat's heart. Lachie's people would have the employment he sought.

Lachie leaped the castle steps two at a time to meet the car as they arrived. He appeared relaxed and comfortable in his kilt and white shirt with the sleeves partially rolled back. Cat's heart thumped as though she'd climbed five flights of stairs.

She'd gone and fallen for the man. What would he say when she told him there were now plenty of *Simones* for his pâté production? She couldn't wait to see his reaction.

29

Chapter Twenty-nine

It was like there was a shift in the universe when Lachie encountered Cat's smile. He struggled to find his balance as energy and excitement pulsed through his body.

His sisters scrambled from the car and headed inside the building while Cat carefully eased Isla to her feet. The older lady stumbled, but Lachie caught her.

"Oh, thank you, Angus. I've got my wobbly boots on, I reckon."

"And verra pretty ones they are too." Lachie intercepted a wry smile from Cat. "What?" he asked in a quiet voice.

"She means she's ever-so-slightly tipsy from the champagne, Angus." Cat grinned.

"I see." He winked at her. "Well, shall I carry ye up the stairs, so yer boots don't wobble too much?" Lachie offered.

"Mmm. That would be nice." Isla slumped against his body.

He swept her into a firm hold then negotiated the stairs with ease. When he reached her room, he took great care in depositing her on the bed.

Satisfied Isla was comfortable, he advanced toward Cat and tipped her chin to his face with one fingertip. He bussed her mouth. He wanted to hold her, but one quick kiss was all he allowed himself until he had her on his own.

"It's nearly time for dinner," he said. "Ye'll come to my study for a pre-prandial nip?"

She chuckled when he waggled his eyebrows, nodded, and directed her attention to her sleeping grandmother.

Lachie headed down the stairs to his office. Having Cat home again was grand. The place was more like a home when she was here. She'd not made any promises to stay on and help with the pâté, but she'd become familiar with many local people affected by the production slowdown.

The soap idea was an excellent one too, and Caelan provided a positive report on the viability of using the excess goats' milk for it.

He poured whisky into two squat, heavy crystal glasses and sat on the sofa in front of his desk. The old leather wrapped around his back and side like a comforter molded just for him.

He rolled the glass between his hands, then raised it to take a small sip. Unconsciously, he assessed color, nose, palate, and finish. It was a fine drop. It should be; it had rested in oak for over twenty-five years.

"Gran's asleep for the night," Cat said, ambling into the room. Lachie bounded to his feet.

"Is she quite well, lass?" He tried to keep his tone neutral while his heart beat a tattoo in his chest. He guided her to the sofa, and she took a seat.

"Yes, if you'll remember from Melbourne, though, it doesn't take much wine of any variety to have her feeling the effects." Cat sat as Lachie retrieved the second whisky glass from the dark oak coffee table.

"Here ye go," he passed the glass to her, then resumed his place on the sofa. "How was yer week in the big smoke?"

Cat's mouth tipped into a crooked half-smile. "Edinburgh is a lovely village." She sipped the liquor.

"Village?"

"I live in Melbourne. It has ten times Edinburgh's population. They don't let you out much if you judge Edinburgh to be the big smoke." Her chuckle sputtered out.

Lachie rubbed his chin, dipped his head, and raised his gaze to meet hers. "Aye, I see what ye mean. What did ye do for the week? Did Iny and Ness entertain ye well?"

The dinner gong drowned his own voice for the last part of the question. He stood and extended his hand.

Cat passed her glass to him. He placed it with his on the coffee table and offered his hand again to help her out of the chair.

"We'll talk later," she said.

They entered the dining room where the smaller family setting was laid. The table was a section of the larger, formal board and able to be reinserted when required. The family preferred the more intimate placement for six to eight rather than dealing with the massive dimensions of the main table.

After the staff cleared the soup course, they presented the appetizer: pâté served with crisp triangles of toast and garnished with cornichons.

Lachie beamed. "It's grand to have the pâté on the table again. Did ye make this today, lass?"

Cat glanced across the table at his sisters before answering his question. "Yesterday. Do you like it?"

"Aye, it's well tidy scran. I've told ye before," Lachie said.

"Is the flavor right?" Cat asked.

"Oh, aye. It's perfect."

"Good." Cat's gaze flipped to his sisters again. They were holding in giggles.

"Is something wrong?" Lachie raised his eyebrows in query.

"Quite the opposite," Cat said. "There was a problem getting it just so, but we got it sorted. Did I tell you they're already erecting the Christmas lights in Edinburgh? Christmas lights with Halloween stuff seems an odd mix."

Recognizing the redirection, he recounted tales of the hijinks his sisters got up to around the Christmas tree in the city when they were small, confusing their poor father when each denied she was the one stealing the baubles from the lower branches. He couldn't punish either for fear of choosing the wrong twin.

His sisters chipped in with their own anecdotes of Lachie inciting them to mischief until finally, they all rose from the table. Iona and Agnes wandered off to their own entertainment while Cat and Lachie strolled back to the study.

Lachie closed the door behind them, drawing her into his arms. "Ah lass, I've missed ye." He lowered his mouth to hers.

Cat cupped his cheek. The touch of her hand against his five o'clock shadow added to the other sensations swirling around him.

She melted against him, but gasped as he tightened his arms around her. He sprang back.

"Shite! I forgot yer ribs. I'm sorry, lass. Come and sit." He slumped into the sofa and cuddled her on his lap. "Now, tell me what ye did this week while I was waiting here like a lost puppy."

"You were?" She leaned back to gaze into his eyes.

"Ye appreciate what I feel for ye, Catriona. Aye, I'm surely a lost dog without ye here." He lay his heart on the line.

"You understand I'm going home next week, don't you?" she warned.

He dragged the back of his forefinger down her cheek. "I can't help hoping ye'll want to return and not for the pâté."

"If I come back, it won't be because of chicken livers, though I'd be happy to help from time to time," she grinned.

Was she saying she wouldn't work on the pâté? He'd reasoned she at least understood the need to provide work for the villagers. According to Simone's decree, she was the only one who was able to do it.

"I'm happy to report you can get your production on track with or without me," Cat said, snuggling into his chest.

"What do ye mean?" he asked. "Ye'll come and do it?" His heart rose in hope.

"You wanted to hear what we did this week? Gran and I taught Iona, Agnes, Daphne, and Sheila to make pâté. You don't need me for that anymore. Simone's tradition can live on without me."

Lachie stiffened beneath her. He lowered his arms to his sides. The thud in his gut was like a doomsday knell. "Ye've no right," he growled.

Cat slid from his knee and faced him. "I have and I did," she asserted.

Propelling himself from the sofa, he towered above her. "What ye held was sacred, and ye passed it on to whoever wanted it? It was yer legacy. Simone meant for her descendant to maintain her own income, and ye've thrown it away."

"You want to shout at me? Well, thanks!" Cat's voice raised to match his. "I can make pâté if I want to. I don't need to. I learned recently my father has left me a wealthy woman. Probably not to your standards, but enough. I don't have to work at anything, ever, if I choose. Furthermore, there is nothing stopping me from teaching any of Simone's female descendants how to cook chicken livers.

"I did not make the pâté we ate at dinner. Gran did not make it. The pâté was produced by either Agnes or Iona. You weren't able to tell the difference. They've worked tirelessly to perfect the techniques during the last five days to make the legacy more secure than it was a week ago. Now there are six *Simones*. When Gran and I leave, there will still be four here. It'll be damned hard for some moron like Darro McGill to erase the Salignac legacy."

"The recipe was only to be handed from mother to daughter. Ye've been disloyal to Simone's wishes." Lachie's fingernails grazed his scalp.

"I've warned you previously about bloody kiddy-whispers," Cat said. "This is a case in point. It's the reason I wanted to read Simone's journals for myself and not have someone else's half-arsed interpretations. Damn it all," she yelled and pivoted, putting some space between them.

"And ye can read old French, can ye?" He humphed.

"I can, and Gran can too. She's better at it than I am because her mother taught her throughout her life—reading, writing, and speaking. Have you read them?"

"I told ye I had," he reminded her.

"You only read what you wanted to because—"

"Simone made it clear the recipe should only be handed through the female line. Ye betrayed that. Ye made solemn promises to yer mother and grandmother ye would hold the recipe safe. Ye've been disloyal to them and to Simone. I have to wonder, madam, what other promises ye would make and have no qualms to break."

Cat reeled as though he physically struck her rather than hammering her emotionally, slashing at her integrity.

There was a brief knock at the door to the room, then Agnes swept in. She stopped, as if sensing the tension. "Oops. Am I interrupting?" Her gaze skittered from one to the other.

Lachie shook his head without speaking.

"Roderick called. I'm to head to town in the morning. I wanted to say goodbye to Cat in case I'm gone before she's up," Agnes said.

Cat's jaw clenched. "What time are you going?"

"Probably eight-ish. I'll give the road a chance to thaw before I leave."

"Can you give Gran and me a lift? There's lots more we want to do there before we head home," Cat said.

Ness beamed. "Of course. I'll get to have you both to myself. Wonderful. Good night." She twiddled her fingers in a wave then left.

Cat spun to face Lachie. "We have nothing further to say to each other except for me to thank you for your hospitality. Goodbye, my lord."

The sneer she threw at him would have demolished him completely if he hadn't been so darned angry.

Pirouetting, she strode in Agnes's wake and out of his life.

30

Chapter Thirty

Cat bounded up the staircase as if there was a rabid dog on her tail, or maybe a rabid laird. She hadn't time to unpack her bag before dinner so there wasn't much extra preparation to leave with Agnes in the morning.

Cat turned the doorknob to her grandmother's room. Isla was sitting in bed wide awake. "Hello Catty."

"Hi Gran. Is everything okay?"

"Ooh yes. I'm a bit hungry. Iny is making me some eggs."

"That's nice," Cat said. "Gran, I've asked Ness to take us to Edinburgh in the morning when she goes. You wanted to visit inside the castle to see the Scottish crown jewels, didn't you? We'll stay at the townhouse and relax. We can have a day or two to do the things we've missed. What do you say?"

"I warned you it wouldn't be an easy road, my dear." Isla's broad smile faded.

"What do you mean?"

"You're tighter than a bowstring and paler than a saucer of milk. I'm thinking either your favorite kitten has died—and you haven't had a cat for years now—or you've fought with the boy," Isla said.

Cat fell to her knees beside her grandmother, burying her head in the blankets. "He says I've betrayed the legacy by teaching the others. He believes I don't respect the promises I make. Why would he think that? I did this for him. I want to be gone, Gran."

"Then we'll go. What can I do to help?" Isla asked, stroking one hand over Cat's hair.

"Nothing, you rest. Eat your eggs. I'll make sure everything is organized." Cat scrambled to her feet, slashing her hands across her eyes as Iona edged her way in the door with a meal tray.

She settled the tray across Isla's legs and turned to Cat. "Ness tells me ye're going to town tomorrow?"

"Uh-huh," Cat murmured. "It's for the best. When you, Daphne, and Sheila make pâté on Monday morning, there'll be no question who's doing the work. The blow-in Aussie *Simones* will have blown out again. You'll do well."

"What about my brother?" Iona's frown was severe. "He cares for ye, ye know. Did ye lead him on?"

Cat struggled to keep her face from crumpling again. "Um, excuse me."

She swallowed hard and dashed from the room into her adjoining one. Slamming the door behind her, she darted straight to the bathroom and retched into the toilet bowl until there was nothing left in her stomach. She stretched one hand to flush the odor away and huddled on the cold floor beside the pedestal.

The man she loved believed she was faithless and disloyal, perfidious even. Iona, the woman she regarded as a friend, did too. Tremors wracked Cat's body. Her heart was being stretched, rent, destroyed. She banged her forehead against her knees, over and over. At some point, the pain in her skull overrode the pain in her heart. She held still for several moments, then dragged herself upright.

She tugged the clothes from her body and stepped under the stinging spray of the shower. The water beat on her shoulders. Eventually, she circled around and lifted her face for the water to sluice away any trace of her tears.

Phillip, the lawyer in Melbourne, warned her not to trust the McKells implicitly. Yet she'd gone and given Lachie her heart. She could only blame herself. She'd been hurt before by a man and survived. She would again. But Lachie? She stumbled. Well, she'd get past him, too.

She threw on a nightdress and wrapped herself in her bathrobe, then padded to her grandmother's room. The food tray was gone. Isla was asleep.

Back in her own room, she threw herself onto the bed. Emotional exhaustion overtook her, and she slept dreamlessly till dawn.

~ * ~

By the time they arrived at Melbourne International Airport, Isla was distressed. Fortunately, the airline arranged for a wheelchair to help her into the terminal and a golf cart to spirit them along the corridors to baggage collection and immigration. It was one advantage of first-class travel, Cat found, to be ushered past the lengthy queues of travel-weary passengers, especially with Isla's confusion growing. A haunted, hunted look marred her expression, but there was little Cat could do to make things any easier.

They exited the arrivals hall to find their hired car driver holding a phone with her name displayed. From the time they landed, they'd accomplished the trip to the house within an hour, despite roadworks on the freeway.

Being in familiar surroundings again was surreal for Cat. The house looked and smelled the same. The worn carpet was still worn, the faded curtains still faded.

There was nothing here to suggest her financial situation was any different from months ago. The court case, the visit from Brad Cameron's lawyers, the trip to Scotland—it was like it'd happened to someone else.

Except meeting Lachie.

When would she learn? When Steven promised her the world, she'd laid bare every cent she'd saved assiduously, and she'd opened her heart. He'd trodden on it and scurried off with the cash.

With Lachie, it seemed same-same. Again, she'd offered a treasure for his sake. She'd passed on the pâté-making secret to someone who was not her daughter, four someones, in fact. He hadn't received the knowledge as the cherished gift she'd intended. Instead, he pilloried her for what he considered her faithlessness.

She was glad she hadn't overtly offered him her love. It didn't help her hurting any less, but it contained the humiliation factor.

~ * ~

"When you return to Scotland..."

Isla's voice broke into Cat's thoughts. "What's that, Gran? I was off in my own world for a few minutes there."

They were lounging side by side in the shade of the large magnolia tree in their backyard, Gran's favorite spot to rest outdoors. Even in the shade, though, the day was quite warm. Melbourne was gearing up for summer.

Isla seemed to tire more and more easily since their return from Scotland five weeks ago. Perhaps it had been happening for a long time. Cat remembered the afternoons she would find Gran snoozing in her chair at the care home.

"I said," she started again, "you must remember to take the jewelry when you go to Scotland."

"I'm not sure I'll be going back to Scotland." Cat glanced up at the clear blue sky, avoiding her grandmother's gaze and the longing she was sure was there in her face. Her chest ached like part of her soul had been wrenched away and wouldn't heal.

"Honey bun, you'll never be whole in your spirit without the boy, just as he'll be a walking zombie without you." Isla heaved a great sigh, rolling her head from side to side, stretching her muscles. "Iona told me the villagers deemed you the bee's knees. They were anticipating the laird's wedding."

"They shouldn't have assumed there'd be a wedding," Cat snapped.

"Maybe they did because the boy had never taken anyone to his community coffee morning. He made sure everyone knew who you were, and he held your hand in the street in full view of the village..." Isla's eyes drifted closed. Cat waited.

"They think he's wonderful. He made the sacrifice to marry a local girl even though she was already pregnant. The rumors said the father was someone other than the laird. Then he suffered the deaths of her and the baby." She sighed. "They want him happy."

A light breeze ruffled her fine hair. It brought slight relief from the stifling heat and carried the honeysuckle scent from the vine covering the side fence of the property.

"You can make him happy," she said, at last. "And he's the one who makes your aura whole. You need to forgive him, petal."

"He believes I betrayed my birthright. He needs to acknowledge I did nothing wrong. I acted in the spirit of Simone's own wishes according to what she wrote in her journals," Cat said, taking her grandmother's hand.

"His sisters told him he got everything arse-about-face. Don't you fear. They're wonderful girls, aren't they?" Isla's lips lifted in a quiet smile, and she patted Cat's arm.

"Iona can be ferocious. She warned me not to hurt her brother. Maybe not in so many words, but enough for me to understand her meaning." Cat grinned.

"I told Iny right away the hurting was the other way around. Make no bones about that."

"Well they got what they needed—the pâté recipe. Now we're off their radar. There's been nothing further from them." Cat pursed her mouth and dragged her hand back to her lap.

"The girls phone me every other day. Usually, it's when I've gone to my room for the night. They're giving Lachie a hard time. Iona says he's like a bear with a sore head, trying to stay away from everyone except to snap orders. He's ruing the fact he's blown the best thing in his life."

"You didn't tell me the girls were in touch." Cat's body went rigid. Isla drew a heavy breath.

"Oh, they believe you wouldn't want contact with them even though they care for you. My hunch is Iona feels guilty because she made you cry when she blamed you for hurting her brother..."

Cat's shock didn't lessen as a tingle of apprehension flowed through her. She leaned forward on her lounger, flicking her legs to the side as she pivoted to her grandmother. "How does she know I cried?"

"Your ensuite backed against mine, honey bun. We heard everything."

"Oh." Heat flooded Cat's face.

"You were right to get us out of Dodge when you did, child. But it's time for you to return now," Isla said. It seemed like she gave as much force as she could muster to her voice.

"I haven't been invited, so we need not worry."

"You don't need an invitation to your own house in Edinburgh, Catty. Inform Ness when you arrive. She'll take it from there."

"Shall we plan a trip for the New Year? Get Christmas done and go? Would you like an onboard suite again?"

"Oh, I won't be going, dear. In the end, I'm happier here where I can be close to my Jimmy. You plan it for yourself. When you go, take the jewelry."

"You mean the parures? They're not mine."

"Everything is yours now, sweetheart. I planned to give them to you on your wedding day. They're like a dowry gift," Isla said. "Wear the diamond one for your wedding, like Simone. It will tell the world you belong. Promise me." She was suddenly anxious, almost distressed.

"If there's a wedding day, I'll wear Simone's diamonds."

"You'll take the other sets to Kellburgh too?"

"Yes, for your sake, I'll take them to Kellburgh," Cat promised.

"Good. Remember, I love you honey bun, always. You are the treasure of my life."

"Gran?"

Isla screwed her nose to one side. "Don't fret, I'm just an old woman being maudlin. It's too hot outside. I'll go in to rest."

"Come on, then," Cat said, easing her grandmother to her feet. "In the lounge or on your bed?"

"I'll sit in the lounge with the air-con and watch the telly."

Cat settled Isla with a rug across her knees since the air conditioner cooled the room significantly. "Do you need anything? Shall I make us a cuppa?"

"Maybe in a little while. I'll have a nap now."

"Okay. I'll go to the kitchen to see what the freezer has to offer for dinner," Cat said. A few minutes later, she swung around the kitchen doorjamb. "Fish or chicken, Gran. What would you prefer? Gran?"

Her heart stopped for a moment before a keening cry rose from within her chest. She rushed to her grandmother's side. Isla was lying on the chair with her head at an odd angle. Her face was bloodless. "Gran?" Cat sobbed as she searched in vain for a pulse on her grandmother's neck.

She found her phone in her pocket and dialed emergency services even though any help was already too late.

Gran was gone.

31

Chapter Thirty-one

"Ye'll have to strap on yer balls and make yer peace with Catriona. Ye realize that, don't ye?"

Iona's bombshell remark reverberated around the dinner table. Thank Christ there were just the two of them present.

"Why would ye say such a thing?" Lachie asked. "Ye heard what I said to her. There's no going back. She'll never forgive me for being an arse."

"I wouldn't blame her for it, myself. Isla has a different view." Iona scooped up a forkful of mashed potato.

"Ye've spoken to Isla?" His body stiffened, his grip tightening on his dinner knife.

"Aye, both Ness and I talk to Isla. We can't contact Catriona until ye make yer peace. Both ye and she would judge we were being disloyal to ye even after all she's done for this family. Isla says Catriona has been doleful like ye for the last month or more."

"That would be my fault too. Would ye forgive a man who accused ye of being cavalier with yer sacred promises?" Lachie flung his cutlery onto his plate.

"Not without a hell of a lot of groveling from said male. Though, I'm not the one in love with ye, ye big lug." Iona rolled her eyes.

"Aye, and there's another thing. She's such a wee thing, like Meredith, and my size scared Meredith half to death."

"Meredith, huh? No one ever understood why ye married such a weak woman and claimed her babe. Ye make too much of yer bulk. Meredith was a wimp, Lachie. She was never yer true match. Ye married her for convenience—her convenience. Yer size doesn't concern Catriona. She'd no problem snuggling on yer lap so far as I saw." Iona chewed her food for a moment. "Do ye love her?"

"Aye, ye know I do."

"So go after her."

He glanced at his half-eaten meal for something to focus his attention. "I canna. I hurt her badly. I'm ashamed of myself for even contemplating she would do such a thing."

"What a cop out. For a strong man, ye're being awfully weak on this. She understood where ye were coming from, eventually. Isla says Catriona's moved past it now. She's comfortable with the notion she did the right thing in teaching us to make the pâté. She figured ye'd work it out in time too. She's in the dumps because ye haven't been in touch. She thinks ye never loved her, that ye were only after a pâté maker."

"She can't believe that." Lachie clenched his fist on the table.

"She can. Ye wanted her when she was the only one with the recipe. Now there are others, ye don't need her anymore, so ye've let her go."

"Shite!" He threw himself against the backrest of the chair. "That's not how it is at all. I fell in love with her the moment she peered along her wee nose at me at the café where she worked."

"Good. Then stop analyzing things through yer big toe or whatever is the most brainless part of yer anatomy. She taught us to make the pâté to get the issue off the table between ye." His sister's scowl bored into him.

"Aye, ye and Ness have banged it into my thick skull, but I threw it in her face, and she left," he said.

"She didn't go far. She and Isla went to Edinburgh for the week. My opinion is she was expecting ye to come to yer senses."

"I disappointed her there too." His shoulders slumped.

"She owns the townhouse and the one next door. Did ye know?" Iona asked.

Lachie nodded. "She learned only recently her father left her a wealthy woman. If I go after her now, will she think I'm after her money?"

"Good grief, Lachie." Iona turtled her neck toward him and flattened her hands on the armrests of her chair. "Is there anything else ye can heap on yerself while ye're having yer pity party? Ye're a bag of misery. My brother, the person I love and admire, always finds the good side to things. He's not ye right now. Pull yerself together. Drag yerself from this hole and soon. People are noticing. The villagers are asking when Catriona will return. They expected yer engagement announcement straight after the community meeting. Then Darro McGill attacked her. They assumed ye put things on hold until Cat was better. Ye've got to make things right for ye and for her. Ye're the only one who can."

He dragged his gaze around to meet his sister's. "I don't know how."

"Ye do." Iona folded her arms and rested them in front of her. "Ye've been fixing other people's messes yer whole life, including the mess Gramps left the business in. Do it for yerself. Fix yer own mess. Get yer butt on a plane. Talk to her face to face. She can't reject ye 'til ye put yerself in front of her. She can't accept ye until ye do either. Go see her."

His stomach dropped. Iona was right, but if Catriona rejected him again, he'd be doomed forever.

~ * ~

Well after midnight, the phone rang on Lachie's bedside table. He wasn't asleep, trying to find a way back to Catriona. He'd done the same every night since she left.

"Aye?" he barked.

"It's Catriona."

At the mere sound of her voice, he catapulted into a standing position.

"Gran died an hour ago. Please inform your aunts and the others."

"Aye, lass. What can I—" The phone emitted a strident beeping in his ear. He sagged onto his bed, his fingers kneading his forehead.

He'd wanted to hear Cat's voice, but not like this.

He raised the phone and pressed the speed dial for James Gallien in Melbourne. "James, Catriona's grandmother has passed away. I want ye to go to her. Do whatever ye can to help; funeral arrangements, death certificates, wills, whatever. I'll get the first flight I can."

"She's an independent sort. What if she doesn't want me there, sir?" James's voice was hesitant.

"If she doesn't need ye, she'll tell ye. Stay close as ye can until I get there. Call me with any updates. Keep me posted on what's happening. Good man."

Lachie hung up and then dialed his sister's number. Her rooms were in the opposite wing of the house. She wouldn't appreciate his banging on her door in the middle of the night.

"Iny? Isla has died. Ye've got yer wish in a way. I'm going to Australia. There's a flight to Dubai first thing in the morning. I'll aim to catch it."

"Shall I come, too?" Iona asked. "I'd like to be there for Catriona in case ye put yer size twelves in the muck again."

"Come when ye can. Get things organized here. I don't want to ring the aunts at this hour. I'll leave ye to tell them and Ness. Ye can bring them to Melbourne, too, if it's what they want."

"Okay. I'll book yer flights. Ye pack."

Iona phoned back in less than ten minutes. Lachie was adding his toiletries to the suitcase on the bed. "I've got yer flight details. I've texted them to ye. Ye'll be in Melbourne twenty-four hours from when ye leave Edinburgh at six this morning. I've booked ye in first class. Ye've a suite in the same hotel in Melbourne as last time for three nights. Ye can extend the time if ye need. Emerson will be at the door in twenty minutes with the Rover. Ye need to leave now because the roads will be icy. Ye'll need extra time. I've given Emerson the day off when he gets home as compensation for the moonlight flit."

"Iny, ye're a blessing."

"Lachie, Cat and her Gran have been the best things to happen in this family in a long time. Tread warily, take care with her."

"Aye, I will," Lachie said.

"I love ye, big brother. Travel safely."

~ * ~

James Gallien answered Lachie's knock on Catriona's door in the late afternoon the following day. "Come in, sir. Several ladies from Mrs. Jenkins's former care home are here to pay their respects. Miss Cameron is struggling."

Lachie walked to the lounge room where a pale Catriona was surrounded by older women. She glanced toward the door with panic in her eyes. As recognition dawned on her face, she stepped back from the group and sped across the room. "Lachie!"

He slammed his arms around her, and she burst into tears against his chest. "Wheesht now *m'eudail*," he said, holding her close. Over her head, he spoke to the women. "Ladies, thank ye for coming to check on Catriona. Do ye have transport to the facility or shall I hire a cab for ye?"

A woman, who was not much taller than Catriona, strode across the room. She raised her gaze to him as she stroked whatever part of Cat's back she could access. "You'd be the McKell? You have the look of them," she said. Her accent was Australian with underlying Scots tones.

"Aye, madam."

She switched to Gaelic. "Well lad, you be careful with this poor wee thing. She was always kind to us with few visitors at the care home. She's alone in the world now."

He responded using the same language. "She is not alone. She has the McKells. I thank ye for caring."

The woman changed to English. "You'll do all right, lad. Our mini-van is parked on the street. We've kept the driver waiting long enough. Come on, ladies."

The room cleared in minutes. Catriona eased from his arms when James came into the room.

"James, thank ye for being here. Catriona and I appreciate yer help," Lachie said.

"My pleasure, sir. If there's nothing else, I'll be on my way." James closed the front door behind himself.

Finally, they were alone. Lachie urged Cat across to the lounge and drew her onto his lap. She lay her head on his shoulder with one hand resting on his chest. She was like heaven in his arms. "You came." Cat's voice was a whisper.

"Aye lass. I wasn't sure if ye'd want me. If ye didn't, I figured ye would say it to my face," he said.

She snuggled her nose closer to his neck, saying nothing.

"I'm truly sorry for not understanding the precious gift ye gave to my family, *mo ghràidh*. Because of my hubris, ye came home to Melbourne. It left ye alone when yer Gran passed. Ye should have been with us, with the people who love ye and who loved Gran."

She pulled back against his arm to peer at him. "What is 'mo gride'?"

He cuddled her against him. "Ye're *mo ghràidh,* my love, my darling." He rested his cheek on her head.

"Well, mo gride, you accept then, teaching the others to make the pâté did not betray the Salignac legacy?"

"Aye, I do. My sisters both laid into me for the way I treated ye. They told me I was ignorant of Simone's wishes. I studied the journals myself. When I accessed them previously, I read what Simone wrote through the lens of what I believed was the truth, that the legacy was a mother-daughter thing. Ye made me realize what Simone really said was the pâté was for any of her female descendants, not only the daughters of daughters," he conceded.

Cat flopped against his chest. "Hmm. Good. Gran loved your family, too. I'm glad, though, we were here at home when she passed. Now, we can lay her to rest with her beloved Jimmy. I never knew him because he died quite young. Gran never stopped loving him. I want a love like hers someday." Her voice sounded sleepy, and her body relaxed fully against him.

Lachie tightened his hold on her. He rested his cheek atop her head. "Aye, *mo ghràidh,* I'll make sure of it."

32

Chapter Thirty-two

In hindsight, Cat recognized her new life began the moment she woke in Lachie's arms that evening in Melbourne. His limbs must have been numb from holding her.

She brought his face close to kiss him in the sweetest merging of souls.

"Well then, laddie, are we going to marry?" she asked.

His chuckle reverberated through her. "Ach lass, there ye go again. It's like the car door. Popping the question is my job."

"Pop ahead." She grinned.

"Shouldn't we wait until after yer grandmother's funeral? To show her some respect?" He tilted his head.

"If you feel the need to do so, fine," she shrugged. "Gran wouldn't be bothered. She knew our future was a done deal when she met you and told me our auras were connected. You remember, when she said you would be part of our family? Our last conversation was about you. She said you'd be a zombie without me. I wouldn't want to condemn you to such a non-life, even if you are self-righteous, opinionated, and bossy." Cat delivered a soft punch to his shoulder.

"A zombie I have been, lass." He shook his head. "There is no life in me without ye around. I was ready to ask ye to marry me when ye came home from Edinburgh. Instead, I sent ye away. What an arse, eh?" There was a desolate sadness in his eyes.

"Yep. I won't deny it. You were. You didn't call. I figured once you got what you wanted with the pâté production, you didn't need me anymore."

"Ah lass, I couldn't phone ye. I was too ashamed." He ran one hand through his hair in the way he always did when he was upset. "That I would treat ye so? That I would speak to ye in such a manner? I didn't deserve ye. Why would ye want me? A big, hulking brute with no finesse. No, ye were better off with me excised from yer life."

She climbed from his lap. "It's not the first time you've referred to your build. Why do you do that?"

Color washed into his face. His eyes wouldn't meet hers. "I never had relations with my wife because she feared my size. She wouldn't sleep in the same bed in case I squashed her; her words."

"Lachie look at me. Am I afraid of you? Any part of you?" Cat probed.

"Not afraid exactly, though ye left when I got angry."

"Because you were an arse, to use your expression. You called me faithless, a person who would betray my most sacred vow. I don't need that shit in my life. I wasn't afraid. I was hurt, and I was mad. With Meredith, did you ever stop to think any man would have frightened her, not you specifically? She'd been attacked and raped. It made sense men scared her. Her fear wasn't personally directed at you. Darro McGill hurt her, not you."

Finally, he brought his gaze back to hers. What she saw there was confusion, like a puppy who'd been whipped without knowing why, but hope too.

She raised her brows. "So, are you going to get on with the question-popping thing or not?"

His face cleared, and he pulled himself to his feet. He took her hands in his as he looked at her. "Lass, I love ye. First, I have a confession to make."

"Will it affect my answer, do you think?"

He scratched his forefinger along his jaw, then bit his bottom lip, all the while holding her gaze. "I'm a marquis. You'll be a marchioness. Our children will have their own titles."

Blood rushed from every part of her body to pool in her gut. She slumped onto the couch, folding her arms across her chest. "Holy shit. You really are a lord, then. I thought…"

"I don't use the title except for ceremonial occasions, but it's there, and it will affect who you become. You've been clear about your views on the aristocracy."

"But you were cleaning out the pens the morning I was attacked. What kind of lord does that?" Her voice squeaked out.

He sat beside her, unwrapped one of her arms from its tight knot and took her hand in his. "The Scottish kind. We work alongside the people in our community. The title doesn't change the person I am. It doesn't change the fact that I love ye. I have done since the moment we met. I've wanted ye since the first time ye put me in my place. I fell in love with ye the very second yer lips met mine. I'm addicted to ye."

He dropped to one knee, still grasping her hands as if she were his only hope of salvation in a stormy sea. "Catriona Cameron, would ye do me the greatest honor by becoming my lady, my life, and my most beloved wife?"

Tears eased their way from Catriona's eyes. "Laochailan McKell, I have loved you all this time, too. Ironically, my mother believed I would have to learn to be a lady some day. Amongst the last gifts she left for me was a diamond bracelet for such a time. Your title doesn't change how I feel about you, so, yes, I will marry you and we'll face whatever comes together." She tugged on his hand to bring him to his feet. Then banded her arms around him. "On that note, the first item on the agenda is to prove we'll be compatible sharing a bed. My room is this way." She clutched his hand to lead him from the lounge room. "And I don't give a damn whether you have protection or not."

"Aye, I have protection, lass. Ye've already taught me that lesson." His sexy chuckle was a warm balm to her soul.

~ * ~

Lachie didn't leave her side for the rest of the time he was in Melbourne. They refrained from formally announcing their engagement until they returned to Kellburgh.

Isla's funeral was almost lighthearted. The celebrant drew on the stories Cat told, along with some from Lachie and his sisters, creating a delightful ceremony to acknowledge and remember an amazing grandmother and a wonderful woman. They buried her in the plot with her husband.

Cat learned from Ben Jones that Brad Cameron's ashes were interred in the columbarium at the same cemetery. Given what she'd learned of her father's love for her mother, Cat took the urn containing her mother's ashes and placed it in her father's wall vault.

She twisted from the mirror, now, as her best friend, Lori, ran an assessing gaze over the picture she made. Lori, Iona, and Ness were helping Cat put the finishing touches to her wedding dress. She was devoid of jewelry except for a small tiara holding her headdress in place and the diamond tennis bracelet her mother left for her that last Christmas.

"Thank you for your help, guys," Cat said, fingering the bracelet. "There's one thing left to do. Lori, can you get the box, please?"

"Ooh yeah! Come to mama, you sparkly good things." Lori bent to withdraw one square black box from the top drawer of Cat's dressing table.

Cat grinned at Ness and Iona. "If you help me with these, I'll be ready to go."

The McKell women leaned in with amazement shining from their faces when Catriona opened the box to reveal Simone's diamond parure. "Where did you find this?" Ness asked in awe.

"It came from my great-grandmother. She was the eldest daughter and received it from her mother for her bridal gift. I promised Gran I would wear it on my wedding day."

"Does Lachie know?" asked Iona in a high-pitched voice.

"Not yet," Cat said.

"You'll blow him away," squeaked Ness. "Right, let's get this done."

The necklace sat framed by the low curve of the dress's bodice. Lori replaced the decorative tiara with Simone's diamond one. It sat heavily on Cat's head. The earrings, too, were weighty. The *pièce de résistance*, for Cat, was the beautiful Scotch thistle brooch with the sparkling amethyst. It exuded energy and well-being. Just like it was for Simone, the thistle was a symbol of Cat's new home, of family, of love, and she was proud to wear it.

The twins and Lori took a few paces away to review the finished image.

"Cat, ye're like the portrait," Iona said. "Don't ye agree, Ness?"

"Perfect, simply perfect. Let's go. I can't wait to see Lachie's face," Ness said.

The troupe juggled their way down the staircase, with Iona and Ness managing the bridal train. Cat struggled to keep her head upright to hold the tiara in place as she negotiated the stairs. Lori held her hand to balance her.

Emerson was waiting with the limousine to drive them the short distance to the church. He beamed as he held the door open for her.

"We're all so delighted for you, miss. We hope ye'll be happy here amongst us."

Cat's throat tightened with emotion. "Thank you, Emerson. I'm sure I will be." It took some moments of careful positioning by her attendants to make sure her dress was protected from crushing, and then they were on their way.

When they arrived, Iona stood inside the church door to signal for a change in the music. Ness checked they'd arranged the bridal train as it should be, and then she shadowed Iona's slow promenade to the altar. Lori faced Cat. She tweaked the bridal veil and adjusted the tartan sash on Cat's shoulder. "This is the start of the best days of your life. You get that, right?"

Cat smiled. "I'm glad you're here to be my matron of honor, Lori. It means a lot to me."

"First class airfare—who would say no? It's something to remind Drene of when she's grown up." She heaved a sigh with an ecstatic grin on her face. "I wouldn't have missed it for the world, Treena. Love you." She bent to give Cat a quick air kiss, spun on her heel, and followed the path of the bridesmaids.

Lachie was standing erect at the top of the aisle, flanked by Enzo, a friend from his university days, and two cousins. When the three bridal attendants were in place, he pivoted to face the back of the church where Cat was preparing to move toward him. His mouth gaped slightly when he saw her. His eyes shone with love and pride.

She bit her lip to stop from crying happy tears. She gripped her bouquet of spring roses, purple thistles, and a ribbon of Lachie's tartan. With the parure in place, as she promised Gran, and her mother's gift around her wrist, Cat sensed the presence of the women who'd raised her. Their love surrounded her as she focused her attention on the spot where Lachie waited.

Catriona drew a deep breath, smiling behind her veil. She set one foot in front of the other, elegantly stepping the length of the aisle, her gaze holding his.

An eternal companion to this wonderful man? She couldn't wait.

33

Acknowledgements

Stories don't come into the world fully formed. The first draft is full of plot-holes, inconsistencies, and poor expression.

My husband, David, is my first critic. No, he doesn't read romance. He's much happier with an annual report than a work of fiction, but he is fantastic at finding plot holes. We might be in the car and chatting about where one of my stories is going and he'll challenge me on the plot, the location, the premise. It's a bit like sitting an academic *viva voce*, but the story emerges stronger for it, when I must defend my characters and their choices, or I'm forced to see there might be a better approach. He gets to know the characters, too, and is comfortable talking with me about these figments of my imagination as real people.

My friend, Kathy, my sister, Audrene, and my mother, Audrey while she was alive, were my next line of defense. They read the work and made suggestions, demands, and noises of dissent. As seasoned romance readers they were quite willing, determined even, to tell me when something wasn't working. Because of them, the story expanded, two-dimensional figures developed depth, and tension became stronger. When they thought it was ready, I edited it again and sent it out to the world.

Cassiel Knight from the former Champagne Book Group snatched the story out of a PitMad twitter feed on an early foray for the book to find a publisher. I'm so grateful for her support and advocacy, for offering the assistance of her team and introducing me to the CBG community of authors. Most particularly, I want to thank Jodi Christensen, editor extraordinaire, who edited with an iron fist in a velvet glove and polished the work to a magnificent sheen.

Finally, I must acknowledge the home team: my husband, David, whom I've mentioned, our children, Bryn and Michaela, their partners, and our grandson, Jamieson. None of them reads romance, but I wouldn't have the space, time or courage to sit down and commit my stories to paper without their love and support. I'm forever grateful I have each of them in my life.

About the Author

Caenys (think Denise with a K) Kerr grew up in a household of mostly women who all enjoyed reading—usually chain-reading romance. Books have been her escape, her inspiration, her sanity and her brain candy (when she was writing her PhD). The university librarian dubbed them brain candy when she was entertained by Caenys' foraging for romances rather than studying the current journals in her academic field of study.

Ideas for Caenys' novels can come from anywhere. There was an occasion when Caenys and her husband, David, visited a French restaurant in Melbourne, Australia, and enjoyed a delicious and distinctive pâté. The meal occurred soon after their return from a trip to Scotland where they'd visited Culloden. They'd been reminded of Scottish history, including attempts to engage the French to help the Scots ward off the English. The confluence of pâté, French, Scots, and Melbourne sparked an idea that became Cat and Lachie's story, The Salignac Legacy.

Caenys lives (with David) by a canal on the southern end of Australia's Gold Coast. She has two adult children (and their wonderful partners) and one precious, newly-adult grandson.

Caenys loves to hear from her readers. You can find and connect with her at the links below.

Website/Blog: https://caenyskerr.wordpress.com/

Facebook: https://www.facebook.com/profile.php?id=100018682002439

Instagram: https://www.instagram.com/caenys/

~ * ~

Thank you for taking the time to read *The Salignac Legacy*. If you enjoyed the story, please tell your friends and leave a review. Reviews support authors and ensure they continue to bring readers books to love and enjoy.

Read on for a sneak peek at Book 2 in the Priceless Heritage Series, *The Beaulieu Birthright.*

Sneak Peek

The Beaulieu Birthright

Prologue

Iona McKell shouldn't have been dreaming about her brother's best friend, tonight of all nights, but he kept intruding. Every time he did, her heart bumped as if the sexy Frenchman stood right there with his movie-star smile and a voice to make her body go quivery.

She slid her feet into the red and white slides she'd bought especially for the occasion. For her eighteenth birthday, she aimed to exude her mother's sophistication.

Facing the patinaed antique mirror, a fixture in her bedroom for her entire life—probably since the accessory was invented two hundred years ago—she adjusted the dangly red clip-on earrings, a perfect match with the shoes. For her, presentation was about the footwear adding several inches to her deficient height.

Her twin sister pushed open the heavy oak door, barging into the room. "Ooh! I'm excited. We're eighteen. It seems to have taken forever."

"Eighteen years is my estimate," Iona said.

"Droll. You know what I mean. We can go to pubs, clubs, do all sorts of stuff without a 'responsible adult'." Agnes twiddled her fingers in air quotes. Her irrepressible *joie de vivre* was in full force.

Physically she was Iona's replica—one fifty-five centimeters in height, green eyes with a hint of blue, along with mid-length straight black hair framing a heart-shaped face with cupid-bow lips. They were different in every other way.

Agnes' outfit contrasted with her twin's trendy though conservative, tonal-gray, above-the-knee tunic, paired with dark gray footless tights. Instead, she wore black leggings tucked into calf-and-a-bit kick-arse boots, a black singlet top to display her midriff, one long earring in her left ear, a stud in the other. She was always the one with the flamboyant confidence to flout convention and take on the world.

"We've been tasting alcohol since we were kids, Ness," she said reverting to the more familiar version of her sister's name. "What's the big deal?"

"Tasting, yes. Drinking, no." Ness grinned from ear to ear, throwing herself backward onto the springy four-poster bed. "Sipping whisky to check the flavor is a long way from oodles and oodles of champagne." She propped herself onto one elbow. "So-o-o will you kiss Enzo tonight, now we're grown up?"

"Why would I?" Iona's shoulders stiffened at the suggestion.

"Because you've been in lu-u-urve with him since he first came here four years ago."

Warmth flooded Iona's face. Enzo never showed any interest in her, apart from her being Lachie's sister. He was twenty-two with girlfriends by the score if the fashion mags were anything to go by, an up-and-coming French perfume magnate with mind-blowing charm and an ego to match. Ness' all-guns-blazing approach to life fit the profile of the women he escorted much better than she could. It didn't stop her from dreaming.

"You said Enzo wasn't able to come. He had to fly to Malaysia or somewhere?" Iona said.

"We'll find out, I guess. Are you ready to go? I want to see who's arrived." Ness bounced once, landing on her feet with an arm flung in the air. "This will be great. Yeah!"

Iona grinned. "Okay, but be sensible, please."

Ness bounded across the room to kiss Iona's cheek. "Iny, you're my elder sister by three minutes. You don't get to play 'mother'. Relax. Have fun. Enjoy yourself. We'll make this a night to remember. This old castle hasn't partied this hard since forever." Ness dragged her to the door. "Let's go." Her enthusiasm was infectious.

Exiting the room with a dramatic flourish of arms extended to either side of her body, Ness bounced down the red-carpeted central stone staircase separating the two main wings of Kellburgh Castle. Iona wasn't to be hurried. Pausing at her parents' portrait, she wished they were there tonight. No one could have guessed within weeks of the portrait's completion, they would be killed in a car accident on the winding, icy, highland roads.

From her vantage point, she observed the lavish display in the Great Room.

Their brother, Lachie, the current laird, spared no expense for this party. Liveried waiters held trays of glasses with wine or whisky. The room was decorated with ribbons, balloons, and massive floral bouquets. Sparkling crystal candelabras lit the room. The dining area, arranged at the end farthest from the door, provided seating for two hundred and fifty guests.

Halfway along the long wall, a string quartet performed on a makeshift bandstand. Later in the evening, when most older guests retired, a DJ would replace the musicians.

Everything required careful planning and execution. Ness reveled in it. She'd involved herself in the preparations for the party weeks in advance. Iona's pragmatic response, that the day was the same as any other, made no dent in her sister's enthusiasm. When take-on-the-world genes were handed out, Ness got her share, along with her twin's.

Taking the last few treads to the parquet floor at the base of the staircase, Iona arrived in the Great Room in time for the early guests. Agnes already held her first champagne flute, engaging the younger set walking through the door.

Iona stood with her brother, focusing her attention on the older relatives. It was what their mother would have done—to make everyone welcome. At least, it had been Peta's practice before dementia carried away her mind and the car accident stole her life.

After an hour's socializing, she gestured for Ness to withdraw into the foyer to be with her and Lachie. The Master of Ceremonies called on the visitors to stand at their table places for the formal welcome of the guests of honor.

Waiting while the emcee concluded his speech, Iona glanced over her siblings. Love and pride for each of them welled in her chest. Lachie was a giant compared with most of those around him. No one could doubt he was the laird, resplendent as he was in his formal attire: kilt, sporran, Prince Charlie jacket and vest. He'd included their father's *sgian-dubh* knife tucked into the top of his kilt hose.

Iona linked her arm through his. Ness did the same on his other side. Together, they paraded the ballroom's length to arrive at the high table.

Lachie made a ceremony of introducing them, first Iona, herself, because she was the elder, then Agnes. "I do this, tonight," he said, "because some of you might not recognize which twin is which. There are others who still believe they are the sweet young things they used to be." Their guests chuckled in response. Lachie raised a glass of McKell's whisky, saluting Iona's glass with a grin and then turning to Ness, before facing the crowd. *"Fáilte a chur roimh.* **Slàinte mhath!"**

The crowd gave a rowdy response to his welcome, returned the toast, drank, then sat. Grateful to be out of the glare of attention, Iona relaxed into her seat. As with every bit of Ness' organization for the party, the meal was faultless, with each course arriving with military precision to every table in the hall. When dessert and coffee were cleared, people moved from the tables to circulate or to dance.

Wherever she was in the room, Iona's focus darted to the main entrance. *Thank goodness Enzo didn't make it to the party.* His presence would have made her a total wreck. His absence was almost as bad, like waiting for a surprise, though unsure if it was a good thing.

Enzo Beaulieu. She'd been fourteen when Lachie first invited the dark-haired Frenchman home from university for the holidays. The first time she'd met Enzo, her body went hot and cold, excited and scared at the same time.

When he'd gazed at her with his deep-blue eyes, her breath stopped. He was not as tall as her brother, but bordering on one seventy-five centimeters, with a slim build and an innate grace and self-assurance unique to him.

Ness teased her for being in lu-u-urve. Iona denied it, of course. She was a kid. At eighteen, he was a man. She was mortified to imagine he'd detected her reaction.

He'd been in and out of their lives on a regular basis in the four years since. Iona would 'accidentally' appear in unexpected places, where he would be, to draw his attention. His mouth would form a perfect smile. When he spoke, it would be only to say, "There you are, *ma petite*." His sultry tone rumbled low in her belly setting up an addictive reaction of liquid heat.

She wished she shared Ness' confidence to go after what she wanted. Instead, she'd mutter something in reply before scurrying away, only to repeat the process at the earliest opportunity.

Allowing the man to breach her consciousness amid the party was unsettling. No matter how much she tried to banish him from her mind, he was persistent. His eyes, the timbre of his voice, and the trim athleticism of his body all conspired to hold him present.

She needed a break. Slipping out, she headed to the rear of the building. A tall figure appeared to her left, arriving from the garage area. She hesitated in case the latecomer required direction.

He strode toward her, his gait confident, head held high.

Enzo.

"*Mignon*, you have left your party?" he asked, taking one of her hands in his.

She froze, then was instantly hot all over. Fourteen years old again. *Damn it, you're an adult now. Get it together.* "For a moment, to get some air," she said.

Her heart thumped. He was there. He'd flown half-way around the world to be there for her party. And Ness', of course. The butterflies in her chest stomped a happy dance.

"I shall come with you. Into the maze?" he asked, intertwining his fingers with hers.

"Aye, there are seats there." Her pulse hammered.

He tilted his head toward her. "You are particularly beautiful tonight, *mignon*. You make my heart beat faster with your loveliness."

She was beautiful to him? Squee! "Smooth talking Frenchman." She twisted the fingers of her free hand into the fabric of her tunic.

"It is true." He grinned. "You are a vision, an angel sent to me. I have watched for four years as you grow more lovely." He frowned. "You are Lachie's sister. I should take you back to your party." He let go of her hand.

"Don't. I need some time. You can go on, though," she said, hoping against hope he would stay.

"And miss a single moment of being with you? Non. Come."

With his palm at the small of her back, they entered the private space afforded by the maze. *Oh God, don't let him feel me shaking. It's so uncool.* He turned her toward him, resting his hands at her hips, sending zinging whispers of happiness through her soul.

Here in the dark, his eyes gleamed in the little light available. They drew her in. Her heart ricocheted in her chest. Nervous shivers agitated her body. She couldn't move either toward him or away. Mesmerized by his nearness, she held his gaze. He lifted one hand, grazing her cheek with his knuckles. Her head canted to capture the soft touch.

"*Ma belle! J'ai attendu si longtemps pour chuchoter de doux riens, pour e tenir et pour faire cela,*" he whispered. *Was it true he'd been waiting to kiss her? To whisper sweet nothings to her?*

She took one small step backward. What would Lachie say if she kissed his best friend? Ness would gloat, say I-told-you-so. Stretching to meet him, Iona's hesitation was brief. She wanted this.

He lowered his mouth to hers—slow, gentle, heightening her awareness and expectation.

This was her dream, her private fantasy. Enzo. Her chest expanded. She leaned into him.

When he pulled her closer, the feather-light joining firmed into a possessive statement. She put her heart and soul into the kiss, giving back as good as she got. He loved her as she loved him.

His tongue danced with hers, his hands roamed her back. Her one moment of resistance melted away. He could do with her whatever he pleased. Heedless of her clothes, her makeup, or any other arbitrary thing, she reveled in the kiss. Her hands speared into the silky waves of his hair, her nails clutched at his scalp. She rested her head against his shoulder to draw breath.

Easing her from his embrace, he held her away by her upper arms. He cast a frown at the shrubbery around them, then back to her. His expression was abashed, stricken almost. He raised his eyebrows, his lips widening into an exaggerated smile.

"*Et voilà*, Agnes. A kiss for your birthday. I must say, *cherie*, you are good at kissing. You must have practiced a lot." He smirked, winked, and dropped his hands. Without another word, he pivoted, then headed toward the party.

Iona remained riveted in place for several moments. Her dreams, her heart, her body deflated with a *whoosh*. Stumbling to the garden seat, she tossed off the red and white shoes, and hooked her naked heels on the edge of the bench's timber frame.

She wrapped her arms around her shins, dropping her brow to collide with her knees. The pain shooting through her head paled compared with the shattering hurt in her heart.

He believed she was Agnes. He pronounced it 'Arn-yes' like he always did. He most definitely did not say 'Iona'. Couldn't he tell her apart from her sister even now? Really?

Iona didn't cry. Crying offered no solution. She'd learned the hard way when her parents died.

The chilly air swirled around her until Ness' voice called into the darkness for her to come cut the cake.

Iona lifted her head, breathed in the air's fragrant stillness and smoothed her hands across her face before scrambling to her feet. If the ignorant idiot thought she was her twin, there was no need to hide and certainly nothing to acknowledge.

Gathering the last of her dignity, she slid her shoes onto her feet before slipping inside through a side door. The bright lights, the cacophony of voices and music, and the chink of glasses hit her battered senses full on. Uncertain, she paused.

Iona McKell, be the grownup. Exude your mother's grace. Raising her chin, smiling at no one in particular, Iona joined her sister in their celebration.

The Beaulieu *blaigeard* could choke on McKell's finest whisky. She was over him—just like that.

Chapter One

"*Merde,* Papa!" Enzo Beaulieu's fist collided with the tempered glass, horseshoe-shaped table which commanded the opulent, extensive, boardroom space. "This is the twenty-first century, not the 1800s. You cannot force me to marry to suit your whims."

The meeting of their company's directors finished half an hour ago. Everyone except him and his father were gone.

"You have two months." Thierry Beaulieu's lined, bitter face was granite. "If you haven't demonstrated you are mature enough to take sole responsibility for the perfumery, I will accept Flowerpot's lucrative offer."

"Flowerpot! They've been our competition for fifteen years. You'd hand the business to them? They use inferior fragrances. It would destroy the name we've labored to rebuild."

His father shrugged in the irritating way he did, telegraphing his arrogant 'I-don't-give-a-damn' attitude.

Enzo stared at the exotic floral arrangement at the far end of the room and out through the clear glass outer wall to the Parisian views beyond. "Two months? You could have warned me." He refused to betray the slightest weakness in Thierry's presence. "You didn't marry until you were fifty. Why should I?" he asked, redirecting his scrutiny to his parent.

Thierry clamped his lips into a flat line, narrowing a glare at Enzo. "You've maintained your playboy lifestyle without regard for your reputation. The company depends on reputation for its allure," his father's reedy voice continued. "Marriage will settle you."

"*Casse-toi.* My 'playboy' activities have not hindered our growth. Since I've been CEO, I've built the business from a venture on its knees to a multi-billion-euro enterprise." Enzo clenched his jaw against shouting how the company had lost its way under Thierry's leadership, leaving it near bankrupt.

"Perhaps. I'll grant you have considerable skill. I can negotiate with Flowerpot for you to have a role in the new company." The senior Beaulieu steepled his fingers under his chin, his rheumy gaze fixed on his first-born.

"*Baise-le!*" Slamming his hands onto his hips, Enzo leaned toward the older man. "I don't want a role with Flowerpot. Beaulieu is my company. *I* built it from ashes." His index finger rammed into his chest.

"And I'm the one who paid for your education, allowing you to do it," he said, flapping one hand as if to ward off Enzo's implied criticism. "You demean yourself with your profanities, *mon fils*. If you don't want a role in the new business, it's your choice. You have the option to retain the company. It would be a pity to lose what your forefathers began two centuries ago, though times change." Thierry traced a fingernail along the table's edge. "All you have to do is find someone willing to marry you to raise my heirs. I don't expect a love match. You're far too shallow. If your behavior was any indication, you were more in love with some little Scottish piece when you were eighteen or nineteen, than the women you've escorted since. Your money will buy a bride," he said, shrugging again. "If you succeed, I'll hand the business to you on your thirty-third birthday. If not, on that day, I will sign the contract with Flowerpot."

"They approached you, or did you make the overtures?"

Thierry shook his head. "They've been sniffing around since the last magazine article about you was published. It's the old strategy—if you can't beat your competition, buy them out."

"You're willing to facilitate it?" Enzo snarled.

"It's you who will do so."

Enzo spun on his heel to stare through the window-wall. From the fortieth floor of the iconic building he'd commissioned in his seventh year at the company's helm, he focused his attention on the Eiffel Tower, a serene structure to symbolize hope and optimism—his touchstone in stressful times. Blood rampaged through his veins.

When he turned back, Thierry was on his feet. "It doesn't matter to me what decision you make. I'm old. I've lived too long without your mother. I will survive my last few years *sans* the Beaulieu birthright. You'd do well to consider your alternatives."

Enzo folded his arms across his chest, staring at the bent, wizened man who raised his brows once before shuffling from the room.

Bon sang! Enzo was the one who built the company from the scraps Thierry left. It was *his*—except on paper. Anger and trepidation roiled within Enzo in equal measure. He'd suffered his father's stubbornness his whole life, though nothing like this. He'd lost his mother through Thierry's demand for a daughter, even though the complications that caused her death in childbirth were a known risk. Enzo blamed his father, too, for the loss of his brother's companionship, along with the connection to his mother's family after she died.

His existence was choreographed by the old man—what Enzo studied, where he worked, even his friends had to pass Thierry's stringent standards. He'd demanded to meet his best friend's family in their home in Scotland. Despite the laird being a gracious host, the episode left Enzo writhing in embarrassment.

He snapped his mind clear from the wayward memories.

Where would he find someone within two months to agree to marry him? He didn't want a soulless 'bought' marriage, especially one required to produce heirs, as per Thierry's decree.

His father was right on one thing. The only person he'd ever loved was a petite Scottish lass he'd met when he was eighteen years old. She was fourteen. His best friend's sister—it couldn't happen. Enzo struggled against his feelings for four years until he put the final nail in the coffin of their potential love on her eighteenth birthday. He'd kissed her like his life depended on it, in that moment it did. Deliberately, he'd called her by her sister's name, killing her passion—and his—stone dead.

The time wasn't right for him to fall into a relationship. His focus was on rebuilding the perfume business his father was now intent on giving away. It might have damaged his friendship with Lachie, his one true friend—the only person who knew Enzo well.

He conjured any number of excuses. The truth was, then and now, she affected him in ways he couldn't control, drew from him a love he had no way to handle. So he'd destroyed it. She'd never forgiven him.

Iona McKell.

The lilt of her name was enough to stampede the regrets lodged in his soul. He'd written coda to his lingering attachment to her when, a scant year after her party, Lachie informed him she was seeing someone in Glasgow. It seemed serious.

She'd moved on from Enzo.

He ignored the jolt in his gut. He was never short of a partner. In fact, Iona never crossed his mind for a moment unless he spotted a face like hers in the crowd or detected a Scots accent in a café, or when Lachie mentioned his sisters in passing. Then Enzo would be back in a hole of longing and regret, berating himself with the 'what-ifs' he'd abandoned with no understanding of the consequences.

The last time he'd seen her was when he'd flown to Scotland two months ago to salute the arrival of Lachie and Catriona's twins. Iona wasn't a biddable teenager anymore. Instead, she was a woman sure of herself and her value.

Like him, she hadn't married, despite opportunities to do so. She wasn't attached either.

His secretary, Michelle, poked her head around the door to the board room. "Monsieur Beaulieu, the store manager is waiting in your office."

"Thank you. I'll be there." A few minutes with the beautiful Marguerite might be the panacea for the day. She'd clear wayward dreams of Iona from his heart.

Marguerite wanted a commitment. Christ, they'd only been dating for two weeks. Marriage was not on his agenda, despite his father's plans. His momentary idea the store manager might help him through this problem with Thierry died a sudden death with her demands.

The day got no better. Enzo was distracted, not able to focus on crucial business. Searching for alternatives to Thierry's scenario, Enzo dismissed each one. Starting again was not an option. Flowerpot would demand a caveat preventing Enzo from founding his own company in opposition to them.

Without the Beaulieu name, the birthright would die. His life was built on the foundation that any sacrifice was worth preserving the birthright for future Beaulieu generations. He must keep the business alive somehow. Where was his father's mind?

He strode to the discreet bar at the far end of the room, poured himself a Scotch, gulped it, poured another. Lachie McKell made great whisky.

Enzo's mobile phone rang on his desk. Carrying the heavy crystal glass, he strolled to answer the clanging instrument.

"Enzo," a voice boomed in his ear, "where in the world are you to-day?"

Speak of the Devil. "*Bonjour,* Lachie. Today, I am in the charming city of Paris. You? Are you at home in Kellburgh?"

"Aye, I am. Since the babies arrived, my darling wife and I try to spend more time here. I use the technology's wonders for meetings where I can. Some things, though, are too significant. Will ye have time if I come to Paris tomorrow? I've something important to ask."

"I'm afraid I fly to Florence in the morning, *mon ami.* I'll be back here on Friday, if it helps." Enzo was already considering strategies to alter his plans to accommodate his friend. If Lachie needed him, he'd do what he could to be available.

"Naw. Friday will be too late, given the urgency. Look, I'll ask ye now. Catriona and I would like it if ye'd agree to be godfather to the girls."

It was not a request he'd anticipated. "You remember I am Catholic? Won't it preclude me from assuming the role?"

"Only if it's a problem for yer faith."

"Non! Not at all. Your pastor might have an issue with it."

"He'd better not, if he knows what's good for him. Besides, I don't reckon God is too bothered by arbitrary denominational boundaries."

Enzo snickered. There were times when Lachie played the laird well. "In that case, I'm honored. It is a special request. *Oui, mon ami.* I am delighted to be godfather to your beautiful twins. Must I talk like this?" He attempted a growling imitation of Marlon Brando as the eponymous godfather character in the 70s classic movie his father used to watch on repeat. "*Non?*"

"I don't believe it's a requirement." Lachie's robust chuckle rattled through the phone. "One problem, though. The christenings are this Sunday. Catriona called the minister, and this was the only spot available for months. She took it. My wife will always make things happen to her timetable when she can."

"Sunday is fine with me. Perfect, in fact," he said, a plan burgeoning in his head. "I will fly into Edinburgh on Friday. Your wife, she too is well?"

"Never better. Motherhood suits Cat to perfection. She sings weird songs to the *bairns*, like "Click go the Shears" and "Waltzing Matilda". Whoever heard of using such music as lullabies? But, aye, she's well." Lachie's tone reflected the love and awe he held for his beloved Catriona.

An envious whorl skittered through Enzo. He pivoted his body to focus on the tall, steel triangle in the distance.

"Need I remind you, *mon ami*, my mother was also Australian. I remember the music from when I was young." *Barely.*

His mother died when he was ten, setting in motion myriad changes in his pre-adolescent life. He recalled only snippets from the songs she sang.

He rubbed his forehead. "Your sisters? Will they be at Kellburgh also?"

"Aye, they'll be your counterparts. Ness is in Edinburgh for now. She'll arrive before Sunday. Iona's already here. She's having a ball making soap with our excess goats' milk."

"This is something new for her, oui?" Enzo said. "Is it serious, this pursuit?"

"Aye. She wants to make her mark separate from our other products. She's struggling a bit with getting the fragrances just right, or at least to her standards. She experiments until she gets it close to what she wants."

Parfait!

"Interesting. I can talk with her about fragrances. Thank you for the honor to be the godfather, *mon ami.* I will be with you on the weekend. *A bientôt.*"

Had the angels gifted him a miracle?

Carrying his glass, Enzo walked to the window behind his desk. It was the same view from the boardroom on the lower level. He moved his stare from the Eiffel Tower to the La Défense streets beneath him.

Despite the activity in the Parisian business district, which would, any other day, command his attention, his mind was elsewhere, busy formulating a plan.

Thierry hadn't specified Enzo needed to be *married* by his birthday to claim the business, only to demonstrate it would happen. Perhaps he might convince Iona to set aside their history—his cruelty—to act the part of his fiancée for two months in a sterile transactional arrangement.

She would receive private tutelage in perfumery, from a three thousand scent *nez* no less, and he would satisfy his father's demands until the business was in his total, unassailable control. Benefit would accrue to them both if Enzo could persuade her to agree.

On the other hand, being seen to play fast and loose with his best friend's sister would destroy the things he held most dear on a personal level. He trusted the McKells. Surely, he could explain his situation in a logical manner so he could proceed without harming his friendship with Lachie.

Enzo would also be disrupting the barren acquaintanceship he'd developed with Iona to disguise his guilt, want, and need.

Should he risk asking her? Would she do it? Would his heart survive a week with her, let alone two months? There was only one way to find out.

Chapter Two

"You'll never guess who's coming to the christenings!"

Iona lifted her attention from studying the lye calculator on her computer to her enthusiastic sister-in-law. Catriona kept her apprised of most acceptances for the celebration for the babies, but no other reply elicited this much excitement.

"Hmm?" Iona arched her back to stretch the locked muscles, focusing on the woman before her.

Cat shared similar features to Iona and her sister—dark hair in a messy chignon, small stature, blue-green eyes, more blue than Iona's or Ness'.

"Enzo Beaulieu. He's drool-worthy." Cat fluttered a hand against her chest. "Not a patch on your brother, of course, though even a married woman can appreciate the gorgeousness of a debonair Frenchman."

Iona's spine snapped straight. Cat's words were not welcome—not because of her Australian accent—Iona had grown used to it during the past eighteen months. Cat still couldn't pronounce her husband's name in the Scottish way. Instead, she called him something like 'Locky'.

She used Australian expressions Iona didn't understand. Nevertheless, the castle was a much happier place with Catriona in it.

No, the problem was not the accent. Rather, the notion of Beaulieu returning to the McKell estate was what was tying her in knots.

"He says he'll fly into Edinburgh on Friday. Would Ness collect him?"

Oh, aye. Iona's twin would love it. The idea grated across her mind. "You could ask her. I'm not sure when she was planning to travel herself."

"Cool. I will. The only problem is… I've allocated rooms for the other acceptances we've received. Our wing is chockas. He'll need to be in your area. Or should I reallocate your cousin Eilish's family to you?"

The megaphone family? Not on your life! "Naw, it's okay. You can put him in the room next to Ness. He'll be fine. It will be quieter." *And at the far end of the hall, away from me.*

"Thank you, Iny. You are wonderful. I never anticipated a simple christening would generate this much interest." Cat rubbed her cheek.

"Well," Iona said, "everyone saw how happy you and Lachie were on your wedding day. My guess is they want to discover if the glow has faded with your daughters' arrival. We've not celebrated a christening in the castle since Ness and me. Meredith didn't believe in it, so Lisbet was never dunked."

"Poor Lachie—to lose his wife and the baby."

"Lachie married Meredith for the business' sake, not because they loved each other. She was already pregnant by someone else."

"Not her fault."

Iona jerked her chin up. "I'm not saying she asked to be attacked—"

"I would hope not, since the same derro tried it on me!"

"What I *am* saying is she was never a wife to Lachie. My heart broke for my brother. He deserved much more." She raised her brows.

"Then your great-aunts went to Melbourne and found me." Cat grinned.

Iona dragged both hands down her face. "Oh aye, my puir brother was sunk!"

"Yep! No hope for the man. He loves me. What more can I say?" With twinkling eyes and a broad smile, Cat threw out her arms, pirouetted to the stairs leading to the central part of the house, before calling, "See ya!"

Iona chuckled as her sister-in-law-slash-great-friend left.

The suggestion for making soap to use excess milk from their goats came originally from Cat. Iona jumped at the chance to try something new, something she could establish for herself beyond the family's whisky and premium pâté businesses. For her own self-worth, she needed to make her mark outside the shadow of being the laird's sister.

She'd found her niche and her passion—discovering new fragrances and creating her own using natural sources, not manufactured facsimiles of jasmine, lavender, rose, or any other.

Perfumier, she wasn't. She'd been doing this for less than two years. Perfumiers were born to it. They spent a lifetime becoming a *nez* or a 'nose' who could recognize hundreds of individual scents. *Could you imagine?* She was only an enthusiastic amateur, willing to learn.

A helpful perfumier would be a knowledge trove. The only one she knew, though, was Enzo, whose family's history making perfumes in Grasse, France, spanned two hundred years. Huh! She wouldn't ask him for the time of day after the way he'd hurt her teenaged self. Who says you couldn't hold a grudge for ten years?

He was Lachie's best friend. They talked to each other for hours about how to repair the enterprises their respective predecessors let slide.

Despite her head's damning assessment of the man, her heart still bounced when Enzo was near. She kept her emotions close, shrouded behind an ironclad hostess veneer. She psyched herself for a week when he was coming. This time, she had two days.

Blaigeard! Why couldn't he stay the hell away for once? She would love to enjoy a family celebration in peace.

~ * ~

Enzo eased himself from Agnes' compact car early Friday evening.

"*Bonsoir, mon ami.* It is good to see you. Marriage and the sleepless nights with babies have not soured you?" he asked his host.

"Enzo, my man. Welcome back. For myself, I'm happier than I've ever been." Enzo's hand was engulfed by the Scotsman's paw.

Squinting at the canopy above his head, Enzo said, "This is new. Did you lose the damned portcullis over the front door?"

Lachie's laugh rang clear. "My dearly beloved said it was bad *feng shui* for it to threaten everyone who entered. Instead, she wanted covering from the car to the door to protect the babies from the weather.

The portcullis was doomed. It's in an outhouse in case the next generation wants to reinstate the original fittings. Come on in."

Enzo pivoted his head to his driver. "Thank you for meeting me at the airport, Nessie, and for your most interesting conversation."

"Huh, don't bother toadying to me." She flopped a limp wrist at him. "Your conversation kept the boredom of the familiar road at bay. We'll agree there are things on which we'll never be eye-to-eye."

Agnes reached on her toes to kiss her brother's cheek before she passed into the house.

"What is the issue?" Lachie asked.

"It's our same old argument. Agnes believes color and sparkle rule the world, whereas, for me, fragrance makes life worthwhile."

"Huh," Lachie said. "Ye'll get more support for your argument from Iona. She's developed a passion for fragrances. Here she is now. She'll show ye to yer room. It's not yer usual because we're full to the brim, or 'chockas', my wife would say. When ye're ready, we'll sample a wee dram before dinner." He stepped away, allowing Iona access to their guest.

"Enzo. How lovely to see you. Welcome back to Kellburgh." Her voice was cool, dispassionate.

His gut tightened anyway. It always did when she was near. He held her soft hand in his as he air-kissed her on both cheeks. Her fingers flexed against his, ready to withdraw. He resisted for a moment. Any reason he could manufacture was never enough for him to touch her.

He could sit arguing with Agnes for ninety minutes, as he'd done on the drive, without an emotional connection. The second he saw her identical twin, it was another matter. Her beauty shone from an inner glow, drawing him in, building the want and need he had for her. His soul was scarred by the emotional distance between them and the belief he meant less than nothing to her.

There was a time when he'd resented her hold on his heart. He'd pushed her away—cruelly. It didn't stop the ache she caused in him—an ache which had never quieted in the decade since.

"*Ma belle,* Iona." He brought her hand to his lips. It jerked, and he nearly lost his grip. She wasn't immune to him. "Your brother says I am to follow you, *ma petite.*"

"Aye. We have you in the room next to Agnes. May I help you with your bags?"

"*Non, merci.*" He shouldered a backpack, grasped his suitcase handle, then followed her along the covered walkway into the house.

"The footmen are run off their feet right now," she said, dodging children playing hide and seek. "We've been overwhelmed by the family and friends who've arrived. The last time there was this number to stay was for Gramps' funeral. Not even the wedding brought so many houseguests. Are you fine with the stairs, or would you prefer the lift?"

"I like the stairs. The exercise helps to keep me fit for my preferred physical pursuits," he said, setting foot on the first tread. He turned in time to catch a slight blush staining her cheeks.

Iona rested a hand on the rail, boosting herself up the stairs ahead of him. He raised a brow, which she wouldn't have seen, and smirked. She wouldn't have seen that either, though it gave him some satisfaction.

"You'll notice we've made many changes since Catriona arrived," she said. "She's enlivened the place. With the babies, there seems to be a lot more activity and noise.

"Catriona inherited some townhouses in Edinburgh. Agnes modernized the colors and furnishings. Now, although the properties still appear to be part of a Georgian mansion from the outside, they have modern interiors. The renovations were so successful, Cat decided to do the same in the castle. She's updated the rooms on this side of the house. She hasn't touched the west wing yet. You'll find the room you have is not much different from the one you've used in the past."

He was well aware of the refurbishments. He'd been here only two months ago. Perhaps she was using it as a neutral topic of conversation to avoid… what? "Are you nervous, *petite?*"

The vision before him stumbled, grabbing the banister to prevent a fall. She glanced over her shoulder. The blush was in full force this time. "Nervous? Of *you?* I've known you half my life."

"*Oui*, so…" He canted his head.

"Don't be arrogant," she drawled. "I'm bringing you up to date with the household, that's it."

"Yet you show a beautiful blush to go with your commentary."

"You're ridiculous, *monsieur.* Here is your room. Will you be able to find your way to Lachie's sitting room? He'd like a quiet drink before dinner."

"I'm not sure, *ma belle.* As you say, I am not familiar with this wing. Perhaps you could wait to show me the way?" There was no need to remind her that he and Lachie explored the castle in minute detail for weeks when they were teenagers.

"In your suite? Not on your life. What would your latest lover say? I'll give you fifteen minutes." She tilted her pert nose at him before spinning on her heel to leave him standing.

Satisfaction expanded in his chest as he walked into a well-appointed apartment. She wasn't impervious to him, neither was she eighteen anymore. She had ten years to find someone else but was still unattached.

The christenings provided a convenient excuse for his visit. It was an honor for him to be the babies' godfather, though not his primary reason to return.

Being close to Iona again, finding the same level of awareness he'd always had, the die was cast for him. Enzo was there for her, his dragon-lady tour guide.

www.ingramcontent.com/pod-product-compliance
Lightning Source LLC
Chambersburg PA
CBHW070318190726
48291CB00014B/2256